Praise for John L. Swann's third
Charlie Chan Mystery
Beyond Murder

"Another fine effort, very enjoyable. If this had been written by Biggers back then, it would have definitely been made into a film. So, if you only know Charlie Chan from the movies, you could easily jump into this series and have a great time."
  Eric Caruso

"You get drugs, smugglers, boats, planes, automobiles, babies, nurses, and, of course, murder. John L. Swann hit one out of the park, again!"
  David Strickler

"I had the pleasure to read this third book in John L. Swann's *Charlie Chan Returns* series, and I for one believe HE NAILED IT! I did not think anyone would ever attempt to continue the 'Chan Canon,' but John has continued where Biggers left off."
  Lou Armagno, editor of The Wisdom Within Earl Derr Biggers' Charlie Chan

Also by John L. Swann

Charlie Chan Returns Series
Death, I Said
The Tangled String
Beyond Murder

Nonfiction
From the Mills to Marcy
Meditations for a Baby Stoic

Wheels Within Wheels

A Charlie Chan Mystery

John L. Swann

Nicholas K. Burns Publishing
Utica, New York

Nicholas K. Burns Publishing
130 Proctor Boulevard
Utica, NY 13501
www.nkbpublishing.com
nickburns@nkbpublishing.com

First Edition

ISBN 979-8-9991899-4-3 (paperback)
ISBN 979-8-9991899-5-0 (ebook)
Library of Congress Control Number: 2026940392

The following is a work of fiction inspired by the characters created by Earl Derr Biggers. Any resemblance to actual events or persons, living or dead, is entirely coincidental. All the characters and events described herein are wholly fictitious.

Book and Cover Design: Nicholas K. Burns Publishing

CONTENTS

PREFACE

Like many fans of the famous fictional Chinese-American detective, I discovered Charlie Chan through the dozens of films that once were a staple of weekend and late-night programming on more than a few American television stations. Intrigued by the character's origins, I then discovered and devoured the six Chan novels authored by Earl Derr Biggers, whose death in 1933 ended the internationally popular book series.

The Chan movies (and other adaptations on TV, radio, even comic strips) did much to contribute to the character's enduring popularity, which shows no signs of waning (at this writing, a Canadian TV Chan reboot is reportedly in the works) a hundred years after the first Biggers novel, *The House Without a Key* (1925), introduced the modest, self-effacing sleuth to fans of detective fiction. In many ways the film Chan became, and remains, far better known than his print counterpart.

For me, Charlie Chan's various film characterizations—while those of Warner Oland and Sidney Toler are mostly excellent—pale in comparison to the Biggers original. Hollywood's Chan and his action-prone sons had to solve a case in less than ninety minutes. Biggers had more time (and more words) to contextualize his creation.

Chan in print was more fully realized than movie-Chan. Biggers gradually (over the course of the series) made him a more fully human character: a middle-aged man who mused over his at times uneasy bridging of East and West; a Chinese-born policeman striving to succeed in his American profession; an immigrant father lamenting his far-too-Americanized offspring's vulgar slang. And a bold opponent of those who devalued him because of his heritage, one quick to deliver philosophy and wit that put them in their place.

I have always wished that Earl Derr Biggers had lived longer and written more. When his best-known character fell into the public domain I began to think of a way to—perhaps—pick up where Biggers had left off, with 1933's *Keeper of the Keys*. The approach of the Chan centennial year, 2025, provided an additional impetus to test the literary waters. If a new Charlie Chan novel appeared, one written in homage to Biggers, one that continued his timeline and his version of the detective, would anyone care?

I'm happy to report that a great many people responded with enthusiasm, and it is because of their continuing interest and support that *Death, I Said* (2023), *The Tangled String* (2024), and *Beyond Murder* (2025) are now joined by a fourth entry, *Wheels Within Wheels*. I have kept Charlie in the nineteen-thirties, a time that suits him very well, I think, and one familiar to fans of some of the better films in the Chan series.

For as much as I have tried to keep to the Biggers path, I sometimes feel (and more than one reader has told me) that the Charlie Chan in these books sometimes speaks and behaves as the character did in the movies. For many, any version of Chan is Chan. His various incarnations blend into one another to realize the beloved character that overcomes ignorance and prejudice as he solves baffling crimes in the neverland of Golden Age detective fiction.

Some critics and scholars see Chan as a flawed creation of a white writer, and they have condemned Hollywood's casting of non-Asians in the role (apart from the two Japanese and one Chinese-American actors whose portrayals are little known today), but others, like scholar-author and Guggenheim Fellow Yunte Huang, disagree.

"However," as the detective himself observed in *Charlie Chan Carries On* (1930), "talk will not cook rice." Thanks to the continuing indulgence of Nicholas Burns at NKB Publishing, and the constant encouragement of family and friends, I am pleased to share with you another Charlie Chan mystery. I hope that you find in it some enjoyment, perhaps a few moments of amusement, and a little time to escape the cares of the current day by spending a little time with Honolulu's best-known fictional police detective.

Chapter One

SINCERELY, FREDERICK SCANLON

Frederick Scanlon hung up the telephone and leaned back with a sigh.

His was an executive's office. Dimly lit by a single chandelier, the room's dominant feature was a massive desk littered with papers and books but no personal touches—no photographs, trophies, or mementos of youth. There was the hushed atmosphere of a cathedral, albeit one devoted to the worship of the debenture rather than the divine. Nothing gaudy, to be sure.

The walnut-paneled walls, free from ornamentation, had a subtly rough-hewn quality complemented by a patterned rug that covered nearly the entire floor. It left bare only a flagstone hearth in front of a large fireplace at the room's far end. Facing the blazing fire, two empty wingback chairs waited for whatever momentous conversation they might host.

Glancing at the fire, Scanlon swiveled the leather high-backed chair, turning away from the oaken desk and looking out the floor-to-ceiling corner windows of his forty-fourth floor sanctum. The view was stunning and rare. Not many companies, and not many companies' chief executives and founders, could boast of such a rarefied perch in the middle of Manhattan. The heart of the city lay beneath him, but Scanlon had seen it too many times before. It had no charm for him now, if it ever had.

Scanlon was of medium height, but his broad-shouldered frame made him seem taller. A clean-shaven face was still unmarked by time, and his pronounced jawline and cleft chin were complemented by a small but sharp nose. Above these features, inquiring dark eyes gazed at the world, topped by dark, bushy brows beneath an unruly head of graying hair.

The smell of woodsmoke reminded him of the places he preferred to be and temporarily banished the business woes of a middle-aged magnate. When he spent months away from the city at his Adirondack lodge, Scanlon looked more nearly like the son of the north country woodcutter that he was, rather than the financial titan he had become since leaving the great forests for the city's promised fortunes.

In recent years he had retreated annually to the woods he loved, often for months on end. Dividing his time in such a fashion, between there and here—this steel and concrete wilderness—gave him the space he needed to thrive in both. But even in this urban environment, something in his persona hinted at the inner man. Change his daily costume from gray flannel suit to denim and flannel shirt, and he would be transformed into his unrealized alter ego—a man more comfortable among the towering trees of the Adirondacks than the man-made canyons of Manhattan.

Dismissing such unprofitable thoughts, Scanlon swiveled back to face his desk and its ever-present calendar. On a notepad he ticked off the first six calls of the day—it was hardly mid-morning, and he had already been hard at work for several hours—and mentally reviewed each one. His thoughts flew from subject to subject in no particular order: *Laidlaw and that commodities deal, best to buy in now rather than later ... Riverside Drive; a good project, but Knoxton? No, the man's definitely not qualified ...*

And so it went: As he did every day, Scanlon reviewed his most recent conversations. Some, he approved and advanced; others, he marked for elimination or simply put on hold—"no further action," he told himself. This morning's names swirled and recombined in his head like the unwieldy shingle of a non-existent law firm: Laidlaw, Knoxton, McTillery, Beddle-man . . .

. . . and C.W. The last call of the morning, the last partner in his imagined legal practice.

"Old fool," Scanlon murmured affectionately. He opened a desk drawer and pulled out several sheets of writing paper, his personal stationery, each page bearing at its top a kind of family crest. From the same drawer he withdrew a dip pen and an old cut-glass inkwell.

For the better part of an hour the titan of industry and commerce wrote and rewrote a remarkable letter. Normally, his correspondence was a formal affair, dictated and typewritten for his signature; but this was no normal missive.

The scratching of his pen's steel nib on paper alternated with its visits to the old-fashioned inkwell. Occasionally the writer paused to reflect, light a cigarette, reconsider a phrase—and then he continued.

Having completed the letter Scanlon took several more sheets of paper and composed a series of invitations—all with similar elements, but each containing unique touches to personalize it. A methodical man, he constructed the missives in alphabetical order, but first he dashed off an interoffice memorandum to a Miss Ida Botts.

To: Miss Ida Botts
From: Frederick Scanlon
Re: Weekend Gathering

Please add to the calendar a weekend gathering October 3-4 at the Great Lodge on Big Moose Lake, New York.

I have invited a group of friends, family members, and business associates to discuss matters of mutual and collective interest.

I will be unavailable Friday, October 2, and Monday, October 5, to allow for travel to and from the meeting site.

The writer paused to light another cigarette, then picked up a second sheet.

Dear Dan,
It's been far too long since you and Muriel visited my favorite hideaway from the madness of the world, the Great Lodge on Big Moose Lake.

Please plan on spending the first weekend of next month, October 3-4, at the lodge as part of a small conclave I'm assembling to discuss matters of particular interest to you both. I should add, Dan, that it will be an opportunity for us to clear the air. I hope that we can move beyond the distant past.

You know the lake area well, so I won't bore you with an enthusiastic sales pitch. Instead, I'll close by wishing you both good health until we meet in the woods.
Sincerely . . .

Scanlon tapped the ash from his cigarette and quickly wrote the next several invitations, keeping to the same plan but altering a word or phrase here and there. Most of the remaining compositions were more perfunctory; he had known Dan and Muriel all those years ago.

Dear C.W.,
You're cordially invited . . . Great Lodge on Moose Lake . . . first weekend of next month . . .matters of mutual interest . . . you surely need a rest, you old sawbones . . .
Affectionately . . .

Dear Alex,
I'm writing to invite you . . . small conclave to discuss matters . . . October 2-4 at Big Moose Lake's Great Lodge... see you that Friday . . . itinerary enclosed . . .

Dear Walter,
You're invited to a weekend . . . Big Moose Lake . . . small group convening . . . financial matters that will interest you . . . all expenses paid . . .

Dear Monsignor . . .

Scanlon put out his cigarette and sighed. *The old boy probably still bears a most unholy grudge,* he thought. *Ah, well.*

. . . Please be my guest October 3-4 at the Great Lodge on Big Moose Lake . . . Sincerely . . .

Putting down the pen and stretching his cramped fingers, Scanlon opened the bottom drawer of his desk and withdrew a bottle and glass. Pouring a liberal libation of old bourbon from the former into the latter, he took a healthy drink and swallowed gratefully.

Now, he thought, *for the last of these!*

Dearest Edna,
I realize that this communication will come as something of a surprise to one I have neglected for so many years. Please accept my apologies for past sins and personal transgressions.

Certain vital matters lie unresolved between us, and among our circle of friends, family, and associates. To address these in a manner that will be satisfactory to all concerned, I am inviting a group to the old lodge at Big Moose Lake for the weekend of October 3-4.

Please extend this invitation to Bill and let him know that his presence is vital.
Yours . . .

Scanlon put down his pen and picked up the glass, but it was empty. Pouring himself another restorative dose, he sipped it thoughtfully.

She can jolly well ask Bill to come along, even though he needs no invitation in this case.

For some reason the thought amused him.

Doubtless he would show up anywhere that free food, liquor and accommodations can be had. Anyway, he concluded, lighting another cigarette, *one less invitation for me to write—and he's not worth a three-cent postage stamp.*

Frederick Scanlon looked at this handiwork and was pleased. Although he was not in the habit of mailing his own correspondence, a trip to the post office this afternoon was clearly in order. But first, there was one more call to make.

He reached for the telephone and dialed his secretary.

"Miss Botts, please get me the overseas operator, will you?

"Thank you."

The territorial governor was a busy man and still relatively new to his lofty position, but he was not unused to high-level decision making. After youthful endeavors in logging and ranching in Oregon and Montana he had decided on a career in the law, eventually serving as Beaverhead County Attorney, attorney general for the state, and as a federal district judge. And now, as Governor of Hawaii these past few years, he pursued different kinds of justice—good governance and fairness for all were the watchwords of his administration.

Above all, he practiced what he preached—especially when it came to personal loyalty. The chief executive of an American territory finds new and eager friends easy to acquire, he had found, but the older ones—those who knew him when he was just another face on the frontier—he valued above all others.

"You were listening on the extension, I trust?"

The governor turned his gaze upon an ever-present underling who served as both secretary and major-domo of a limited residential staff. This person had thrust his head inquiringly into the office for instructions as soon as the call ended.

"Yes, sir," the diminutive man replied. In appearance he was mild and unassuming, his usual pose until called upon to execute his boss's will. "Shall I prepare a letter for your signature?"

"Certainly," the Governor replied without hesitation. "The usual carbons, one for our files, one for the caller, and the original . . ."

The assistant looked up from his notes.

"Yes?"

"Goes to the subject of the letter," the Governor concluded, his mind returning from its brief visit to Montana. "But hold off on sending that original for a few weeks. Best if he hears about this from someone he knows personally."

The assistant scurried away to begin the task as directed. The Governor absentmindedly picked up a rustic-looking desktop wooden box, running his hand over the bas-relief carving of a formidable-looking moose on its lid. Opening it he extracted a cigarette and a wooden match, scratching the latter on his thumb to light the former.

The box had been a gift from a loyal friend in bygone days, Fred Scanlon. The Governor's expression softened as he recalled the Montana logging camp where he had worked as a youth. Fred had been the wayward son of an Eastern tycoon who had sent him "out West" one summer as a last attempt at reform. The young ne'er-do-well had saved a future governor's life that summer, and now—in a small way—he could return the favor.

The Governor picked up the telephone on his desk and called the switchboard operator.

"Doris? Yes, please—get me the police station on Butler Street, the chief's office."

"Dear Inspector Chan," the letter began.

I write to thank you for taking on an assignment that will require a lengthy journey to a place far from your familiar surroundings. Please accept my apologies for arranging what must seem to you something of a command performance. It seems to me, a man of middle age, that little time is left to hope and plan for one's schemes to ripen. "Needs must," as the old saying has it, and your territorial governor was kind enough to oblige his old friend in securing your services to gratify my wishes.

I hope that you will enjoy the more picturesque of the several modes of travel necessary to transport you to your destination. As has been communicated to you by this time, all arrangements have been made. For much of the journey you will be unencumbered by your usual duties, free to see the sights along the way.

Once on board the train from New York to the mountains, you will receive a communication containing a précis of the essential facts and descriptions of the persons you will meet—some of them en route, others at your final destination.

I consider this method of preparation for the task ahead better than providing too much information too soon. Thus, while my thoughts about the matter are still fresh in your mind, you will encounter and judge for yourself all that I have described. I wish you every success and have made the

necessary arrangements for appropriate remuneration at the conclusion of your investigation.
I remain,
Respectfully yours,
Frederick Scanlon

Charlie Chan's wife, Chan Chun Shee, brought evening tea to him. The little lanai outside the family bungalow was pleasantly cool under its sheltering algoraba trees, and as he sipped the pale steaming liquid, Chan considered this most unusual assignment. He re-read the letter the Chief had handed him that morning.

"Not exactly how I prefer to assign my best detective," the Chief had admitted. "Politics and favoritism have no place in our work—you know how I feel about that, Charlie. But in this case . . ."

The man Chan most admired for his integrity was at a loss for words.

"Each of us has a boss," Chan had reassured him. "Even the head of police department must answer to higher authority."

Chapter Two

NO TIME FOR SIGHTSEEING

Despite the most up-to-date travel innovations of the 1930s, Charlie Chan found that a trip from the Territory of Hawaii to the State of New York was no easy matter. He silently thanked the fates—and Mr. Scanlon—for making it possible. *The rich man's whim guides the poor man's travel*, he mused, *like a great wind blows a single leaf to its destination.*

To go from Honolulu to New York was an expedition of several stages.

First, by air: the Clipper, from Honolulu to the mainland, was followed by a series of flights from California to New York. What the detective saw of that famous city was glimpsed through the window of a taxicab that whisked him from Newark Metropolitan ("busiest airport in the world," a fellow passenger had told the detective) to Manhattan's Grand Central Station. He had barely enough time to walk through the immense building's ornate hall before the boarding call came.

No matter, he reflected philosophically. Sightseeing was not the reason for this trip.

Grand Central teemed with people on the move at this early hour. After the relative solitude of the overnight flight, Chan found himself swept along by the tide of movement. For someone used to the pace of life in much less populated surroundings, it seemed that all of New York was either entering or departing the station, and Chan found his place on a train filled to capacity.

As he always did when traveling, Charlie Chan examined his fellow passengers discreetly but thoroughly. Many of them—judging from their attire and baggage—appeared bound for distant destinations. Some wore the uniform of businessmen and the serious expression appropriate to their calling, but even they thawed once the trip was underway. After an hour or so, when the grays of the city had given way to a more natural palette, passengers talked with new acquaintances, dozed, or admired the spectacle of forested hillsides. It was the time of year when changing leaves colored the landscape in ways few artists could hope to imitate.

Many of the passengers appeared used to the scenery and ignored it. It was easy for these natives of the region to spot the tourists, the seasonal pleasure-seekers who fairly gawked at the colorful woodlands. Charlie Chan appeared to be one of the latter; he admired autumn's finery in a part of the country he was seeing for the first time. Although he was neither sightseer nor holidaymaker, this assignment was taking him far from home—and he accepted the gift of new experiences that helped make up for the rigors of travel.

Traveling alone, as he usually did, provided the detective a rare opportunity for rumination. His mental exercises usually began with a grateful review of family, especially his wife and their eleven offspring: Henry, applying himself well in San Francisco as an investigator in assistant U.S. attorney June Kirk's office; Rose, newly minted attorney, devoted mother of Gracie, loving spouse of John Winterslip . . . and so on.

The rest of the family passed in review in this mental roll call, ending with the youngest, Barry, as Chan reflected on the continuing Americanization of his children. He found the process bittersweet, especially the tendency of the younger offspring to be even more American than their older siblings.

Pride in their accomplishments was offset to some extent by a regret that they did not, in his eyes, honor their heritage.

Still, he admitted to himself, his own shortcomings in this regard had been brought home to him by more traditional Chinese family members—cousin Chan Kee Lim came to mind—because he wore American clothes and had made a career among what Kee Lim called, "the white devils." That most Western of qualities, pride, battled his preferred philosophical trait, humility, at every turn.

Chan looked out the window at the heavily wooded terrain. He had read of nature's annual autumn exhibition of colorful foliage, but no written account could compare with this first-hand view. The detective had seen many rainbows in the constantly changing skies over his beloved islands, but here was something warm and glowing that sprang from the earth—and returned to it each year. More colors were laid out before his wondering eyes in this scattered, fragmented spectrum found in no Hawaii rainbow. Leaves of brown, gold, red (and shades to which Chan could not put names) in their countless numbers mingled with the evergreens on the hillside facing the side of the train.

The fall landscape looked as though it could go on forever, but at last a cloud cast its shadow on nature's canvas. Chan accepted the dimming as a sign that his first experience of New York's foliage in all its glory was at an end.

"Mr. Chan?"

A dark-faced conductor had stopped in the aisle and looked at the detective expectantly over the tops of steel-rimmed glasses.

"Yes," Charlie Chan acknowledged his identity with a nod and reached for his ticket. "Here is my—"

"That's quite alright," the official interjected. "No need to punch your ticket." He smiled. "You're cleared all the way down the line to your final destination, so you can keep that for a souvenir."

Chan pocketed the ticket and returned the smile. The conductor consulted his watch and pulled an envelope from the recesses of his uniform jacket.

"I was instructed to deliver this to you on this date, at this time, after verifying that you are, in fact, Inspector Charlie Chan of the Honolulu police." The conductor adjusted his spectacles and looked through them, eyebrows raised slightly.

The detective pulled open the left side of his coat briefly, revealing the silver badge pinned to his vest.

"That's fine, just fine," the conductor declared. He handed over the envelope and touched his cap. "Anything you need along the way, Mr. Chan, you let me know."

"So kind," Charlie Chan murmured. "Thank you so much."

He opened the envelope and pulled from it two sheets of paper. The first was a letter.

Inspector Chan,

Welcome to "the other New York," far from the tall buildings and sleepless bustle of Manhattan. The train on which you are now traveling will take you into the remnants of the great forest that once covered much of this continent. In some respects, the Adirondacks has retained its wild, primeval character; tremendous specimens of the black bear are common, and other woodland creatures abound.

This vast region's unique character holds true from its "High Peaks" to its low wooded slopes and fine lakes.

Here, in a peaceful corner of this wilderness, I have arranged for you to enjoy the same accommodations that I have found restorative to mind, body, and spirit for many years. In this setting I have assembled those persons whose lives have overlapped with mine in important respects: friends, business partners, esteemed colleagues; those I love, respect, and admire.

Chan paused to reflect. This Scanlon must have great wealth and influence to move people about like chess pieces, but why? The letter's next sentence intrigued him.

I want you to find out which of them intends to kill me.

The detective closed his eyes for a moment to consider this remarkable declaration.

Most interesting, Chan thought, *that a successful and careful man like Mr. Scanlon writes "which of them," not "which one of them." Perhaps he suspects that multiple persons desire his death?*

"You may, at this point," the letter went on,

. . . wonder why a man of my standing in business and society suspects that he has become a target for assassination. In answer, by way of introduction, I will offer you brief biographies of those you will meet soon at the Great Lodge at Big Moose. I cannot tell you that my suspicions fall more upon one person than another. The fact is, my personal and professional successes and failures alike have given these persons a variety of reasons to do away with one whom they knew many years ago. To some of them these encounters have brought joy; to others, sorrow; to some—I have no doubt—anger, and bitter hatred.

By means of the appended summary, and through your personal experience of those described therein in a setting far removed from their normal haunts, I am confident that you shall find the truth.

I remain,
Yrs. truly,
Frederick Scanlon

P.S. You should know that despite the threat of injury or death I have determined to make my peace with these persons. Toward this end I have extended, and they have accepted, invitations for all of them to spend a few days at a lodge that I have long thought of as my true home. Your expertise, experience, and reputation, I trust, will enable you to get at the truth of the matter.

Chan's thoughts found little to dwell on in the tycoon's vague missive. As in his earlier correspondence, Scanlon offered few concrete details but seemed sure of his purpose. The detective reflected on the famous and wealthy he had encountered in previous investigations. Fame and money, he mused, do not ensure wisdom—or even rational thinking. Perhaps, as his old friend Inspector Duff of Scotland Yard would put it, this Scanlon has a bee in his bonnet.

He turned to the next sheet, Scanlon's appendix. *Here at last,* Chan thought, *we shall see what we shall see.*

The train rumbled on, but Charlie Chan took no notice of the scenery that flashed by. He was focused on the business titan's strange communication.

The second page began without preamble. It consisted of a list of names with a few descriptive sentences following each one.

Dr. Carl W. Collins. *As young men we were close friends until romantic rivalry caused a rift. The woman we both pursued became my wife. I have always sensed that he re-*

sented her choice and was jealous of our marriage. Poised to pursue research at the highest level, instead he took to drink and was reduced to the general practice of medicine. In recognition of our youthful friendship I consulted him on medical matters until his continuing decline made it impossible.

Alexander P. Creighton. *We met in the city some years after university. Alex and I are like-minded in many ways. We are the same age, but he was schooled in the South while I am New York born, bred, and educated. After partnering with me in business, he became my greatest rival after we parted ways professionally. The newspapers made much of the dissolution of our joint interests, portraying it in a more dramatic fashion than was actually the case. One scribbler actually wrote in the* Times *that we were "sworn enemies."*

Rev. Msgr. Leonard Plevna. *My one-time spiritual adviser and chess partner. I am told he would have been made a cardinal if not for his close association with me. Instead, he was shunted aside in the church hierarchy and given a lofty-sounding title and a thankless administrative post. We are no longer close.*

Walter Merriweather. *The company's accountant, a financial wizard whose Wall Street acumen has maintained my company's position even during the darkest times of the last several years. We were great friends at college, and I trusted him implicitly. Lately I had heard that his love of risk-taking has found expression beyond the New York exchange. It was even rumored that he gambles with the company's funds. I recently confronted him with these tales, and he threatened me with ruin.*

Mrs. Edna Scanlon*, my former wife. She was the girl of my dreams, my helpmeet and soulmate. Sadly, we were not blessed with children, and it may be that we grew apart over the years as a result. She hated my business and would have nothing to do with it, calling my dedication to the company an excuse for abandonment. She left me with little explanation, but her few written communications since have placed the blame squarely on my shoulders. Nonetheless, I still consider her my lawfully wedded wife and partner in life.*

Mr. and Mrs. Daniel Bryant*, friends during our wedded years. Daniel and I were close in those days, and I endeavored to interest him in an investment opportunity. Unfortunately his trust in my advice was rewarded by financial ruin, and—although he has recovered some-what—I have always felt that he bore a grudge. His occasional remarks thereafter on my continued success and his recurring struggles seemed to me sinister in their import. His wife, Muriel, has remained friendly with my former spouse.*

William Yantzen*. My former brother-in-law was and remains the black sheep of my wife's family. I have no doubt he resents my rejection of his frequent appeals to me. Often he has sought funding for wild, usually illegal, schemes that—in my judgement—would have enriched him at the expense of others. I suspect that Edna's affection for and devotion to "Brother Bill" was responsible in part for her departure from my life.*

Eight persons, Chan counted. Some with possible motives for murder, according to Scanlon's descriptions. The barest hint of a frown flitted across the detective's usually placid countenance. Where in all of Scanlon's grievances and suspicions does he find some indication that his life is in danger?

Too few seeds make a poor harvest, he thought, and looked out the window again. Mountainous hillsides and colorful foliage had given way to fields and grazing herds. The fenceline of one such pasture was only a stone's throw from the railroad tracks, and a single cow looked disinterestedly at the passing train, chewing her cud.

Chapter Three

THE FORMIDABLE MRS. SCANLON

As Charlie Chan began to re-read Scanlon's letter its envelope fell to the floor, into the path of a girl making her way down the aisle. She stooped to retrieve it and presented it to the detective.

"You dropped this, mister," she said shyly. "Here you are."

Chan accepted the envelope with a nod and a smile. The dark-haired girl reminded him of his youngest daughter, Anna, when she was of a similar age.

"Thank you, miss," he replied. "Your kindness has saved the creaking joints of an old man. To walk close to the ground is an advantage of youth."

The girl giggled.

"You're not old," she replied cheerfully. "Old people have white hair and wrinkles—"

"Clarissa!"

A well-dressed woman in middle age appeared behind the girl.

"I'm sure you've taken up enough of this gentleman's time," she said briskly. Taking a closer look at Chan, she added sternly, "And what have I told you about talking to someone to whom you have not been introduced?"

Abashed, the girl hung her head, but only for a moment.

"I know, only—he dropped a piece of paper, and I picked it up for him," she replied, a trace of defiance in her voice. "He said I was *kind*."

"Well," the woman said doubtfully. "I'm sure that was very thoughtful of you, but please remember that you are not to wander away from Miss Clarkson—especially on the train."

"Excuse, please, this interruption," Chan interjected. "Perhaps I can fulfill the requirements of etiquette by introducing myself." He rose and bowed slightly. "I am Charlie Chan of Honolulu."

"Where's that?" Clarissa inquired. "I've never heard of it before."

"Clarissa!" The woman was determined to observe the social niceties. "Please excuse the child, Mr. . . . Chan, was it? Allow me to introduce myself. My name is Scanlon, Mrs. Edna Scanlon." She added as an afterthought, "Of New York City.

"I believe you've already become acquainted with my little girl, Clarissa."

Chan smiled at the two as they took seats immediately behind him. If he was surprised by one of the names from Frederick Scanlon's list coming to life before his eyes he gave no outward sign.

"I am pleased to become acquainted with persons from the great city," he replied. Resuming his seat, he turned to continue the conversation. "Someday I hope to make a longer visit there, perhaps to see the world's tallest building and other famous sights.

"May I satisfy your young companion's geographic curiosity?" Chan looked at Mrs. Scanlon for permission. She nodded dismissively. The idea of conversation with a perfect stranger, and one clearly of exotic origins, was not to her liking. She turned impatiently and looked behind her as though in search of a missing item, ignoring for the moment her disobedient young one and the foreign-looking man.

"Honolulu, young miss, is the city where I come from," Charlie Chan explained. "Not so large as your city, New York, and very far away from here. Honolulu is on an island called O'ahu—part of Hawaii, a place in the Pacific Ocean.

"Maybe you will study it and other far-off places in school," he suggested. "Maybe," the girl replied skeptically, "but Mrs. Scanlon says—"

"Now, dear, that's quite enough," that redoubtable woman said sharply without turning. "I can speak for myself, and Mr. Chan isn't interested in your educational plans."

Peering down the aisle toward the end of the car, Mrs. Scanlon uttered an exclamation of impatience.

"I wonder where she can be?" she muttered. Chan wondered, too—was she referring to the aforementioned Miss Clarkson or someone else? He looked around the compartment to examine the other passengers. Awake or asleep, they provided him with food for thought.

In the rear of the car, a man and woman of late middle age dozed peacefully. *Long married*, Chan thought, noting their relaxed demeanor at rest: the woman's head, hatless, rested on the man's shoulder; a shawl covered her from the neck down. The husband appeared to snore slightly, his mouth open under a bristling gray mustache. Of the rest of his face nothing could be seen since a battered straw hat was tilted forward over his eyes.

Across the aisle from the sleeping couple a man frowned in concentration as he turned the pages of a magazine before consulting a substantial book. *A professional man*, Chan thought, *one of great learning—even while traveling he stays abreast of developments in his field— law? Medicine?*

Nothing in the man's appearance favored either conclusion, Chan decided. A dark suit and tie offset his thinning gray hair and plentiful mustache, the kind he had heard son Henry deride as a "walrus."

The professional man's frown dissolved into a more satisfied expression as he penned something on the magazine page, and Chan's scan of his fellow passengers was interrupted by a bark from the formidable Mrs. Scanlon.

"Where on earth—well! Here you are at last," she fumed. "Where have you been?"

Her ire was directed at a young woman in dungarees and flannel shirt who had just entered the car from the far end. The new arrival was a petite and energetic person, not yet thirty, with a complexion that spoke of outdoor recreation, and auburn hair spilling out from under a soft, draping beret.

"Gosh! I'm so sorry, Mrs. Scanlon," cried the aforementioned Miss Clarkson, who did not appear at all sorry. The younger woman's smiling face was flushed as though she had run the length of the train, which was only partly true. In fact, before hurrying down the aisle to find the Scanlons she had been viewing the landscape from the caboose platform, and as a result she appeared windblown and a trifle rumpled.

"I was just enjoying the scenery so much that I lost track of things, I guess," she explained cheerfully. "Glad I caught up with the two of you.""Indeed," Mrs. Scanlon humphed. "You certainly lost track of your charge, and you're not paid to sightsee—"

"Gee, I am sorry if I inconvenienced you," Miss Clarkson said contritely. "But I wasn't worried about Clarissa getting lost." There was an impish look in her eye. "Not much chance of that, since we are on a train after all.""This impudence left the older woman speechless for a moment, and Miss Clarkson went on hurriedly.

"Looks as though both of you have made out all right, though, making a new friend here," she smiled at Charlie Chan, extending her ungloved hand. "I'm Gloria Clarkson—pleased to meet you."

The detective hid his amusement at Mrs. Scanlon's apparent discomfiture and introduced himself, shaking the proffered hand gently. He wondered at the absence of the child and the companion's names from Scanlon's correspondence.

"Are you going to Albany on business, Mr. Chan?" Miss Clarkson inquired. "I hear it's a lovely city—not nearly as large as New York, of course, but it is the state capital, so—"

Mrs. Scanlon interrupted brusquely.

"Really, Gloria, I hardly think it necessary to pry—"

Charlie Chan waved away the older woman's concern.

"Youthful curiosity is easily satisfied," he said amiably. "Like many on this train, I am merely a traveler who will pass through the capital city of Empire State on my way to a destination 'down the line,' as railroad language puts it."

Undeterred by her employer's furrowed brow, Miss Clarkson persevered.

"How nice! So are we—that is, going on past Albany," she explained. "We're on our way to a place in the Adirondacks. Not high up in the mountains, you see, but definitely out in the wilderness. It's a place called—"Mrs. Scanlon interrupted again.

"Dear Clarissa!" The little girl had fallen asleep during the tedious adult conversation, and she stirred reluctantly. "You must be hungry by this time, and I am famished." Mrs. Scanlon rose, swaying slightly with the motion of the train. "Gloria, please take charge of the child, and let's go to the dining car—the three of us," she said firmly.

"Good day to you, Mr. Chan." Having delivered the curt farewell the woman strode toward the far end of the car, her determined gait foiled repeatedly by the train's sudden lurching. Reluctantly, Gloria Clarkson departed with the sleepy girl in tow, giving the detective a friendly wave which he returned with a grin and a nod.

Charlie Chan leaned back in his seat and closed his eyes. His travels had taught him to value even the briefest opportunity for rest, and he could sleep (and had) on airplanes, trains, and in automobiles.

Other passengers attempted to nap, and some moved back and forth in the aisle. A few gazed curiously at the sleeping Chinese man dressed for business, not pleasure.

Blissfully unaware of their scrutiny, the detective dozed as the train made its way up the Hudson River toward its next stop.

Awakened by the conductor's voice Chan took a deep breath and retrieved his scattered thoughts. The Empire State Express slowed to a crawl as it screeched into Albany Union Station, and Chan played the part of an eager tourist, gazing out the window at the crowds arriving and preparing to depart. He found the great numbers of people in the East fascinating—such energy, so many journeys of purpose!

He reflected on his own odyssey, wondering where it would lead.

"Just enough time to stretch your legs if you have a mind to, Mr. Chan." The conductor smiled and checked his timepiece. "Not enough time to see the state capitol or call on the governor, I'm afraid. We'll make up a little time here by shortening our stay—but you're welcome to walk or smoke on the platform for a few minutes."

Chan nodded.

"No need for me to smoke," he grinned. "Other passengers who indulge in tobacco habit are always willing to share—inside some train cars and outside, too."

The conductor smiled weakly at this apparent criticism of the railroad, its smoking cars—or both.

"I hope you haven't been bothered by smoke from other passengers, Mr. Chan," the railroad man said earnestly. "No smoking is permitted in this car—but sometimes the smoke, the odor, can travel from car to car, and I want to assure you—"

"Please," Chan interjected gently. "No criticism of New York Central Railroad was intended. I have experienced no discomfort more severe than sounds of gentle snoring from nearby weary passengers.

"Smoke on trains has a long history," he hastened to add. "Burning coal on early railroads made passengers uncomfortable in ways that are only a distant memory now, on this modern train."

Relieved, the conductor returned to his ambassador of the railway character. This Chan, after all, was a Very Important Passenger, it seemed. Best to humor him at all costs.

"You're right about that, and no mistake," he agreed. "My father was a railroad man in the early days on this line, and many's the time he would tell of ash and sparks landing on passengers—burning holes in their clothing, if you can believe it."

Chan assured him that such primitive conditions were believable, and that current-day travel by rail was a modern marvel by comparison.

"Ancient philosopher in my country advised of the importance of taking the first step toward any distant destination," he said cheerfully. "How much quicker his thousand-mile journey would have been on a train."

The conductor laughed and moved on.

Chan rose and considered. A brief promenade on the platform and the promise of fresh air appealed until he recalled that he was not in Honolulu, or any place like it. The passengers he had observed through the window a few minutes ago were bundled up in ways that spoke of brisk temperatures—all the more so for one accustomed to warm breezes and waving palm branches.

A walk to the dining car would suffice to stretch his legs, he decided. No need to disembark only to reenter the train after a few minutes.

Other passengers had similar ideas. The club car through which the detective passed en route to his destination boasted a bar, a few tables, and lounge chairs, and several passengers availed themselves of refreshment and the comfortable seating. The dozing couple (now fully awake) and the professional man, the detective noted, occupied a table for four, but the empty chair and their expectant looks suggested they were waiting for someone. *Were they already acquainted or had they just struck up a conversation as passengers often do?* Chan wondered.

"Won't you join us?"

The professional man stood, gesturing toward the vacant seat. Above the bushy gray expanse of his mustache, a pair of dark eyes twinkled at the detective in friendly fashion.

"So kind," Chan returned, taking the proffered chair. "But you are, perhaps, waiting for someone?"

"Indeed we are—you," said the other man, nodding his head vigorously.

"Now, Danny," the woman cautioned. "Let's not get ahead of ourselves—"

"Ahead of ourselves?" Danny blurted out. "Why, it's perfectly clear. Hell's bells—I'd wager any amount of money he's the only Chinese fellow on the whole train—"

The other man cleared his throat.

"Under normal circumstances we would begin by introducing ourselves," he smiled—or appeared to, since the great white mustache hid much of his expression. "In this instance, though, I'm sure you'll pardon me for first inquiring: Are you, in fact, Inspector Chan of Honolulu?"

"I am happy to confirm your astute observation regarding Chinese fly in New York ointment," the detective grinned. "Exact number of my countrymen on board this train, however, remains unknown to me—like the number of angels on the head of a pin."

All three of Chan's new acquaintances spoke at once, and their words of apology and protest mingled unintelligibly. Their audience of one raised both hands.

"Pleased to make acquaintance of three passengers at once," the detective reassured them. "No need to apologize for stating the obvious fact, and be assured that no offense was received."

Danny hastened to set matters aright.

"And no offense was intended, Mr.—Inspector Chan," he said firmly. "Just my way of blurting the first thing that comes into my mind. Daniel Bryant's my name, and I'm a sore trial to my wife—may I present Mrs. Bryant?"

The object of the introduction colored visibly, aiming a raised eyebrow at her outspoken husband. Chan acknowledged the introductions with a nod and smile, then turned to the other man expectantly.

"My name is Collins—Carl Collins," the professional-looking man said, his mustache quivering in apparent amusement. "Physician—mostly retired from practice now—"

"Oh, I forgot to present my professional credentials," Daniel Bryant interjected. "I'm by way of being one of those investors on Wall Street and elsewhere, the kind the newspapers blame for the 'state of things today.' Not entirely retired from my business endeavors—still poking about a bit, here and there."

Chan's demeanor was gracious, but his eyes were watchful. Evidently Scanlon intended at least some of his listed friends and enemies to encounter the detective well before journey's end. The detective thought the arranged meetings and his role in them seemed like a play on a stage—one in which he was both audience and actor.

"Pleased to make the acquaintance of a businessman referred to by more than one writer of headlines as 'tycoon,'" Chan acknowledged. "Reputation, like a faithful dog, follows close behind the man who travels far from home."

Dr. Collins coughed to conceal a short burst of laughter as Bryant's expression darkened, his lips a thin line. His wife blushed an even brighter pink; she rummaged in a small handbag and pulled out a small silver case. Fumbling for a lighter, she lit the chosen cigarette and blew a modest cloud of smoke toward the ceiling.

"More like a bloodhound, my so-called reputation." Daniel Bryant gritted his teeth in the semblance of a smile. "No matter how much good you do in the world, how much success you achieve, some people are only interested in sniffing out your missteps."

He shrugged dismissively. A white-jacketed porter arrived with drinks for three; Chan ordered orange juice. "Never understood that word tycoon," Bryant went on, lighting a cigarette and glancing at his whiskey and soda. "Except that apparently there's no such thing as a good one—so being called a tycoon is hardly a compliment."

"Newspapers fill themselves with words—yet very few compliments find their way into print," Chan observed. "But I am filled with curiosity. Businessman, wife, and physician on pleasure trip greet unknown policeman by name—why?"

The silent Mrs. Bryant had taken a healthy sip from her pink lady. Fortified, she wagged a contradictory forefinger at the detective.

"Hardly unknown, Mr. Chan," she chirped. "The dogs of reputation have tracked you as well. Still—well, I'll let the men tell the tale." She smiled archly.

"There's no great mystery about it," Daniel Bryant said smoothly, casting a warning glance at his wife. Oblivious, she gestured toward the passing porter and indicated the need for a second pink lady. "Muriel and I encountered Dr. Collins as we boarded the train—we were acquainted years ago but had lost touch with one another—and Dr. Collins informed us—"

"—that I was told by, er, a friend of my youth to be on the lookout for you," the doctor cut in.

Chan's eyebrows raised inquisitively.

"I refer, of course, to Frederick Scanlon," Collins went on. "He telephoned me recently—told me that he had recruited you to join a small group at his lodge for this weekend gathering."

The detective nodded.

"Correspondence from Mr. Scanlon to me mentioned you, and Mr. and Mrs. Bryant, as well as others he invited," Chan replied. "The presence of a physician is always welcome—no doubt health and well-being follow in your wake."

"I make no promises," smiled Collins. "As for this lodge weekend assembly—I don't suppose Fred enlightened you as to its purpose? We were just mulling that over—the three of us—when you arrived on the scene," Bryant told Chan, nudging his untasted drink toward the physician. "Here, Carl, you drink the damned thing. Don't know why I order whiskey and soda when I can't stand the concoction. You look as though you could use another one."

Indeed, the doctor's glass was empty, and he accepted Bryant's drink with a nod and a smile. Chan tried again.

"Mr. Scanlon kindly arranged for me to travel to a mountainous destination to encounter several of his friends and business acquaintances," he explained vaguely. "Doctor Collins—you spoke to Frederick Scanlon on the telephone—yet you remain puzzled by his invitation?" The doctor grasped his glass, swirling its contents with a practiced gesture. Chan's question seemed to worry him; he set down the glass and smoothed the bushy gray mustache before replying.

"I don't know that Fred Scanlon's weekend invitation to God knows how many people is at all puzzling to me," Collins countered. "In point of fact, nothing that he might think, say, or do would surprise me."

He downed half of the drink and continued.

"You see, Mr. Chan, I've known Fred since we were boys. In our younger days we were friends. When I was a young doctor starting out he consulted me, and I was his personal physician back then.

"Not that there was ever anything particularly wrong with him," he grumbled. "Healthy as a horse and strong as a bull—all that time in the woods, I suppose—but he would worry about every little thing. Imaginary ailments.

"However, even then . . ." Collins trailed off and attended to the rest of his drink. Catching the eye of the nearest attendant he pointed meaningfully at his empty glass.

The doctor's audience waited, but there was no more.

"We never knew Fred to be ill, did we, dear?" Mrs. Bryant twittered at her husband. She was halfway through the second pink lady, and the effects were evident.

Daniel Bryant shrugged and pulled the table's ashtray toward him. The white ceramic receptacle's round bowl proudly proclaimed, "New York Central Fast Early Bird Freight Service," and the slogan surrounded the cartoon-like image of a jaunty cap-and-kerchief-clad avian consulting a wrist-watch.

Bryant examined the advertisement for a moment, then stabbed the cheerful bird with the remains of his cigarette butt.

"Hmm? No, not that I can recall," he said vaguely. "Didn't know that there was any question about—say, why on earth are we discussing the man's health? As I said a moment ago, I haven't even seen him for quite some time."

"Idle speculation sometimes reveals information," Chan asserted, "like attempted bunt resulting in base hit."

The detective grinned.

"Please excuse the intrusion of sporting-talk," he went on, "a habit acquired from my cousin Willie Chan, captain of Honolulu's all-Chinese baseball team—his vocabulary is large but occasionally vulgar."

Polite laughter greeted Chan's remark. Dr. Collins shook his head.

"I don't know that there's anything to be gained by any verbal jiggery-pokery," the physician said sharply. "The fact of the matter is that the Great Man has summoned to his mountain fastness a number of his . . . friends? Acquaintances? Enemies?

Those assembled are to be examined by Mr. Chan—for reason or reasons known only by Mr. Frederick Scanlon, Esquire."

"I'm sure none of us meant—" Mrs. Bryant began in a bleating voice. "That is, we have no reason to—"

"Precisely," the doctor cut in. "None of us has any reason to surmise that Scanlon's physical or mental wellbeing has any bearing on this peculiar gathering, and I'm sure that when we all see him in the flesh—"

Chan extended a hand across the table.

"Pardon the interruption, please," he broke in. "Are you certain that Mr. Scanlon will welcome us to our destination in the northern woods?"

Collins stared at the detective for a split-second in mock disbelief.

"Surely, Mr. Chan, you don't mean to suggest that we are all on our way to a weekend without a host?" He shook his head, briefly awakening the more unruly strands of his mustache. "What would be the point of such a meeting?"

"That," Chan said softly, "is a question even speculation cannot answer."

Chapter Four

AN UNEASY REUNION

The train jerked into motion and slowly left the station. Some of the passengers who had sampled the chill air of the Albany platform during the brief stop made their way into the club car, and Chan spied a few familiar faces. So did his tablemates.

"By gad! Edna!" Dr. Collins rose unsteadily from his seat, extending his hand toward the oncoming Mrs. Scanlon. The woman appeared startled at the sight of the doctor, Chan thought, but quickly recovered her normal demeanor by turning round and snapping at her two followers.

"Miss Clarkson! Please don't crowd me in these close quarters—and mind the child, for goodness' sake." The child, Clarissa, and Gloria Clarkson were close—apparently, too close—behind Mrs. Scanlon. Unfazed by the unnecessary reprimand, Miss Clarkson took Clarissa by the hand and retreated to a corner table for two.

Mrs. Scanlon turned back toward the doctor and his associates. She grasped his hand with all the muted enthusiasm of an isolation ward visitor.

"Doctor Collins. How charming to see you after all these years," she intoned in a distinctly uncharmed voice. "How nice," she concluded, turning toward the others at the table.

"Mr. . . . . Chan, I believe?" The detective acknowledged the lukewarm greeting graciously, and the steely woman's eyes flickered as she continued to survey the party.

"Daniel! And—Muriel Bryant." Mrs. Scanlon's heretofore grim countenance betrayed some emotion, Chan thought, but her tone was brittle. "How lovely."

At last, Chan thought. *She Who Must Be Obeyed reveals a softer side.*

Mrs. Bryant crooked an unsteady finger and pointed at the seat next to hers.

"Edna, Edna, Edna," she said happily. "Come join us!"

It was, Chan observed, a reunion of sorts. He rose and sought to excuse himself, but his offer to depart was rebuffed.

"Stay right where you are," Daniel Bryant insisted. "Seems we're all bound for the same destination, and we may as well become better acquainted along the way."

Chan resumed his seat, and Bryant ordered more refreshments for the table.

For a few minutes, the conversation was general; the Bryants and Mrs. Scanlon brought each other up to date. The doings of the three and their mutual acquaintances passed in summary. The round of drinks arrived, and Daniel Bryant lit another cigarette.

The train rocked from side to side for a moment, and the group fell silent.

"What did you mean, Daniel, that we're all on our way to the—'the same destination,' I believe you said?"

Mrs. Scanlon's question was accompanied by a hard look, her unblinking eyes aimed at Bryant through his lingering cloud of cigarette smoke.

Bryant's eyes dropped toward the ashtray. Grateful for the diversion, he tapped his cigarette unnecessarily on it in an unsubtle play for time.

"Bless my soul," he exclaimed, more loudly than necessary. "Did I say that? Unwarranted assumption on my part, perhaps? I just thought that—"

"You thought," the steely-eyed woman returned frostily, "that this could hardly be a chance meeting. That I had also received a kind of 'invitation' (the word was uttered with disdain). That all of us, including this—Mr. Chan, have been summoned to some kind of ghastly—"

"Now, Edna," Dr. Collins said in his best bedside manner. "No need to look at it in that light. Of course, you have the right to see things in a slightly different manner than the rest of us, since—"

"You're right, Carl," Mrs. Scanlon hissed across the table. "I have the right, the reason—the justification for viewing the matter in any way I please."

"Edna, please don't—don't—" Muriel Bryant was quite pink in the face, but her inebriation only reinforced the plea.

"Don't what?" Mrs. Scanlon's stony expression softened as she turned to her old friend. "I don't blame you, dear, not even Walter. Nor you, Carl," she turned toward the doctor. "I should apologize for letting my anger show, but it can't be helped. The person responsible for my ill-tempered behavior is absent, and the very idea of revisiting the past in this public manner . . . it's galling.

"Excuse me," she said, getting to her feet and leaving the drink untasted. "I really think I would prefer to—to—leave this little reunion now. I'm sure we can reconvene later, when we *all* arrive at our destination."

Ignoring faint protests from the Bryants and the doctor, Mrs. Scanlon left the car hurriedly, gesturing imperiously to Miss Clarkson. The younger woman took Clarissa by the hand and followed her employer dutifully, if not enthusiastically.

Chan made his excuses and left the rest of his new acquaintances, returning to his seat. With names from Scanlon's list coming to life before his eyes he was glad to have some time to consider their behaviors. Perhaps he could begin to divine their attitudes toward the enigmatic businessman whose fear of death had brought about this strange odyssey for a Chinese detective five thousand miles from home.

He looked out the window, but none of nature's beauty registered. His mind was busy replaying the bits of conversation between his fellow passengers, the names on Scanlon's list.

First, he considered Mrs. Scanlon—the former wife of the man who, according to his memorandum to Chan, still considered her the love of his life. Yet Scanlon professed some doubt as to why she had left him, beyond her strong distaste for his business. Her demeanor and her exchanges with the Bryants and Dr. Collins indicated equally harsh feelings about the strange gathering of which she was to be a part.

And Scanlon had described his former wife's relationship with Muriel Bryant—or vice versa—as "friendly." Chan thought there was little real warmth in the two women's attitudes toward each other just now. Perhaps Frederick Scanlon's characterization was outdated or otherwise inaccurate.

Dr. Collins. Nothing in his behavior in the brief encounter Chan had witnessed smacked of a man still carrying a torch for his long-lost love. Still, such emotions often were buried deep, Chan knew from his study of human nature. Daniel Bryant—was some long-ago bitterness concealed well below his affable exterior?

Chan wondered.

Still much to observe and even more to learn, he counseled himself. *In time, what is concealed will be revealed.*

The conductor had returned to Chan's side with a gentle reminder.

"My instructions are to make certain that you leave us at the next stop, Mr. Chan," he said regretfully. "Wish you could stay aboard for the whole run to Buffalo, but you'll want to collect your things. We'll be arriving at Utica in just a few minutes."

Utica!

Chan thought of the Roman history he had read while attempting to fill in the gaps in his education. Utica was the great city of the ancient Phoenicians, of Carthage, and, before its slow destruction, of Rome. *Scholarly men must have settled here in long-ago wilderness of so-called New World*, he thought. The conductor had earlier remarked that the train was passing near Ilion—another name for ancient Troy—and that Rome was several miles distant from Utica.

I alight after a journey of five thousand miles at a modern city with an ancient name, he mused, *before the final leg of this trip takes me to a wilderness with, perhaps, more wild animals than civilized persons.*

The detective clutched his suitcase and followed the other disembarking passengers off the train and into the tunnel that led to the station: *Union Station*, a sign proclaimed.

Making his way through waves of humanity that seemed to ebb and flow in the station, Charlie Chan found a seat on one of a series of long wooden benches and marveled at his surroundings. He was in a great hall of marble walls and an ornate ceiling supported by dozens of marble pillars. The detective craned his neck; the ceiling must be forty or fifty feet high. This impressive structure reminded him of an old Roman temple he had seen in a photograph.

Chan thought it fitting that a place named for an ancient city of empire should construct such a magnificent place for travelers. The minutes flew by as the detective let the sounds of the crowd and its myriad conversations wash over him. He realized that he could spend hours here, just observing the passing scene.

A metallic voice boomed from a loudspeaker and dispelled any such notion.

"Passengers for Remsen, Forestport, Woodgate, Otter Lake, McKeever, Thendara, Big Moose, Beaver River . . ."

As the announcement continued its litany of unfamiliar names, Chan picked up his battered suitcase and headed toward the point of departure. The names of these destinations reminded him that he had arrived at a kind of jumping-off point. He had seen the California desert country and its snowy mountains, and the cities of San Francisco and Boston. Far from his beloved islands, he was now about to venture further north than he had ever been before—into an unfamiliar wilderness—at the behest of a man he had never met.

The detective glanced at the waiting train; it was shorter by far than the one he had boarded in New York hours ago. Only a handful of travelers were waiting to board this little train headed for the mountains.

The northbound train pulled away slowly from the gray exterior of the station. Charlie Chan looked around him at the other passengers. At first glance most appeared quite ordinary. He smiled to himself at this presumption. No doubt it was *he*, thousands of miles from his home on Punchbowl Hill, who appeared out of the ordinary—a strange figure to these folk bound for the northern woods and mountains.

Charlie turned from his examination of passengers to a genial conductor standing in the aisle. As he had earlier in the day, the detective automatically reached for the envelope with his tickets, but the official hastened to assure him.

"You're all paid up, so to speak—everything taken care of in advance," the uniformed man informed him. "Proud to have you aboard, Inspector," he continued. "I've read something about you in the newspapers. Not often we have someone of your reputation on this line."

Chan nodded, acknowledging the compliment.

"Reputation grows like pagoda tree bark—sometimes thin, sometimes thick," he remarked. "So ancient saying of my countrymen puts it."

He grinned.

"Newspapers also have been known to remove bark and cut down trees to print news," he continued. "For now, at least, bark remains intact."

The conductor laughed.

"Well, it's a pleasure to know you, that's for sure," he beamed. "And I'm pleased to make your acquaintance on a special like this—gives me a little more time to chat."

"It is perhaps unusual for a special train to travel this route?" Chan said politely.

"Well, it don't happen every day, that's for sure," the railroad man laughed. "And a very few of us are fortunate enough to be on this run, owing to the nature of this particular special.

"There's only one passenger car—the one we're in right now—and, I believe, nine passengers counting you," he went on. "The car ahead of us is for the crew and our gear, then there's the coal car and locomotive. Behind us—" he pointed toward the back "we have a club car and dining car, plus the caboose, of course."

Hearing the train whistle past a crossing, the uniformed man consulted a battered gold watch. "And it looks like we'll make it to Big Moose before dark.

"That's good for you, being a first-time visitor here," he went on, snapping shut the watch and pocketing it. "You'll get to see the last stretch in daylight—prettier that way."

The official departed as the train whistled its way past a crossing. Chan looked out the window in time to see a man at the reins of a horse-drawn wagon loaded with logs. It was the first person the detective had seen along the way for some miles; the train seemed to be bound for some earlier place in time, far from noisy humanity.

Chapter Five

ON THE WAY TO BIG MOOSE

As Charlie Chan had expected, the Bryants, Dr.
Collins, and Mrs. Scanlon's party of three were seated
in the carriage. The detective noted a few new faces in his
brief survey, including a younger man seated across the aisle
who offered a friendly look before speaking.

"Mr. Chan—er—Inspector Chan?"

The detective quietly acknowledged his identity, and the
younger man smiled.

"I'm Matthew Trenville—I work at the lodge you'll be
visiting," he explained. "The staff—well, it's quite an unusual gathering, a private party—and when we heard that
you were going to be staying with us, why . . . "

Chan smiled to put the fresh-faced young fellow at ease.
He seemed like a product of the countryside through which
they were passing, the detective thought: enthusiastic, rustic; a clean-shaven, fair-haired youth of about thirty just
finding his footing in the wide world.

"I am happy to make the acquaintance of one who is
familiar with the lodge and its neighborhood," Chan returned. "Perhaps you could enlighten me while we travel
toward your place of employment—my home for a few
days."

"Sure! Glad to trade stories about the ol' lodge and the
Adirondacks in exchange for, er—that is, maybe you could
tell me about some of the cases you've handled," the young

Trenville continued eagerly. "I'll bet there are plenty that haven't even made the papers this far east."

"Tales of past cases are what my daughter Evelyn calls 'old news'—meaning uninteresting for your generation," Chan smiled. "For the young, more current events hold greater interest."

"Not at all," the younger man cried. "Why, your exploits—your adventures over the years would make great reading material, or—or—Hollywood, the pictures. Say, people would love to see a mystery movie with some famous actor playing you!

"Anyway," he concluded, "I'd love to hear some of your stories this weekend—if you have time. And if you have any questions about the lodge or the area, fire away."

"To begin," Chan said, "it would be most helpful to hear a description of your fellow workers at this lodge. How many are they and what are they like?"

Trenville smiled.

"That's easy," he declared. "Not too many there, most of the time. For a fairly large party such as this weekend's, some temporary staff are brought on—local folks who can help with the cooking and housekeeping and so on..

"The full-time staff are just three. There's Zachary Clemden, the caretaker. Big fellow, quite a few years older than me, kinda rough looking, big beard. He's sort of in charge, more or less, because he's been there the longest, I guess. But really he's a kind of one-man maintenance and repair department for the lodge—even keeps the fleet in running order."

"Lodge on lake has multiple boats?" Chan inquired.

Trenville laughed.

"No, 'the fleet' is what we call three old flivvers that the lodge has collected over the years—they're available for guests who want to take a drive and see the sights. On top of everything else, Clemden keeps 'em in good repair. He's certainly a peculiar fellow, too."

"Peculiar in what way, please?"

"Well-l-l . . ." Trenville hesitated before continuing. "For one thing, he's almost a hermit. Keeps himself to himself at the lodge, for the most part, and in the winter he goes off into the woods by himself for months at a time. Supposedly lives off the land—he's a great believer in roughing it that way.

"Winter's usually quiet at the lodge, very few guests, so we get along fine without him," he went on. "Then, come spring, he comes out of the woods in plenty of time to get things ship-shape for the season ahead." He laughed. "Like a grumpy ol' bear waking up from hibernation."

Chan nodded.

"Then there's Ma Warren," the younger man continued. "I call her Ma—usually not to her face—that's just how I think of her, I guess, since she's surely old enough to be my mother. I don't think she ever had any children of her own," he mused. "She jes' seems kinda like somebody's ma—cookin' and bakin' and fussin' over a fellow to eat more. Anyway . . .

"Ma runs the kitchen and keeps house in a general way," he went on. "She hires and supervises the local help that's needed in the lodge, indoors, when things pick up in the summer. For this weekend she's brought in an upstairs maid to do the guests' rooms, a Mrs. Glas from Eagle Bay. I don't really know anything about her," he finished apologetically.

"You said the man Clemden has been at the lodge the longest," Chan interjected. "The woman, Mrs. Warren, she has been there as long as he?"

"I don't really know for sure," Trenville admitted. "Ol' Clemden—seems like I heard him say one time that he'd been tramping through this part of the country for twenty years or more, but I don't know if he meant the lodge—or just the country around it. And Ma, well, I asked her once why she had stayed so close to where she grew up, in Eagle Bay, and she said she was offered the position at the lodge by 'Mr. Clemden,' as she called him.

"So I guess she hasn't been there quite as long as he has," he reflected. "And that brings us to yours truly—not much to tell, in my case."

"You are, possibly, from this part of New York state?" Chan inquired.

"That's right, if you mean the part of the state that's not New York City. I guess you could tell I'm not from the city," the young man said sadly. "Not a cosmopolitan bone in my body, I'm afraid. Actually I was born and bred in a place called Speculator, not far from the mining that goes on."

"Miners seek coal there, perhaps, or precious metals and gems?" Chan inquired politely. The young man's personal history was more detailed than he had expected, but the detective believed that all knowledge could be useful in some way.

Trenville smiled.

"If you're thinking of doing a little prospecting during your visit, Mr. Chan," he informed the detective, "I'm afraid you'd be disappointed. No gold, or silver, or diamonds.

"Just one precious stone comes from that neck of the woods—the garnet," Trenville continued. "Biggest garnets in the world, they say. They call them 'Gore Mountain Garnets'—the big mine is not too far from where I was born. Mostly industrial uses, the particular type of stones they dig up there."

"Anyway, that's not what you want to know," Trenville sighed. "Any aspirations to take on Manhattan someday don't bear on the present situation, namely your questions about my position at the lodge.

"I went to the college at Albany and was graduated with a bachelor's degree in frustration, I guess you'd say," he continued glibly. "Studied business and history, but came away without a clear sense of—of what I wanted to do.

"Well, dear old dad put up with his undecided son for just so long, and then he launched my career in, er, hotelkeeping in the woods," the young man smiled. "Thanks to somebody he knew, I landed a job at first one lodge, then another. Big Moose is my third such, er, engagement."

"You are a newcomer compared to fellow workers Clemden and Warren," Chan commented. "What duties occupy you at the lodge?"

"That depends on the time of year, of course," Trenville explained. "But I'm by way of being Clemden's second in command. When he's there for the season, he tells me what needs doin'—keeping up the grounds and tending to what needs repairs, inside and out. A lot of carpentry, painting.

"Usually he'll have a kind of to-do list for each season, big projects and little, that he'll give me in the spring," Trenville went on. "He would rather spend time away from the lodge, 'tramping in the woods' as he calls it. So he's gone a lot of the time, and I work solo on maintenance and such.

"I'm also the front-desk man when the occasion calls for it," he continued. "Checking in new arrivals, answering questions, giving directions. Lots of folks want to take a boat or a canoe out on the lake or take a hike in the woods. So if they haven't visited before, they want to make sure they don't get eaten by a bear, for instance."

The detective's eyebrows rose.

"Large woodland creatures make meals of lodge visitors rarely—or frequently?" Chan inquired. "Consider this substantial policeman from far-off island as one of these first-time visitors who burns with curiosity."

Trenville laughed.

"Not frequently, not rarely—not ever, as far as I know," he said reassuringly. "Even Clemden has never said anything about bears giving much trouble to people up this way. These are black bears—not quite as mean as the grizzlies out west.

"The best advice I can give you is this: Don't leave any food outside where they can find it, and make sure you never get between a mother bear and her cubs."

Chan nodded and beamed.

"I thank you for your wise advice—same words of wisdom probably apply to other mammals, including humans.

"One more question, please," he went on. "You have, perhaps, some knowledge of the gathering planned at the lodge this weekend? For example, you knew that I would be one of the guests—can you tell me what you and fellow workers have been told about this unusual private event?"

"Not a lot," Trenville admitted. "Ma, that is, Mrs. Warren told me that Clemden got word to expect a dozen or so guests, but she didn't say who told him to get ready. Last time I saw him, he told me to spruce things up inside and out—any painting or freshening up that needed doing—because the bigwig owner had invited a bunch of people up."

"Mr. Clemden did not indicate whether the man with the 'large hairpiece' would also attend the gathering?" Chan queried.

"I guess I just assumed that if he invited his friends that he would be here to play host," the young man replied, puzzled at the question. "I mean, why wouldn't he—especially after going to all the expense for two days and nights.

"As for who the guests would be, I didn't hear anything specific about any of them," the younger man went on, "except you." He grinned. "That's because Ma had read about one of your investigations in San Francisco—it was one of those features in the Sunday paper a while back, she said. And when Clemden said this was to be a high-class kind of event, people of means and famous folks, some of 'em, he told Ma that you were one—to impress her, I guess.

"She was impressed, that's for sure," he laughed. "Told me to make sure of everything—including your room, one of the better ones on the second floor. Even asked me to oil the door hinges that were squeaking the way they do in old houses.

"She told me she's going to make sure that the food while you and the others are visiting is 'just so'—something special," he recalled. "She's a tremendous cook, and bakes bread, and cakes, and pies, and—"

"Please," Chan held up a hand in mock protest. "Too many foods for middle-aged detective would only increase already ample proportions. You must consume more than your share of Adirondack delicacies this weekend so that I can avoid enjoying them beyond reason."

"You needn't worry about that," Trenville assured him gleefully. "I always eat my fair share, but in this case I'll be glad to go above and beyond. For the sake of your waistline," he added hastily.

"Very commendable," Chan replied. "In return, I will share 'old news' of some past case when time permits."

"That's great," the younger man said abruptly, getting to his feet. "It's been a pleasure, Mr. Chan, and I'll be sure to remind you about that at the lodge. For now—I've got to be running along," he said abruptly, and strode down the aisle toward the rear of the carriage.

Charlie Chan smiled to himself. Like Trenville, he had observed Miss Gloria Clarkson with Clarissa in tow headed toward the back of the car.

Young man who pursues romance on a train could be one of those written about by the famous English writer of plays, the detective thought. *Journeys end in lovers' meeting'.*

"I beg your pardon—is this seat taken?" Matthew Trenville addressed the young woman he had followed from a discreet distance to the next car back, and Miss Clarkson looked up in surprise. She occupied a window seat, and the aisle seat next to her was empty since Clarissa had taken up residence one row back. (The little girl liked to pretend that she was quite grown-up and traveling by herself.) Seeing that her questioner was both young and reasonably handsome, she assured him that the seat was available—and that he was welcome to take it.

Thank goodness Mrs. Scanlon has gone back to the dining car to her 'old' friends, the young woman thought gratefully. *There's practically no one on this trip under a hundred, and here's someone I can talk to for a few minutes who was born in the same century, at least.*

These thoughts rattled through the girl's mind even as she automatically introduced herself and Clarissa, who ignored the two young adults importantly.

"Don't mind her," Miss Clarkson confided. "She likes to pretend that she's traveling by herself—very independent."

Trenville nodded and pronounced himself pleased to meet both of them.

"Are you going far?" he asked innocently, hoping that the answer would be 'no.'

"Only to a place called Big Moose," the young woman replied. "Is it far? I've never been this far north before, and I'm looking forward to seeing the woods and mountains and, oh, everything."

"Not far," Trenville responded absently. "It's not much of a stop, but if you're going to the big lodge—"

"Oh! Yes, that's right," Miss Clarkson exclaimed. "How did you know?"

"That's just about the only reason someone from the city, from New York, would have for taking the train to Big Moose," he explained. "You are from the city, yes?"

"Born there and grew up there . . . and I'm still there." Was there a hint of regret in her voice or simply a lack of enthusiasm? Trenville wondered.

Anyone so enthusiastic about gamboling through the woods in search of wildflowers would hardly be the right girl for me, he lamented inwardly. *And despite that character flaw, she is a nice looking girl—seems pleasant enough.*

"I've always wanted to live in Manhattan," he divulged. "Don't suppose I ever shall—some people have all the luck."

"Not exactly luck, just an accident of fate," she returned tartly. "A person can't help where they're born, can they?"

Trenville admitted that fate and fortune were no one's fault, and short silence ensued.

Nice looking, but probably like the great crop of eligible men who think that their fortune lies on Wall Street or elsewhere in the city, she decided. *Anyone who thinks Manhattan is paradise needs to go soak his head.*

Unaware that his head was a possible candidate for immersion, Trenville smiled pleasantly and attempted to make polite conversation.

She may not be my type, he thought, *but other than the little girl she's the only person under my parents' age on the train.*

Chapter Six

AN UNSCHEDULED STOP

After making its way up a long, steep grade, the train was picking up speed on the downhill side of a substantial slope. Late-afternoon shadows cast by the treeline were starting to darken the view for passengers scanning the now fast moving scenery.

The train screeched, slowing abruptly, and passengers were thrown toward the front of the car, while baggage slid from overhead racks. Startled cries and more than a few oaths added to the general chaos, and an unfortunate conductor tumbled at the forward end of the aisle and collided with the door. After what seemed an interminable time the train ground to a halt.

Charlie Chan had braced himself at the first sign of trouble and was unhurt. He stood to survey the situation.

The small group seated in neat rows—some talking, others reading, a few sleeping—had been thoroughly disturbed. It was as though a giant hand had grasped the car, tilted it, and given it one good shake. Chan was glad to see that no one appeared to be seriously injured.

Cries of relief and distress gradually subsided as Chan and his eight fellow travelers collected themselves and retrieved hats, handbags, eyeglasses and other items that had been displaced by the unscheduled stop. The conductor was quick to recover, and he moved rapidly through the car to assess the general state of people and things. To his relief, the only injuries sustained were bumps and bruises. Most passengers were also relieved—"It could've been so much worse," Trenville remarked—but not all.

The voice of a nearby passenger cut through the noise of recovery.

"Conductor! I say—conductor!"

Chan stole a glance at the speaker, a well-dressed man gesturing with a rolled-up umbrella. His dark topcoat and gray homburg hat struck a discordant note in a train headed for a less settled region. Of the nattily attired man seated a few rows away, all the detective could see were a goatee, pencil-thin mustache, and pince-nez with dangling black ribbon.

The man had half-risen from his seat and was waving his long, black bumbershoot imperiously at the beleaguered official. The conductor's uniform cap had been battered by its abrupt introduction to the car door, but his official expression was that of the long-suffering servant of all who rode the rails. He had seen and heard everything in the course of his career, and such experience enabled him to answer the umbrella-waver's question before he posed it.

"Trouble on the line," he announced laconically. "Trouble on the line," he repeated, walking steadily down the aisle toward the rear of the car. "We'll be on our way in a few minutes."

The well-dressed complainant snorted in disgust and looked around him, but all eyes were averted. Finding no one to whom he could vent his ire, he resumed his seat and looked angrily out the window. The umbrella he held tightly, as though preparing a defense against any marauding wildlife that might find their way aboard.

Chan thought the conductor's announcement both premature and optimistic. The detective was no railroad expert, but the chaotic stop felt like no minor incident. His face maintained its characteristic calm. *Fate settles all things, great events and small,* he reflected. *Even the arrival of a train in the mountain country.*

Charlie Chan returned to his reading. Several minutes passed. Murmured conversations from his fellow passengers were punctuated by an occasional mechanical clanking from somewhere underneath the train.

"Folks, could I have your attention, please?" The conductor had reappeared, and the expression on his face mixed frustration and resignation in equal parts. "Just a brief announcement—we're going to be delayed here longer than expected, so I would ask that you make yourselves as comfortable as possible—"

A few of the passengers grumbled, and the man in the homburg hat stood up and interrupted angrily.

"We've already been jostled about and delayed for some time," he pointed out, waving the inevitable umbrella. "How much longer will we be stranded in the middle of this damned forest? I have business to attend to!"

Scattered mutterings met this complaint, and more than a few dark looks were aimed at the umbrella waver. Chan observed that Trenville objected to the characterization of his beloved locality as a "damned forest."

"Now, then—please, just a moment." The beleaguered official held up his hands in supplication. "There's no good way to say this, so I'll just tell you what I know. The train stopped because the track is blocked, and we're waiting for help to arrive to remove the—er—blockage on the line. Seeing as how we're more than a few miles from the nearest station, it'll be several hours before we're able to proceed—"

At the words "several hours," more than a few voices were raised in protest. At least one voice angrily consigned the conductor, the engineer, the "blockage," and the entire railroad corporation to a much warmer and more distant destination than the Adirondacks.

"Folks—folks! I don't like it any better than you do, and I'm just as sorry as I can be, but we're just all going to have to make the best of it." The conductor raised his voice, struggling to be heard over the din. "When there's something new to report I'll be back to tell you the latest."

The noise subsided to scattered swearing and grumbling as the red-faced official, uniform cap askew, made his way through the connecting doors at the front of the car, and was gone.

"Beggin' your pardon, gents. And ladies."

A voice like the low growl of a bear pierced the silence. Chan and the others turned toward the sound coming from the rear of the car.

A heavily bearded man dressed for the coming winter stood tall in the dim light just inside the door to the next car. No longer young, he looked as though he had lived in the mountains for many years. Above his prodigious beard, his eyes were overlooked by shaggy eyebrows that had apparently never encountered a barber's scissors. Stray locks of unkempt hair peeped from his earflapped fur cap. From his worn brown boots on up he looked to be part hunter-gatherer, part hermit.

The rest of his outfit, weathered by many seasons of exposure, consisted of patched dungarees faded to an indefinite color, a once-colorful flannel shirt, and a full-length coat made from the hide of some animal. A pair of cowhide gloves stained from much wear was strapped to his belt, and the handle of a fearsome knife peeped from its sheath, barely visible under his coat flap.

"It's gettin' on toward nightfall, and from what the railroad man just said I'm guessin' that they won't be able to clear the tracks till tomorrow," he rumbled, his voice rising and falling to compete with the group talking among themselves. "All of you, I do believe, are bound for Big Moose Station—maybe you're stayin' at the big lodge?"

Several heads nodded.

"Name's Clemden. I'm caretaker at the lodge, and I know the woods here'bouts as well as any man, I reckon," the bearded man said flatly. "I'm not one for spendin' the night in a railroad car, and probably none of you is so inclined, neither. So if you'd like to join me for a little hike through the woods, we can make it to the lodge before dark."

This offer was met with a mixture of relief—tempered by skepticism from some quarters.

"How can we be sure you know your way around in this blasted wilderness?"

Chan turned toward the by now familiar voice of the homburg hat man. The little man had lost some of his earlier poise, apparently unnerved by having to choose between two evils: sleeping in a railroad car in the woods or tramping through woods filled with unknown terrors.

"How can you be sure? You can't," the bearded one grunted. "No such thing as a sure thing in the woods—in the mountains.

"Howsomever," he continued. "They do say time spent in the outdoors is healthful, and I'd wager a ramble through the woods would do you no harm. Looks to me like you've been cooped up in an office for many a year. Of course," he shrugged, "it's all the same to me whether I go it alone or—"

"Please excuse this interruption," Charlie Chan stood to address the would-be guide. "I am interested in the distance from here to accommodations—and the difficulty of the potential journey for those less able than yourself. Perhaps you could enlighten fellow passengers on these points before asking them to decide."

"Well, sir," returned Clemden, rubbing one side of his bearded face vigorously for a moment before continuing. "As the crow flies we're closer to the lodge than to the depot. See that rise?" He pointed toward the right side of the train, and a few persons looked through the windows at the steep hillside. "If we was to climb up and over that, we'd be there in a very few minutes.

"As to the actual distance I couldn't tell you for cer-tain-sure," he went on. "Some of the country here'bouts is rough, I won't deny it, but even those with fancy shoes should make out all right."

Leaving the little group to consider his offer, Clemden retreated to the club car, perhaps for some liquid stimulant. Intrigued, Chan retrieved from the upper luggage rack his topcoat—a gift from daughter Rose during his last visit to San Francisco—and joined those gathering outside the train.

It appeared that all nine passengers were willing to follow the woodsy-looking Clemden. A short line had formed with Mrs. Scanlon, the child, Clarissa, and Miss Clarkson, in the front, followed by Dr. Collins and the Bryants. The man in the homburg was pushing toward the front, umbrella in hand.

"Alright folks, follow me please—not too close," their guide boomed in a gravelly voice. "Give yourself and the next fellow—er, or lady—some room, in case anybody trips or falls," Clemden cautioned. "Don't want one of you to send the rest down a hill like dominos," he muttered under his breath.

The group had taken only a few steps before officialdom intruded.

"Mr. Chan—Mr. Chan!"

The conductor who had recognized the detective earlier rushed to the front of the line and stopped to catch his breath.

"Pardon me, Inspector, but I was looking for you on the train when I realized—"

The official gestured toward Clemden and his departing group, and touched his cap respectfully.

"The fact is," he said in a low voice, drawing close to Chan in a confidential manner, "that is, we have a situation, and I—the railroad—would appreciate your assistance. If you would be so kind—"

"Now, then," Clemden rumbled darkly. "I'm taking this gentleman and these folks to the lodge so's they don't have to spend the night out here. Seems to me the railroad can take care of its own without our help."

The conductor wilted before this hairy opponent, but Chan interceded.

"I am grateful to you for offering guidance through approaching darkness," he assured Clemden, "but my duty lies here." He gestured toward the locomotive. "Best that you lead this group to journey's end, and I will make my way to lodge in due course."

Clemden's face may have darkened in anger, but he was so heavily bearded and his woolen headgear hung so low onto his brow that it was impossible to tell.

"Suit yourself," he growled. "Rest of you, follow me. Like I said before, not too close."

Like a shepherd guiding his sheep, Clemden led the now slightly diminished group of eight up a hill and vanished into woods glowing in the fading afternoon sunlight.

The conductor was effusive in his gratitude.

"Thank you, Mr. Chan, for staying behind—very generous of you! We have an unfortunate—a terrible situation on our hands, and I'm afraid we're far enough away from official authority, from the nearest settlement of any kind, that—"

"Happy to assist the railroad company and its workers," Chan interjected mildly, "but please explain the need for this unofficial policeman far from home to help repair a stalled train."

The conductor smiled weakly.

"If you'll follow me, I think you'll understand why we need a policeman. Or a detective. Or maybe both," he said nervously.

"There's a body on the tracks."

Chapter Seven

OUT OF THE DARKNESS

The conductor—he introduced himself as Jacob Mc-Vay—led the detective along the cars, down the incline to the bottom of the hill where a few railroad workers stood in silence, smoking and waiting for someone to take charge.

"You have taken steps to notify local authorities of death?" Chan asked McVay.

"No, that is—"

The uniformed man's black boot slid on a patch of dry leaves, and McVay narrowly escaped an ungraceful fall down the hill. His footwear was not designed for hiking in the woods.

"We haven't—we do know what the proper procedure is," he continued, slowing his pace to avoid any further missteps. "It's just that we're some distance from the station, and the sheriff—if he's in this part of the county today—is a few miles farther away than that, at his outpost in Eagle Bay."

"Group that just departed for the lodge—perhaps one of your men could follow and ask the bearded gentleman to telephone authorities from the lodge?"

"Say, now—that's an idea! They can't have gone too far."

The conductor and Chan approached the little knot of men awaiting developments. McVay tapped one of them on the shoulder.

"Parsons—would you do us a little favor? This is Inspector Chan, a police detective who was on the train, and we've been discussing how best to get some official help down here."

McVay scribbled a note for his messenger, and Parsons scrambled up the hill in pursuit of Clemden and his flock. "Nothing about this run that's normal, I guess," the conductor continued thoughtfully, "a body on the line—that's the kind of thing that don't happen very often."

"Speaking of unfortunate deceased person . . . " Chan gestured meaningfully.

"Oh!" McVay exclaimed. "Yes. That is, if you don't mind?"

The conductor led the detective around the railroad men, exchanging nods with his fellow workers and performing a single introduction.

"Boys, this is Inspector Charlie Chan, of the police force in Honolulu—that's in the Hawaii territory, and he's a long way from home—passenger on this train, bound for the lodge at Big Moose Lake. I've asked him to take a look at things while we're waiting for the sheriff or somebody local to get here and tell us what's what."

Chan nodded to the men, who murmured lowkey greetings suitable for the circumstances. The railroad men stepped aside to give him a clear path to the thing on the ground. McVay handed him an old signal lantern that burned silently, providing enough light for the grisly task. The smell of kerosene was strong.

The body of a man clad in a herringbone tweed suit lay perpendicular to the tracks, the head and shoulders under the locomotive's leading wheels. Chan, lamp in hand, leaned in for a closer view to satisfy his assumption.

No one would be able to determine the dead man's identity by looking at his face.

"Can you tell—?"

McVay was keeping a respectful distance, but "who" was the question uppermost in all the men's minds.

Chan shook his head and returned his attention to the body on the ground.

"Unfortunate man's countenance would be unrecognized even by those he knew best," the detective said tactfully. "Still, it is possible to learn much from the body of the deceased—and, perhaps, from his clothing."

Getting down on one knee, he placed the lamp next to the body and spread a clean handkerchief on the ground. As his examination went on, Chan gently removed items from suit pockets and set them on the white square of cloth for future consideration. A closer, better-lighted view would tell a more thorough story than this initial exam.

Chan lifted the arms one at a time to look at the bare hands, which had a bluish tinge, for signs of aging. The well-manicured fingernails pointed to a man of means. The palms and fingertips were smooth and uncalloused by manual labor, but several of the larger fingers on each hand were discolored just above their knuckles.

Apart from the style of the suit—conservative, its lapels and vest indicative of an earlier era—the collarless shirt suggested that the dead man had still favored a detachable, probably celluloid, collar. That item, or what was left of it, was probably under the train, the detective thought.

Chan looked carefully at the body's loosely knotted necktie, its lower ends tucked into the dead man's vest. He examined the knot closely, comparing it to the one that secured his own neckwear—loosening one after the other and then retightening them.

Turning the ends of the necktie over revealed the maker's name—*H.C. Cohn, Rochester*—on the back. Chan replaced the remains of the silk tie as well as possible and turned his attention to the suit. Finally, the detective turned down the cuffs of the dead man's tweed trousers, finding only some lint, then looked carefully at both shoes. These were two-toned wingtips—a fashion choice favored by son Henry—of black and dark brown. Chan ran his hands over the tops of the shoes and shifted the legs enough so that he could see the bottoms of the fashionable footwear.

Chan turned toward the conductor and his coworkers. "Conversation with witnesses is necessary," he said to McVay, "would you be so kind as to introduce the driver of the train?"

"Hank Stedford, our engineer," the conductor said helpfully, indicating a burly man in denim overalls, dark cap, and workboots. "Hank's been with the New York Central for thirty years or more, all over the state. He is the—er—driver of the train—"

"Pleased to meet you, Inspector," Stedford grunted. He was not one to stand on ceremony.

"I am honored to meet one who guides this great machine over vast distances," Chan said formally, before launching into a stream of necessary questions. "To begin, general appearance of the body and its garb—do they seem familiar in any way?"

Stedford looked blankly at the detective.

"Couldn't have been one of the passengers—unless he sprouted wings and flew ahead of the train," one of the men said. The others muttered their negatives.

Chan persisted.

"Perhaps the appearance of this man's woolen suit is familiar—maybe worn by a passenger on previous train, today or earlier this week?"

The men shook their heads—they rarely saw passengers—but McVay's fellow conductor, a man called Reston, looked more closely at the remains and piped up:

"Could be a fellow that was on the downtrain a few days ago. Man from the city—seemed like a city fellow, anyhow—had a suit like that, all salt-and-pepper."

He shrugged.

"Hard to say for sure, but it could have been this—this—" Reston gestured at what was left of the unknown.

"Pardon my ignorance of railroad language," Chan said. "Similarly clad man traveling earlier this week—you said he was on the 'downtrain,' meaning, perhaps, 'down to lower country than mountains'"?

One of the men grinned for a moment before recalling the grim occasion. McVay interceded with an explanation.

"Actually, Inspector, 'downtrain' means away from the big city on the line—'uptrain' means the opposite—so the fellow a few days ago was on one of the trains headed north, 'down the line' from Utica."

Charlie nodded—he had heard 'down the line' already today—and returned his gaze to the engineer, who had been standing in awkward silence.

"Me and the crew, we—it's just the damndest thing," the burly man said in a choked voice. "Something you never get used to, a death on the line." He cleared his throat noisily as a similarly clad coworker nodded agreement.

"Enos Kauser, Inspector—I'm the fireman on this train." Seeing Chan's puzzled expression the man hastened to explain. "Fireman's the fellow who keeps the coal fire burning on a train like this. Got to have steam to keep the engine runnin', you know.

" Anyway, Hank's right," he went on shakily. "Terrible thing when somebody decides to . . ."

His voice faded away mournfully.

Chan nodded sympathetically and waited a moment for both men to regain their composure.

"Experienced engineer has perhaps witnessed other similar incidents in long career," Chan ventured. "The number of unfortunate persons choosing a train as an instrument of death—is it large?"

"I guess you mean, is it common for someone to—well, officially we just don't know," Stedford said grimly. "These, er, incidents, you see, the railroad doesn't tally them up as such.

"Me personally," he continued. "I've seen this kind of thing six times, counting today, since nineteen hundred and five. First time on this line, in my experience."

He paused and cleared his throat again.

"And, as I say, you jes' never get used to it."

Kauser, the fireman, offered Stedford a cigarette, which the engineer lit. He sucked the smoke into his lungs gratefully and exhaled it in a cloud accentuated by the growing chill in the air.

"Dedication of railroad men is well known," Chan noted reassuringly. "Passengers travel to their destinations in a confident frame of mind, knowing they will arrive in safety."

"Kind of you to say so," the engineer returned. "Nobody expects something like this to happen, and, of course, there's no way you can stop in time to—even when there's enough light to see—"

"Please pardon the need to pose additional questions," Chan put in, "but application of brakes—this happened when you saw something ahead on the tracks?"

Stedford closed his eyes in concentration, then took another long drag and exhaled before replying.

"I'm thinkin' now that there was enough sunlight through the trees, and that's why I could see him down at the bottom of the hill. Not movin' at all.

"But if we'd been on schedule, it woulda been nearly dusk—cloudy day like this, trees on all sides, I probably wouldn't have seen a thing and, well, wouldn't have tried to stop. But we were runnin' early—"

"Excuse this interruption, please," Chan said. "This was a train on the regular schedule, but one with a single *reserved* passenger car?"

Stedford ground the last of his cigarette thoroughly under his booted foot; there could be no ember left to ignite dry leaves.

"That's right—unusual arrangement on this line. I've known the railroad to run special trains from the city—New York, that is—up into the mountains, back in the day. But this is just the one passenger car, and fewer than a dozen folks on it.

"Anyway," the railroad man went on, "we were a few minutes ahead of schedule. Normally this time of year it's just about dark when we pull into Big Moose Station, or pretty near to it. And right through here, well, we might think about switching on the headlight—depending on the weather—anytime from this point on into the station."

Chan nodded and thanked both men. McVay removed his battered uniform cap and scratched his head thoughtfully.

"You're thinking that maybe this fellow who wanted to do away with himself was familiar with the schedule—that he figured he could do what he did and the train would pass on by without stopping?" The conductor's face displayed his confusion. "But if a man decides to—to—well, in that state of mind he wouldn't really care whether the train stopped or not, would he?"

Chan's reply was interrupted by a clattering sound from atop the hill in front of the stalled train.

Out of the darkness a small light pointed down the tracks, moving steadily downgrade toward them. A grinding, scraping sound grew in volume as a mechanical apparition approached.

"Looks like somebody's come to call," Stedford remarked. "Probably Teasdale's come lookin' for us."

"Teasdale's the stationmaster at Big Moose," McVay explained to Chan. The detective turned a quizzical glance toward the approaching one-eyed contraption. "Oh, that's a handcar, Mr. Chan. Hard to see it in the dark, but Jack Teasdale uses it to get up and down the line, usually for maintenance or—or—emergencies.

"Say, looks like he's got a passenger," the conductor remarked as the handcar stopped several feet ahead of the locomotive and its grim underpinning. "Well, now, that sure was quick.

"It's the sheriff."

Chapter Eight

"NOT SUICIDE. NOT AN ACCIDENT."

Sheriff Farley Fairden was nearing the end of a long and undistinguished career in minding the affairs of animals and humans. His youth and young manhood had been devoted to the Adirondack Wilderness (as it was commonly called then). He lived simply in a cabin of his own making, fishing, taking game and performing occasional paid tasks when the need for cash-money arose.

At some point he had become a fire warden, one of the hardy men charged with keeping a watchful eye on the woods during the dryer seasons of the year. And when some of the longer-serving wardens became forest rangers, Fairden welcomed the change.

No longer a young man, he had become sheriff of the county when the incumbent died in the line of duty. Although he lacked policing experience, Fairden knew the territory and its people. The job was offered, and he accepted.

"Fellow can't be chasing after fires and poachers forever," he wrote to his brother out West. "Being sheriff in this part of the country surely won't take all my time—I still plan on hunting and fishing and the like, whenever time allows for such things."

The pace of life and the relatively crime-free terrain under his keeping suited Sheriff Fairden just fine, and he relaxed gratefully into the slow pace of acting the part of local peace officer. He was not a very good sheriff, people said, but he was good enough for their needs.

To give him his due, Fairden had been an energetic fire warden and an enthusiastic forest ranger; but he was only a middling sheriff. That was the consensus of the residents who had watched his performance thus far with a mixture of tolerance and amusement. His once wiry frame and vigorous demeanor disappeared, replaced by a middle-aged paunchiness and a slow-moving almost bovine persona.

Like many men in the district he affected a beard and mustache, although neither even seemed to achieve full growth. His sandy-colored hair was streaked with gray, and in dress he resembled a logger or a hunter. A silver badge of office pinned to his coat was enough to let people know who he was, he thought, since practically everyone knew him by sight anyway. His habits, good and bad, were few; but he was an inveterate tobacco chewer. Sometimes it was hard to tell whether his cheek was oddly shaped or just hosting a plug of Red Man.

"Sheriffing in these parts," as Fairden referred to his duties goodnaturedly, was less like the work of a police official and more like the job of a nanny—a genial caretaker tending to the cares and hurts of people and animals. Interceding in marital disputes fueled by homemade "hard" apple cider took up a good portion of his official time.

When the representatives of homo sapiens behaved, the sheriff often was called on to address situations involving larger mammals. The region's wildlife surely outnumbered the human population, and occasional encounters of one kind or another could end in injury or death. Usually the four-legged participants in such incidents were blamed—but not always.

Sheriff Fairden had spent a good part of the day trying to convince the Kenderleys not to assault each other. Nelson and Gladys Kenderley ran the market halfway between Big Moose and Eagle Bay; "market" was an inadequate term for their establishment. An indispensable resource for residents and visitors, Kenderley's Market was a general store of the old school. In addition to staple food items the couple offered for sale everything necessary to survive in the wilderness, from gasoline to shotgun shells. Nelson dealt mostly in cash, but hard times had resulted in bartering—and whatever items he acquired were usually offered for sale at bargain prices.

Last spring, snowshoes had been sacrificed by some customers more in need of flour, sugar, and bacon than winter footwear. With autumn headed for the exit, last season's snowshoes were prominently displayed near the counter in hopes of quick sales.

Unfortunately for Nelson, Gladys was a hardy woman, quick to anger. A morning quarrel had escalated from words to blows, and the ready availability of wooden weaponry was too great a temptation for the angry woman. Born and bred in the Adirondacks, she could wield a snowshoe with vigor and efficiency, and only the sheriff's timely arrival (concerned customers had called him) saved the storekeeper's skull from permanent damage.

The snowshoe escaped unscathed.

Having restored peace to Kenderley's Market, Fairden was about to depart when the telephone rang.

Nelson Kenderley answered, but the caller wanted something more official than salt pork. Kenderley held out the receiver toward The Law.

The sheriff's disposition was known to be unusually prickly, but his temper surfaced only when provoked. His time with the Kenderleys had nearly drained his well of patience. He grabbed the receiver from Nelson Kenderley and dispensed with the customary official greeting.

"This is the sheriff, and by God—"

Fairden paused as the voice on the other end of the line started talking and kept right on going.

"Sheriff? This is Sam—you'd better get over to Big Moose, to the depot, double-quick—Jack Teasdale called. A VIP special he was expectin' is overdue."

***

Sheriff Fairden's timing was excellent. He had settled the Kenderley dispute about the time an urgent call had been placed from Big Moose Station to his second-in-command at Eagle Bay. Deputy Sam Hirner, knowing that the sheriff was likely still settling things at Kenderley's, had reached him there just in time.

The deputy explained the situation in a few words, and the sheriff replied in like manner.

"Call the station and tell Jack I'm on my way," the sheriff ordered, and hung up the store telephone. "You two," he instructed the Kenderleys firmly, "keep the peace. I've got better things to do than come back up here for the umpteenth time this month."

With that rough valedictory the sheriff departed for the depot, where station manager Jack Teasdale was ready with a two-man handcart. In a few minutes they were on their way.

Teasdale spent a fair amount of time on the station's handcart, pumping it by hand up and down the line for one thing or another, but Sheriff Fairden was no longer in peak condition. By the time they arrived at the scene of the incident the lawman was feeling his age.

The station master brought the cart to a stop ten feet or more from the locomotive. The sheriff, breathing like a man who had run a race, descended slowly and carefully.

"I'll be running this contraption on back to the station," Teasdale informed him. "No need for me to be pluggin' up the works when the time comes for that train to move along."

Glad to be on solid ground again, the sheriff nodded.

"You bet, Jack," he affirmed. "Thanks for the ride."

As Teasdale slowly pumped the handcart up the hill toward the station, the lawman approached the group of men. He knew the train crew, and matter-of-fact greetings were exchanged.

"Hell of a thing, this," Sheriff Fairden muttered. "Any of you know the man?"

A general shaking of heads ensued. Jacob McVay spoke up.

"Sheriff, this is Inspector Chan—one of the passengers." The detective stepped forward into the lantern light, and Fairden's eyes widened. A Chinese man in a topcoat and fedora—the sheriff had never seen anyone like Charlie Chan in this part of the country.

"I asked him to—to take a look at things, unofficially of course, while we were waiting for you," McVay explained. "Truth is, we weren't sure how long it would be before anybody could get to us, and . . ." The conductor trailed off as he realized that he must have violated some kind of law enforcement protocol by allowing a passenger—even one who was a police detective—to examine the body. No one was paying the slightest attention to his explanation.

The sheriff nodded perfunctorily, and Chan inclined his head slightly.

"So glad that an official representative of law has arrived," the detective said graciously. "I am merely a traveler bound for the big lodge. Happy to fade into the background so the sheriff can take charge of this case."

"Case?" Fairden's eyebrows shot up. "Fellow decided to do away with himself, didn't he? Money troubles or woman troubles or—"

"No doubt sheriff will wish to examine the body and personal belongings of dead man," Chan said placidly. "Taking a great liberty, I have arranged contents of unfortunate person's pockets so that you may collect same and examine them in the waning light of daytime."

Not knowing whether to thank or chastise the unfamiliar interloper, the sheriff stood silent and gaped at Chan for a fraction of a second. His mouth then closed with a slight snap; his dentures had been giving him trouble.

"Let's take a look," the lawman said grudgingly. Dead animals he had encountered many times in his career, but this was something new. The four railroad men kept their distance and talked among themselves as Chan led Sheriff Fairden to the locomotive and body that lay near it.

The sheriff's pallor escaped notice in the lamplight, but he felt a trifle lightheaded as he leaned over to get a good look at the decapitated corpse. Stepping back from the place where the man's head ought to have been, he crouched down next to the body to look at the items Chan had set aside.

On the detective's handkerchief lay an empty wallet, gold signet ring, a black bird's feather, and a railroad ticket stub. The wallet was plain in design and made of black leather, and the ring's face displayed what appeared to be an ornate rendering of a thin crescent with a small curlicue clinging to its lower stem. The feather was small and black, the sheriff noted, but despite spending years in the mountain wilderness he possessed no great knowledge of ornithology. The ticket stub for the New York Central line that served Big Moose bore yesterday's date.

Straightening up, he looked up and down the line as though searching for something, then turned toward Charlie Chan and the railroad contingent.

"Well-l-l," he drawled uncertainly. "I guess we'll have to wait on the coroner, but if it was up to me we'd load what's left of our friend here onto the handcart and take him back to the depot. Not much mystery about it," he went on. "Fellow from—well, not from around here, judging from his clothes—fellow from the city comes up here, probably to visit, to see the sights.

"Something doesn't go his way, or—more likely—things haven't been goin' his way for a while now, and he gets the idea that the world could get along jes' fine without him," the sheriff went on, warming to his theme. "Maybe he has no gun, or he doesn't like the whole idea of doin' it that way. Hangin' doesn't appeal to him—awkward business—and he hits on the idea of the train. Quick and sure, put an end to himself and be well out of things, he thinks.

"Checks the schedule first, then comes out here in the woods—not too far to walk from the lodge, maybe he was stayin' there—lays hisself down jes' so, and—"

The sheriff turned aside and discharged a cheekful of well-chewed tobacco, which made a small but unpleasant sound as it landed on the leaves.

"That's how I see it, but officially the coroner will take a look and make his ruling," he concluded. "That's the law—in the State of New York, I mean to say." The latter remark was directed politely at Chan. The sheriff thought the distinction necessary. *Who knows how things work in—in—wherever this fellow is from,* Fairden mused.

The engineer, Stedford, swore.

"Who knows how long it'll take for the doc to get here?" he demanded rhetorically, knowing full-well that the answer was, "No one." Dr. Manston was the local general practitioner and had served as coroner for quite a few years. He was not known for speed, except in emergencies.

"The fellow would be just as dead if you was to haul him to the station, I suppose," Stedford fumed. "But instead we have to camp out here all night, damn the luck!"

"Now, Hank, you know we got to follow the law in a case like this," Sheriff Fairden said quietly, almost soothingly. Mollifying domestic disputants on a regular basis had influenced his *modus operandi* in situations requiring calm. "Even in a case of suicide—"

Chan stepped forward into the lantern light.

"Please excuse this interference from one with no official standing," he began placidly, "but the victim did not take his own life."

Sheriff Fairden's mouth was open, about to receive a plug of tobacco grasped between his thumb and finger. He closed his mouth, licked his lips, and the little brown chunk of Red Man fell to the ground, ignored.

"What's that you say? You don't mean to tell me this was an accident, do you? Because if you think for one minute—"

"Pardon, please," Charlie Chan interjected. The lamplight shone faintly on the detective, flickering in his dark eyes. "Not suicide. Not an accident.

"Murder."

Chapter Nine

A PRECARIOUS PERCH

A woman's shriek echoed through the empty Great Room of the lodge, arousing a sleeping dog by the fireside. Shaking himself briefly, the medium-sized mutt trotted toward the main entrance and added his voice to the continued shrilling from the second floor.

"Help! For god's sake, help!"

This noisy duet greeted the little group entering the lodge after their hike from the stalled train. Leading the way into the room, Clemden paused to soothe the barking dog, Mischief (by name and avocation), then turned his gaze upward.

A woman of about forty, clad in a maid's uniform, was making her way quickly down the last flight of stairs. Her initial outburst had devolved into a sobbing, gasping hysteria that seemed to be inflamed by the sight of the new arrivals.

Rushing down the last several stairs she flung herself into the arms of the nearest man, which happened to be the grizzled and apparently astonished Clemden. The bearded man awkwardly patted the woman on the back before extracting himself from her grip.

"Now, then, Mrs. Glas, what's all this about?" Clemden employed what he considered a sympathetic tone of voice, but to the several former train passengers in his wake the result sounded like the growl of an irritable bear. "No need to take on so—see here?" He turned toward the small group behind him. "I brought you some guests from the train."

This information failed to quiet Mrs. Glas, who responded with renewed wailing.

"Guests—now? I can't! I just can't!"

"Can't what?"

"I always take guests to their rooms, and—"

The woman fell to her knees, sobbing and pointing up the stairs.

"There's a man—up there—he's dead!"

Clemden and the others looked upwards, but the stairwell was dimly lit. A few candles in wall-mounted sconces provided scant illumination.

"By gad, I'm goin' up there to see what's what," Clemden grunted, turning toward the newly arrived guests. "Any of you men want to come up with me?"

The man in the homburg demurred, but Daniel Bryant and Dr. Collins stepped forward. Clemden led the way up the stairs.

The flickering candlelight shone on a half dozen trophy heads, and their antlers cast weird shadows on the men climbing the stairs. The hunting lodge motif went further than stag's heads on the wall. Many-pointed antlers were mounted all along and underneath the banister from the bottom floor to the top landing. Clemden ignored the handrail, but Bryant and Collins gripped it for support and were careful to avoid contact with the antlered decor.

The three men reached the landing, and Clemden muttered an oath as he turned and looked up to the top of the stairs. Bryant and Collins struggled to see around their broad-shouldered leader.

"Come on, Collins," Clemden growled, as he clambered up the last several stairs. "This is somethin' you'll need to take a look at."

The doctor followed their guide more carefully—he didn't relish the thought of a fall at his age—and saw the cause of Mrs.

Glas's hysterics. In his long practice he had seen many grim sights but none so macabre as this.

Bryant gasped and gripped the railing.

The body of a man was slumped facedown over the newel post at the top of the second-floor stairs, arms dangling toward the floor below. Seeing a tiny stream of blood from the body and the antlers mounted along the rail on both sides of it, the three men came to the same conclusion that had sent the unfortunate Mrs. Glas shrieking down the stairs.

The dead man—for all of them assumed that he was, in fact, dead—appeared to have been impaled by one or more points of the newel post's resident trophy. The three men's grim assumption, if true, also accounted for the body's fixed position. Otherwise, it would have slid or fallen from its precarious perch. Clemden was first to reach the grisly scene, but he quickly stood aside for the medical man to render judgement.

Below, the wailing of Mrs. Glas could be heard faintly, but the trio was focused only on the sight that had set her off.

"Here—Daniel—can you bring one of those candles closer?" Dr. Collins gestured hurriedly toward the grim figure. Bryant complied, pulling the nearest wax taper from its mount and holding it at the medical man's direction.

Finding no pulse the doctor conducted a cursory examination, hampered by the inconvenient position of his subject. Looking closely under the body and at the railing above and below it, he examined the scene for a few minutes before turning to the two men.

"Daniel, nothing here is to be touched, and I want you to stay on guard here for the time being until everyone in the lodge is so informed—not just those in the main hall, but there may be guests on the second floor—"

"Understood," Bryant replied promptly. "I'm here for the duration."

"Good," the doctor returned. "Clemden, I want you to deal with the rest of the group you brought here while I telephone the authorities—"

"Sorry, Doc," the bearded man interrupted, "but last time I checked, it was out of order. Nearest phone is at Big Moose Station."

"Damn and blast," the doctor fumed. "In that case, I'll talk to the folks downstairs—and any other guests already in residence—and you, please, make your way to the station and telephone the police."

Clemden nodded.

"That'd be Sheriff Fairden, he's the law out this way," he grunted. "Could be a while before he can get here—I reckon he's still at . . ."

The big man paused for a moment. Dr. Collins looked at him expectantly.

"Well?" The doctor's inquiry barely masked his impatience. "How far away do you think the sheriff is?"

"I reckon he's either in his Eagle Bay office—or somewhere between there and the county seat," Clemden explained. "It'll take some time to get word to him, very likely."

"Then it's all the more important that you should be on your way," the physician said firmly. "And please make it clear to the sheriff that this will also be a case for the coroner."

Clemden nodded and made his way down the stairs and out the door.

Chapter Ten

THE LATENESS OF THE HOUR

A stunned silence followed Charlie Chan's pronouncement. Only the faint noises from the locomotive could be heard for a moment.

The engineer uttered an oath and lit another cigarette. The other railroad men kept their peace, realizing that matters were well out of their hands. The sheriff turned a shade of red that could be seen even in the dim lighting. Apparently his work resolving disputes had produced only a temporary effect, and his irritable nature was about to make a comeback.

"Murder—the hell you say! We—we haven't had anything like a homicide hereabouts for thirty years or more," he declared. "Not since that Gillette fellow made away with the young woman. Saint Peter's keys! We sure don't want that kind of publicity in these parts ever again."

"It put Big Moose on the map—and not in a good way," McVay remarked. "What was that girl's name, the one he—"

"Grace Brown." The sheriff nodded vigorously. "Anyway, I sure hope we don't have another situation here like that.

"Inspector—Chan, is it? What in the Sam Hill makes you think some damn fool would kill a man out here in the middle of—I mean to say, why go to all the trouble of murdering somebody by putting his head under a train?"

"Killer thought method would mislead railroad officials and investigators into assuming suicide," Chan pointed out, "since desperate persons have done away with themselves in similar manner for many years."

"That's all well and good," the sheriff blustered, "but how can we jes' assume it's murder—and not suicide?"

Chan gestured toward the body on the tracks.

"We both examined the dead man closely," he said generously. "Doubtless sheriff is pondering clues that I also observed. Two experienced investigators will reach the same conclusion—one first, the other later. But the result is the same."

"Er—of course," Sheriff Fairden blustered. "Jes' to compare notes, so to speak, what did you notice, particularly?"

Chan picked up the lantern and walked over to the body. The sheriff followed.

"Condition of victim's hands suggests one unused to manual labor, and the style of suit and shirt—missing detachable collar—points us toward a man of a certain age who prefers clothing that is no longer fashionable.

"You agree so far?" Chan turned politely to his colleague.

"Well, sure—I reckon no young fellow would dress like that, and his hands—I see what you mean, makes sense."

"Also note," Chan continued, "that some person other than the dead man has dressed him, probably in haste."

"How do you figure?" Fairden's skepticism was fading, but he needed to keep up appearances. The railroad men were watching the scene play out, and the sheriff knew his reputation was already shaky across the county. *If I'm not careful they'll be spreading the story around till the next election,* he thought, *that it took a Chinese detective to show me my business.*

"Note appearance of my necktie, and compare the knot on same to neckwear of victim," Chan said promptly. "Aging detective living on small island clings to past—always ties simple four-in-hand knot." He loosened his brightly colored tie for the sheriff's benefit, untying it completely.

"Compare with more elaborate knot favored by younger men—according to son Henry, fashionable wearer of same—called Windsor."

The detective crouched by the body, the sheriff leaning over his shoulder. Chan loosened the victim's knotted necktie to demonstrate the difference between the two.

"Dead man favors suit and shirt styles of bygone times, yet ties necktie in keeping with latest fashion. Also," Chan continued, loosening the knot further, "please observe closely the victim's tie, how its ends have been folded left to right to achieve the so-called Windsor knot.

"Now, please, watch this aging policeman tie same kind of knot." Suiting the action to the words, Chan began constructing a Windsor knot. "Note that right-handed man who ties own necktie always folds end of tie right to left—so!" The detective deftly knotted and pulled the tie into place.

"Dead man's tie demonstrates opposite method, left to right," he went on, "As father of eight sons I have had occasion to tie their neckties while facing them—and have done the same. Tying the knot from my perspective results in reverse of folded ends, just as in present case.

"This reversal suggests that killer put tie on victim after dispatching him," Chan concluded.

"Well, I'll be—" Fairden humphed. "You wouldn't hardly notice unless you was lookin' for it—which I reckon you were?" He eyed Chan with the beginning of something like respect. "It's like he was lookin' in a mirror."

"Inspector—not to butt in." McVay the conductor, fascinated by the sight of a detective at work, had been quietly looking on. "I-I was wondering, that is, I'm left-handed—and I tie my neckties left to right. What if the dead man was left-handed? Wouldn't he tie his the way it looks, same as me?"

"Conductor of travelers displays a keen intellect," Chan said. "However, other indications show the victim was right-handed. Right hand is slightly larger than left as is common with the dominant hand. Used more, it grows slightly bigger over time. Small callouses can be felt, little more than slight thickening of skin on fingers and thumb of right hand. These indicate dead man writes a great deal, probably with pen and ink. No such indications on the left hand.

"Placement of watch in left-hand vest pocket also strongly suggests right-handed man," Chan continued, "since custom and habit dictate that most men retrieve timepiece with the hand they do not favor—leaving the dominant hand free. Same with newer wristwatches, the right-handed wear them on the left wrist—opposite practice is customary for left-handed persons."

Sheriff Fairden appeared to be struggling to keep up.

"Let's say you're right about this right-handed fellow and necktie and the watch and so on, and so forth," the lawman replied, "but none of that proves he was murdered—does it?"

Chan nodded approvingly.

"Citizens of this county are fortunate to have sharp-witted sheriff with able mind," he noted. "Proving murder can be a difficult task, but we can start by disproving suicide."

The detective turned to McVay and the other three railroad men.

"How long now since this train made its unscheduled stop here in wooded area now shrouded in darkness?"

Both conductors—McVay and Reston—instintctively reached for their watches, but McVay was quicker.

"Less than an hour, Inspector. I make it fifty-seven minutes."

"Fifty-six and a half," McVay offered primly, "but either way, definitely less than an hour."

Chan turned to the sheriff.

"With no disrespect intended toward unfortunate man," he instructed, "will sheriff please move fingers of dead man's right hand to form a fist?"

Fairden attempted to comply, without success.

"Say," he exclaimed. "I'll be—"

"Please make further test," Chan went on, "and bend the arm of deceased—either arm—at its elbow."

Again, the sheriff tried and failed to move the body as directed. Fairden stood up, disgusted with himself.

"Maybe the folks in this county don't have such a bright-eyed sheriff after all," he grunted. "Don't know what I was thinkin'—should have seen that earlier."

"Old Chinese saying puts it this way," Chan reassured him. "Being late is better than not arriving. Now, we have arrived together.

"Stiffening of body that scientists call rigor mortis occurs bit by bit. Gradual process usually begins two or more hours after death," the detective explained for the benefit of the railroad workers. "If this man came to woods for fatal encounter with train, his body would not now be so rigid. Such a condition would not happen for several more hours.

"Therefore death must have occurred six hours, maybe as many as twelve hours ago," he continued, a grim smile rising to meet the occasion, "and since dead men do not march to forest to encounter train, some other person must have placed body on track sometime before arrival of train now delayed by unfortunate event."

"So you think this fellow under the train—well, what *do* you think?" Fairden was puzzled.

"Thinking deeply—this is something required for any investigation," Chan demurred. "Also, you may wonder at my appearance on ill-fated train. Same is due to private investigation at lodge that brings me to mountains of Adirondack fame."

The sheriff nodded, consulting a battered timepiece as the two stepped back into the lantern-lit scene. The railroad men were eyeing their watches as well.

"Well, I guess we'll see as time goes on whether your job and mine are connected," the lawman exclaimed. "But right now,

I know for a fact that my deputy called ol' Doc Manston right after he rang me. So he ought to be here by now. Unless he got held up by some emergency case, he'll probably be along any minute."

"Glad to hear it," the engineer fumed. "Maybe we can get to the station before dawn. Hell's bells," he went on. "We've still got crew on this train, folks that would surely like to see Big Moose before the sun comes up."

As if in response to Hank Stedford's angry lament, a voice from up on the hill hallooed.

"That'll be our coroner," Sheriff Fairden remarked, shouting in the direction of the distant voice. "Down here, Doc!"

A faint light bobbed and jiggled unsteadily as the doctor-coroner made his way down the hill. In a few minutes, Dr. Cletus Manston, lantern in hand, had joined the group. The sheriff provided introductions.

"Went to the lodge first," the doctor explained. "Thought the trouble was there—not out in the woods. No matter, though," he grinned. "I got there right about the time as some folks from this train were gathered outside the entrance, and they pointed me in the right direction."

Manston was a wiry old man, his gray hair and weather-worn face visible in the lantern light, and he might have been any age between fifty and seventy, Chan thought. The doctor moved with the vigor of a much younger man, and his actions were brisk and purposeful. He was protected from the growing chill by a gray woolen top coat and fur hat, and a dark muffler was wrapped around his neck. In one hand he carried the familiar black leather bag of a medical man; in the other hand, he grasped a long, collapsible canvas bag.

Stooping down, and then crouching on one knee, the doctor examined what he could of the body.

"Now, then," Manston said briskly, after several minutes' work on the corpse. "I'd very much appreciate it, Hank, if you could back your rig up several feet. I need to gather and bag what I can of the, shall we say, detached remains for closer examination in better conditions. Sooner you can do that, the sooner we can all adjourn this little meeting and get things moving on this line again."

The engineer grumbled faintly, but moved with alacrity. He sensed that the unplanned vigil in the woods was about over. The other railroad men moved quickly as well, boarding the train in anticipation of completing the run to Big Moose.

The locomotive grumbled and hissed as it slowly backed away from the body and came to a stop. Having fulfilled the coroner's request Stedford called down from the engine cab.

"Give me the high sign when we can get a-movin', will you Doc?"

The coroner replied with a thumbs-up and got to work.

Once Dr. Manston had completed his grim work, he and the sheriff loaded the remains into the first passenger car. Chan waited as the two men secured the unfortunate freight, and then the three seated themselves at a respectful distance.

"Well, Doc?" Sheriff Fairden demanded. "What's the verdict?"

The coroner laughed shortly before replying. He reached into an inner coat pocket and withdrew a cigarette case. Offering its contents to Chan, who declined politely, Dr. Manston put lighter to cigarette and blew a little cloud of smoke across the aisle toward the sheriff.

"It's a little too soon for a formal ruling, Farley," he replied. "You shouldn't rush this kind of thing, you know.

"However," he added quickly, seeing the sheriff's disgruntled expression, "I could venture an opinion—nothing official, you understand—"

"Nobody's going to hold you to it," Fairden said firmly, "and I sure don't see any lawyers on this train."

"Fine. Then it's my unofficial opinion that there's no way this is suicide, first—"

"So it's murder, then," the sheriff cut in.

The coroner blew a smoke ring that wavered in the dimly lit train car and rose to collide with the ceiling.

"Not necessarily," he countered. "Unofficially."

"Damnation, Doc—talk sense," the sheriff fumed. He stamped his feet—either in frustration or to ward off the frosty air seeping into his boots. The interior of the train had grown colder during the stop. "Surely it's one or the other."

The doctor examined the last of his cigarette thoughtfully before extinguishing it under his heel. Rubbing his ungloved hands together briskly, he turned to the sheriff and the others and cleared his throat.

"First things first," he began. "The body is that of a well-nourished man of middle age. There are no marks of violence on the body apart from the injuries to the head, which were, well—er—substantial.

"At first glance," he continued, speaking as though to a class of middling students, "one might think the impact of the locomotive caused the trauma to the head and, therefore, that death was immediate.

"However, a cursory examination confirmed that rigor is already well advanced, meaning, of course—"

"Stop talkin' like a medical book, Doc," he interrupted. "The body's probably stiff as a board out here in the cold. I'm beginning to feel that way myself."

"Eminent physician's examination confirmed what I observed earlier," Charlie Chan put in. "Well advanced stiffness—rigor mortis, in medical language—indicates that time of death preceded the arrival of this train on this spot by hours."

The doctor stared curiously at the detective before nodding in agreement.

"That's it exactly, Mr.—er—Inspector," he confirmed. "That fact alone indicates that the body was placed on the tracks. The condition of the head suggests the possibility that this was done to obliterate the true cause of death—a blow or blows to the head, for example."

"Does bluish color of dead man's hands suggest other possible cause of death?" Chan queried.

Dr. Manston looked at the detective with increasing respect.

"It could," he admitted. "Barbiturates administered in a substantial dose, for example. Need a blood test to be sure—too many other factors in play here."

"Such as?" Sheriff Fairden was struggling to keep up.

"Well, someone could've drugged him and hauled him out here," the coroner replied. "The presence of certain drugs alone could account for the discoloration of the hands.

"On the other hand—you'll pardon the expression—if he spent substantial time alive out here, perhaps alive but unconscious, the cold could account for it."

"Well, that sure sounds like murder to me," Fairden said stubbornly. "Somebody killed him, brought the body here, and laid it out on the tracks—hoping the next train to come along would take care of any evidence, any clues that might point to the guilty party."

"That's one interpretation," the coroner agreed. "A full investigation, hopefully, will determine whether or not you're looking for one person or more than one. For instance, we can't rule out right now the possibility that someone found him already dead and put the body under the train to conceal his identity."

The sheriff was an uncomplicated man, and he preferred uncomplicated investigations. "Why would anybody in their right mind drag the body out here to the woods so it could be—well, so it would end up under a train?"

"That, Mr. Sheriff," Dr. Manston pointed out, "is what you have to determine."

Chapter Eleven

THE GREAT LODGE

Big Moose Station was a modest affair, a small wood frame structure perfectly suited in size and character to its wooded surroundings. Charlie Chan alighted with pleasure, breathing in the crisp mountain air. The sheriff, coroner, and the crew followed.

"You'll be needin' a ride to the lodge, I suppose," Sheriff Fairden said to the detective. The remark was part statement, part question. "Glad to give you a lift there—it'll give us time to get better acquainted."

"My invitation to the lodge on the lake indicated transportation from this train station would be arranged," Chan replied, looking around. "Perhaps the unexpected delay of the train has caused a change in plans."

Seeing no waiting vehicle, he smiled gratefully. "Your kind offer would be most welcome."

"Oh, I don't know how kind it is," Fairden smiled grimly. "I have a few questions that need answerin'."

The sheriff's battered Model A pickup truck had been his faithful servant in these woods for ten years. He had acquired it while still a fire warden, and the rugged vehicle was well suited to the rough roads in his territory—especially in winter. Fairden hoisted Chan's baggage into the back, and opened the passenger door for the detective.

"Climb aboard," he invited, "and we'll be on our way."

The lawman peppered the visiting detective with questions on the drive to the lodge. Chan was mostly forthcoming, and gradually Fairden became better informed—but not completely satisfied.

"I would very much like to hear what you think of the things you found in the dead man's pockets," the sheriff persisted, jerking the truck's steering wheel to avoid an oncoming vehicle on the narrow road. Chan braced himself, but a collision was narrowly avoided.

"Damn fool," Sheriff Fairden muttered. "Probably some city fellow who thinks he can jes' run over anything that gets in his way.

"Now, what was I sayin' . . . I remember: What do you make of the things you found on the body? The wallet, for example. A man doesn't go around without some cash money or photographs or—"

"Or means of identification?" Chan grinned. "Uncooperative dead man unkindly fails to carry a piece of paper with name, address, and telephone number for detectives to find."

This unlooked for witticism earned Chan an appreciative snort from the sheriff.

"Sure would have made things easier, and that's a fact," the lawman replied.

"Anonymous leather container without contents suggests two possibilities," Chan went on. "Either victim wanted to travel unknown to all he encountered..."

The detective trailed off, his eyes revealing nothing of his thoughts. Fairden had no patience for additional mysteries; an unidentified body was more than enough for the former fire warden.

"Or? What's the other possibility?" he demanded.

Chan blinked and looked at the lawman.

"Or the murderer," he continued thoughtfully, "wanted his victim to remain unknown to us."

The sheriff scratched his head, or tried to; his woolen cap got in the way.

"I don't follow," he said gruffly. "Why kill a man and then go to all this trouble to fix it so nobody can tell who he is?"

Chan smiled grimly.

"The answer to that riddle is tied to the identity of the murderer, like the ancient Greek story of the difficult knot," the detective remarked. "Once one answer is revealed, the other will become clear."

"First," Chan continued. "We must untie the knot."

As Fairden drove along the road near the lake, the moon broke through the clouds and gave Chan his first look at the Great Lodge at Big Moose Lake. From the outside its sheer size reminded him of the Royal Hawaiian Hotel, but there the resemblance ended. Hawaii's famous (and quite new) luxury hotel was pink concrete stucco, a bright and cheerful contrast to the sands of Waikiki Beach.

Dimly lit by the pale moonlight, the old lodge that Chan beheld was a rambling affair of no particular shape or apparent design. A large two-story rectangular structure appeared to have been the builder's original vision, but wings and branches seemed to have sprung outward in almost every direction over many years. A log exterior and metal roofing brought some symmetry to the crude but homely edifice, true. But it was clear to any discerning eye that the builder or builders had grown and nurtured the expanding lodge like an arborist oversees the year-to-year development of some tree or shrub.

Charlie Chan took it all in. The side of the lodge that faced the lakefront was graced by a two-story full-length porch overlooking the lakefront. He could dimly see small watercraft docked on the shoreline and at least one proper boathouse. Near each end of the main lodge its few outbuildings looked as though they had been carved out of a forest, and the detective guessed (correctly) that in daylight the mountain foothills offered stunning views. Even in this half-light of a chilly evening, he was impressed. It was all unlike anything he had ever seen.

On the side of the main lodge facing the wooded hillside, an expanse of lawn bordered a small graveled parking area. As the two men got out of the truck, Sheriff Fairden led the way down a rocky path to the huge structure.

Through towering twelve-foot wooden doors, the lodge entrance opened onto a great paneled room with trophy heads of impressive size looking down blankly from the walls. At one end of the room, logs blazed in a fieldstone fireplace big enough to walk into. Chairs, settees, small tables—one with a chess set at the ready—appeared to have been fashioned from native woods. On a cold night it would be a comfortable and inviting place, the detective thought, but at the moment the atmosphere was strained at best.

Among the people standing in the lobby were some Chan recognized from the train—the Bryants, Mrs. Scanlon and her entourage, and Dr. Collins—and also a few unfamiliar faces. A heated three-way conversation was the loudest feature of the uneasy atmosphere. Mrs. Scanlon was loudly insisting on something to which Dr. Collins strongly objected. The third party, lodge worker Matthew Trenville, was attempting to keep the peace, but his efforts to placate both parties were falling short.

Consulting from memory Frederick Scanlon's list of invitees the detective quickly matched a few names to those in the room.

Surely the older man of calm and benignant demeanor was the priest—the Reverend Monsignor Leonard Plevna—whose inclusion on the list puzzled Chan. From the limited information Scanlon had provided, the detective wondered, what reason could this middle-aged man of the cloth have for dispatching his one-time friend?

The other man Chan looked at with interest. Here, in the person of (he assumed correctly) Scanlon's disfavored former brother-in-law William Yantzen, Chan could see the makings of a scalawag—perhaps a murderous one. "Brother Bill," as Scanlon had called him, looked anything but brotherly, the detective thought.

From his dark brilliantined hair to his fashionable two-toned shoes, Yantzen wore the uniform of the era's bright young men—a well-cut suit of some tan material offset the dark hair, eyes, and thin mustache. Chan thought he saw avarice and cruelty in the man's expression, ill-concealed by a thin veneer of pleasantries and cigarette smoke. Yantzen's eyes were hard—unsoftened by his insincere smiles.

Not far from the priest and the unpleasant-looking Yantzen, the detective saw the finicky man from the train—he had shed his homburg but still, for some reason, clutched a black umbrella.

This enigmatic individual stood alone, studying a framed map of the Adirondack region on the wall opposite the fireplace. Chan was puzzled; the man seemed unlikely to be holidaying in the woods at this time of year. Further, he corresponded to no one on Scanlon's list, yet he had been on the train with the others.

Chan filed away his initial impressions for later consideration and remained at the sheriff's side as Fairden interrupted the argument between Mrs. Scanlon and Dr. Collins.

"Folks—folks," Fairden began, and the room fell silent. "For those of you who don't know, I'm Sheriff Fairden—and this is Inspector Chan, visiting here all the way from Hawaii."

The sheriff would likely have continued the introductions, but Dr. Collins had other ideas.

"Thank heaven you're here," the doctor exclaimed, casting an unfriendly eye toward Mrs. Scanlon. "I'm Doctor Collins, and I've explained to these good people that we're duty-bound under the law to wait for you before—well, before disturbing things upstairs."

"Upstairs?" Fairden's surprise was apparent. "What things? What are you talkin' about, Doctor . . ."

"Collins. Carl Collins," the physician said helpfully.

"Well, Doctor Collins, it seems to me that I don't know as much about the situation as you do, so why don't you or one of these other nice people fill me in?"

"Say, didn't that fellow—Clemden—didn't he telephone you?"

The sheriff shook his head.

"I haven't been near a phone for quite a while, so he may have tried," Fairden explained. "Only reason I'm here is to look into a matter involving the train, the one some of these folks was on."

"Well," the doctor said briskly, "that's fortunate, because we have a man upstairs—murdered—"

"The hell you say!" the lawman exclaimed. "Take me to it.

"You folks—the doctor was quite right in telling you to stay put."

A few voices were raised in objection, and Fairden went on, drowning them out.

"Now, then—I don't want anyone to leave till I've had a chance to take stock of the situation. Mr. Chan, here, will keep an eye out—so don't none of you decide to take a moonlight stroll."

The doctor and sheriff climbed the stairs in silence, Charlie Chan watched the reactions of those assembled in the lobby. Mrs. Scanlon caught his eye and approached purposefully.

"Perhaps you have some influence with this sheriff, Mr...Inspector," she sniffed. "This whole thing is really intolerable, and I for one—"

"Inconvenience accompanies travel always," Chan said blandly. "The two are joined like a man and his shadow. But murder outweighs all other considerations."

Mrs. Scanlon stared at the detective.

"That's nothing to me," she replied coldly. "No one I know has been murdered, and I don't see why—"

"Inspector Chan!" Sheriff Fairden called from the stair landing. "The doctor and I would—that is, I sure could use a second opinion upstairs." The lawman had removed his wool hat and was wiping his brow with a dark blue handkerchief, and his expression was equal parts dismay and disgust.

Making his excuses to the callous Mrs. Scanlon, Chan mounted the stairs. The detective's eyes narrowed at the sight of the body on the newel post, and he looked to the sheriff and doctor.

"Death in the wake of death," Chan said to the sheriff, "like one wave follows another in a rising tide."

Sheriff Fairden's face reddened noticeably.

"What I need at the moment is a little less poetry and a lot more—a lot more—hell, I don't even know what in the Sam Hill I *do* need," the sheriff fumed. "Aside from the identity of the deceased, and maybe a few clues as to how he died. Oh, and the coroner. If I could have all those things, I would be satisfied for the moment."

Chan responded to the sheriff's tirade with a calm expression and encouraging words.

"Perhaps I can offer the second opinion you requested, and slowly—step by step—we will arrive at your desired destination," he assured Fairden. "Man may move a mountain one shovelful of earth at a time."

The sheriff was mollified somewhat by Chan's serene demeanor. He gestured toward the dead man invitingly.

"Feel free to shovel away," he grumbled. "I feel as though we already had this conversation, but Doctor Collins here has reminded me that we oughtn't to move the deceased until the coroner has given us the high sign. Fortunately he sent the handyman Clemden to fetch me and Doc Manston some time ago, so he should be here soon.

"Meanwhile," he said impatiently, "I couldn't see much or do much, but maybe you'll have better luck."

Chan leaned carefully over the balustrade, avoiding the nearby antler points and searching the body's pockets—as many as he could reach. From these he extracted a half-empty pack of cigarettes, a book of matches, and a wallet. With a little more effort he was able to grasp a gold watch and fob, removing the former from its pocket and unmooring the latter from the dead man's vest.

Stepping up onto the top landing, Chan handed the collection to Fairden for safekeeping. The lawman put the items on an occasional table that stood against the nearest wall. The doctor had descended two steps and was making a second attempt to get a closer look at the body's torso, specifically the site of any wound.

"I tried this earlier—you can probably see some amount of blood has stained the lower part of the man's vest," he declared, leaning precariously over the banister, "but I still can't tell if the death wound was caused by one of these—horns? Antlers?—or by something else."

He rose from his awkward position, face flushed with the effort, and stepped up to the landing. The sheriff and Chan were looking at the dead man's belongings, and Dr. Collins was reminded of some words the two had exchanged earlier.

"Say, what was it you two were saying about death following death?" The medical man inquired curiously. "And something about having had the same conversation before?"

"Merely quoting ancient philosopher's writings," Chan said hurriedly, giving the sheriff a pointed look. "Passage means that one death follows another constantly, like endless crashing waves."

"I was just recalling—er—that Inspector Chan and I discussed some of his cases on the ride over here," the sheriff said. "You know, murder scenes where the police have to wait for the coroner to show up, that kind of thing.

"And then, by gum, no sooner do we get here," he continued with greater certainty, "than that very thing happens. Here we are, waitin' for Doc Manston. No offense to you, Doctor, you've been a big help. It's jes' that we need something official from our coroner before moving the man—"

"The name, to be precise, is Walter Merriweather," Chan announced, holding up two items he had found in the dead man's wallet. "Happy to say that the printing on this calling card matches the name on his driving license issued by the State of New York.

"If you would be so kind, Doctor Collins," the detective said to the physician, "your presence below would be helpful to guide coroner here when he arrives—soon, I hope."

"Happy to oblige," the doctor replied promptly; he made his way down the stairs into the lobby.

Charlie Chan watched Collins descend, making sure that the doctor was out of earshot. Then he indicated a small alcove where two wing chairs stood next to a small marble-top liquor cabinet, the latter nearly dwarfed by a large fern that perched on its top.

"Time may be short before the coroner arrives," he said urgently. "Please allow me to share information that we should keep to ourselves for reasons that will become clear."

The two took their seats, and in as few words as possible the detective explained the correspondence he had received from Frederick Scanlon, including the list of names on which Walter Merriweather had appeared.

Sheriff Fairden gave a low whistle.

"So this big businessman thinks the people on the list he sent you have reason to want *him* dead, and now, here's one of 'em—jes' as dead as can be," the lawman pondered. "And then there's the other body." He stroked his jaw thoughtfully. "Nothin' to connect it to this, er, Merriweather, so I reckon they could be unrelated. After all . . . "

The sheriff trailed off as Chan held up a small object he had found on Merriweather's body.

A single black feather.

"Well, I'll be—" Fairden's jaw dropped before he could specify whether he was condemned eternally or of doubtful parentage. "Is that what I think it is?"

Chan nodded.

"This feather in pocket with Merriweather's wallet is the same in appearance as the one found on the body of the headless man on train track," the detective said thoughtfully. "One there, one here.

"Two feathers of a black bird."

Chapter Twelve

"THE PROSPERITY OF THE WICKED"

Charlie Chan gently extracted the feather from the wallet and placed it on the table.

"If you will be so kind as to place other example of plumage beside this one we can compare one with the other," the detective suggested. "It will present only a rough comparison, but *liǎo shèng yú wú.*"

"How's that?" Sheriff Fairden asked, pulling a knotted bundle from his hip pocket and spreading handkerchief and contents on the table. "I—er—didn't quite catch what—"

"Apologies," Chan said, grinning, "I have, as cousin Willie Chan says, 'put the foot in it.' Old Chinese saying means 'better than nothing.' Similar to what English-speaking persons mean when they say, half of one loaf is better—"

"'Than no loaf at all,'" Fairden chimed in. "Well, let's see."

Chan carefully placed Merriweather's feather by the side of the other and pulled a magnifying glass from his pocket for a closer look. He looked first at one feather, then the other, then both together.

The sheriff watched with interest, and Chan handed him the glass.

"Hmm." Fairden repeated Chan's examination; his skepticism barely concealed. After a thorough look at the two specimens, he handed the pocket magnifier back and folded his arms.

"Well, I sure ain't no bird expert, but they look the same to me," he conceded. "I'll give you that. But . . ."

"But?" Chan prompted.

"Heck, they could be the same kind of feather from the same kind of bird—a crow or a blackbird or a raven or what-have you," the sheriff grumbled. "And so what? Furthermore, they could be two feathers from the same damn bird—and that still don't prove the same party killed both men!" The lawman punctuated his conclusion with a hesitant slap of the hand on the table top, then looked up sheepishly.

"Does it?"

Charlie Chan considered the matter in silence. It illustrated a larger issue that he had been considering for some time, deference to local authority. He had no wish to take credit from the clearly beleaguered sheriff—that is, if the gods looked favorably on their efforts. He resolved to employ the same method that had served him well in the past.

"You are the sheriff," Chan said simply. "I am only a visitor, one who seeks to help without meddling. When someday the solution to this matter arises, to you will go all the credit—and rightfully so," he said reassuringly, thinking of a certain San Francisco policeman he had placated more than once.

"Until then," the detective continued, "I will not try to impose all thoughts and opinions on an experienced local lawman. It is enough that I share with you impressions of evidence that we encounter without muddying Adirondack waters with unnecessary poking. I will pursue my line of inquiry, and you will conduct the official investigation. Sometimes our paths will intersect, other times you may think me guilty of running after untamed water fowl."

"Well-l-l . . ." Sheriff Fairden considered the unusual proposition, something new in his experience. "I reckon what you're proposing will help get us to where we need to be, so it's okay by me. Sooner we catch whoever's responsible the better.

"Now, then," he said, getting back to the issue at hand. "What about these feathers?"

Chan shrugged.

"A point of interest, that is all," he admitted. "As you say, their mere presence proves nothing. I will consider them in my own time, and if you think them unimportant then you can probe other more important clues.

"For example," the detective pointed toward the body, "did you observe this Merriweather's fine timepiece?"

He pointed to the handsome gold watch and fob he had retrieved from the dead man's vest.

"The watch itself is old—much older than deceased person—perhaps a family heirloom," Chan speculated, "but the fob and gold seal that hang from it appear of more recent manufacture—note the variations in color and finish."

The sheriff nodded, although he could not see much difference. The lawman's interest in jewelry ranked well below his knowledge of birds.

Chan ran his fingers over the little seal. On its face appeared to be a reversed letter "c" with a small tail like a comma dangling from it. Opening the case with a gentle click, Chan observed that the watch kept the correct time. Snapping the case shut and turning it over, he was pleased to find an inscription on the caseback cover.

"'From M.R. to F.S. with love and affection,'" he read softly. The style of the golden turnip definitely belonged to the previous century, Chan reflected.

Sheriff Fairden pushed his chair back and stood. The sentiments of the long dead held no appeal for him; his interest was in the more recently departed.

"I suppose you can add that item to the things you're going to look into on your own time," he declared. "Right now, I would surely like to know when Doc Manston is going to grace us with his presence—"

"'Talk of the Devil, and he's presently at your elbow,'" a familiar voice announced. The doctor-coroner, Manston, had arrived. Chan rose from his chair and bowed slightly.

"Goodness gracious, sakes alive," the new arrival said jocularly. "I haven't even had time to look more closely at your earlier find—and here you are again, the both of you, with an awkwardly placed body."

Manston put down his black bag and peered up, down, and all around the deceased. Satisfied with this cursory survey, he looked expectantly at the sheriff.

"Well? You don't expect me to get this fellow down by myself, do you?"

Fairden was unfazed; he was used to Manston's grim humor.

"Thought you'd never get here, blast you," he replied with a straight face. "Can't get on with things till you give us your blessing. How do you want to go about this?"

The sheriff followed the coroner's direction, and the two lifted the limp form from the newel post to the floor as Chan stood nearby. Manston took a thermometer and a few other items from his bag and crouched down, aiming occasional remarks at the lawman as he examined the body carefully.

"You know, Farley, the voters will be disappointed in you if this keeps up," the coroner said, unbuttoning the dead man's vest and shirt. "I would venture to say that they are already perturbed, those that know. Two bodies in less than twenty-four hours! I can hear the bold pronouncements of other candidates already.

"Help me turn him over, will you?" Manston paused his political forecast while the two men adjusted the body as needed. "That's fine, thanks."

Taking a razor-sharp implement from his bag, the coroner slit the body's coat, vest, and undershirt from bottom to top in a single motion and pulled the ripped cloth aside in both directions.

"Ah," he exclaimed in an undertone. "Here, both of you," he said, looking over his shoulder at the two men. "You'll want to see this for yourself."

Chan and the sheriff leaned over as the doctor pointed toward an imperfectly round wound between the dead man's shoulder blades.

"Unless I miss my guess," the gray-haired coroner declared, "there's your cause of death—and sufficient reason for a preliminary determination as to cause of death: namely, homicide."

"Not so much blood on his back, though," the sheriff pointed out. "What there is, is on the front of him. What do you suppose would make a big hole like that in a man's back, Doc?"

"Very pointed, not blunt, and quite sharp," the medical man replied promptly. "I can tell you more after an autopsy, but it must have been something like a spear. Whatever it was went into our friend here with sufficient force that it pierced the base of the heart, rupturing the left or right atrium—possibly both—and played hob with the great vessels, the superior and inferior vena cavae.

"In short, it was a quick and brutal death," he said grimly. "And then the 'person or persons unknown' had the cheek to put the poor fellow where he was found."

Manston and the sheriff rose, and the coroner replaced his instruments in the black bag. Chan remained kneeling by the dead man's side, looking more closely at the face and hands.

"The only other thing I can tell you for the moment," the coroner said, picking up his black bag, "is that there's practically no sign of rigor coming on. That and the temperature of the body indicate that this fellow breathed his last a very few hours ago."

He consulted his watch.

"This is just an estimate," he went on, "but it wouldn't surprise me if he died just about the time the three of us were out in the woods tending to—I don't suppose we know *his* name yet, do we? I mean, the fellow whose head I need to examine—what's left of it, anyway. For that matter, how about this one? Does *he* have a name?"

"Walter Merriweather," the sheriff replied absently. "Not from around here."

Charlie Chan stood up slowly, a thoughtful expression on his face.

"Autopsy will include tests for various toxic substances?" he inquired. "I raise the issue because such procedures are perhaps not standard for all post mortem examinations."

The old physician looked closely at Chan and nodded.

"Not standard—that's right," he replied. "Unless we suspect some other contributing factor—apart from the primary cause of death. You have a suggestion to make?"

The detective indicated Sheriff Fairden before replying.

"Only an unofficial suggestion," Chan emphasized. "Formal request would come from the sheriff."

The lawman nodded his approval, and Chan gestured toward the body.

"Large wound in the back attracted our combined attention," the detective said apologetically. "So much so that I almost failed to see what doctor surely observed—curious color of dead man's lips and tips of fingers under the nails."

Manston stared at Chan for a moment, then knelt quickly by the body and confirmed the detective's observation.

"Pale, almost blue—certainly indicative of cyanosis," he muttered. "Possibly due to phenobarbital dosage well above recommended levels."

He got to his feet again, and pursed his lips.

"Well, I'm damned," the doctor-coroner declared. "Thank you, Mr. Chan, for teaching me my business. Maybe I am getting old after all."

"Wisdom comes with age to one so experienced," the detective said warmly. "Myself, I am a suspicious policeman who looks for the worst possible indications at every opportunity."

Manston laughed.

"Inspector, I think Sheriff Fairden is fortunate that you came to visit when you did," he beamed, looking at the local lawman. "And Farley, if Mr. Chan has any more 'suggestions' I'd take him up on them, for damned sure.

"And yes, we'll test for drugs in this fellow's system and let you know the results," he said. "One last thing, Sheriff—"

"What's that?" Fairden replied as the coroner headed down the stairs.

Manston stopped and turned his face upward. His eyes twinkled.

"Try not to let anyone else get killed for a day or two," he deadpanned, "so I can get caught up."

In the lobby of the big lodge, Matthew Trenville did what he could to soothe the restive little gathering. From the maid's first shriek to the sheriff's instructions, the word "murder" had done its work. A stony silence prevailed as those in the room exchanged suspicious glances. Trenville, ever the lodge host, served refreshments from a massive corner hutch that boasted a wide selection of strong drink. His first two grateful customers were the man Chan had identified as a likely scalawag and an older man in clerical garb.

"Pax vobis, Monsignor," William Yantzen said mockingly, raising his glass. "You'll pardon me for speaking English, but I'm afraid 'peace to you' constitutes the whole of my Latin. How—er—nice to see you again after all this time."

"William." Monsignor Plevna's face was expressionless. "You'll excuse me if I don't engage in idle banter, given the unfortunate circumstances."

"Suit yourself," said Yantzen brusquely. "If someone's gone and got himself killed, that's no concern of mine. Since you didn't inquire after my health, let me assure you that I am, in fact, prospering. I believe there's something in your good book about the 'prosperity of the wicked,' and the author may have had me in mind."

The priest, a portly man with graying hair gathered thinly across his scalp, stared at the younger man.

"Old Testament," the ecclesiastic said absently, looking around the room. "I think you may be right, but you may recall that even the Evil One himself quoted scripture. In your case . . . ." Plevna pointedly left his thought unarticulated.

Yantzen smiled thinly, his tight-lipped expression conveying contempt.

"Indeed." He paused before answering. "'He that is without sin among you, let him cast the first stone.' One of my favorite bits of biblical doggerel; perhaps you're familiar with it.

"However," Yantzen went on breezily, "let's not speak of murder and ancient fiction—such dreary things! Am I correct in assuming, Reverend Father, that you are or have been acquainted in some way with my famed brother-in-law, Frederick? Or is it mere coincidence that you and I have arrived in this rustic locale—along with my sister and these other fine folk?"

The priest examined the contents of his glass. The amber liquid's remaining ice cubes were slowly melting.

"Oh, Fred and I knew each other quite some time ago," he said, looking up at the younger man. "In fact, my first assignment after ordination was in this—what did you call it?—'rustic locale.'"

Yantzen looked at the priest with renewed interest.

"Hmm." He lit a cigarette and blew a stream of smoke toward the crackling fire. "Then if you're old cronies, perhaps you can shed some light on Fred's letter of invitation—I assume you got one, too—and its meaning?"

"Meaning is a slippery subject," the priest hedged. "Even a plainly worded communication finds itself parsed in different ways by sender and recipient."

"Don't go all jesuitical on me," snapped the younger man. "Either you know why we're all here or you have a fairly good idea. Well?"

"I haven't the faintest, vaguest notion," Monsignor Plevna said serenely, "and as for the Jesuits and their ways—well, I'm a Franciscan. A thirsty one," he added, "who must leave you now to refill my glass.

"Oh, and one other thing, William," said the monsignor, looking for a member—any member—of the lodge staff. "About the verse you mentioned?"

"What of it?" Yantzen said with a sneer. "Should I begin repenting now—just when things are going along so well?"

"Better not to wait too long," the priest replied. "You forgot the rest of that particular passage, which is: 'The prosperity of the wicked shall be but for a short time.'"

"No heavenly reward, I assume?"

"Highly unlikely, I would say," the priest replied. "Let me see, I'm trying to recall precisely what was written about them—the evildoers, I mean. I'm thinking of a particular translation, you see, one that pointed out that we needn't worry about the likes of you."

"And why not, may I ask?" Yantzen asked jeeringly. "Are we fated to turn aside from the error of our ways?"

"Not exactly, William," the monsignor said as he walked away. "The verse describes rather a different outcome, one that explains why the prosperity of the wicked only lasts a short time.

"'Because the wicked shall perish.'"

Chapter Thirteen

STARTLING NEWS

On the other side of the room Mrs. Scanlon was comparing notes with the Bryants. She had just dispatched Miss Clarkson and her charge, Clarissa, to the kitchen to amuse themselves as best they could.

"Well, whatever induced Fred to invite this little group here," Daniel Bryant ventured, "I can't imagine that it could have anything to do with—with murder—"

"I'm sure that he will explain things when he arrives," Mrs. Scanlon interrupted rudely. "My former husband—well, he's always been good at explaining things."

"Oh, Edna—murder?" Muriel Bryant interjected somberly. "Surely not.

"Anyway," she continued, nodding toward the stairs, "here comes Mr. Chan. Perhaps we'll learn something new about this situation."

The detective, followed by the coroner and sheriff, came down the stairs. Fairden held up an arm and addressed the room.

"Folks—folks, if I could have your attention, please." The room fell silent except for the crackling and hissing of the wood fire. The sheriff cleared his throat and began.

"I'm Sheriff Fairden, and I know that those of you who are staying here are anxious to get settled in your rooms," he acknowledged. "Want you to know that we'll make that happen as soon as possible."

This was met with a low murmur of approval, but the sheriff wasn't done.

"I will have to ask for your patience just a little bit longer, and your cooperation as well." The murmur continued, but an undercurrent of discontent was now noticeable.

"Some of you may have exchanged a few words with Mrs. Glas, who works here at the lodge," the sheriff went on. "She was the one who discovered the body upstairs—quite a shock, as I'm sure you can understand.

"Now, you may as well know right now," the lawman said, "that we've got a serious situation on our hands. A man has been murdered, and that's just the half of it." Chan listened with interest. He guessed what the sheriff was about to say, and the detective was intrigued by the prospect of observing so many reactions to such startling news, all at once.

"Here's the long and the short of it," Fairden continued. "*Two* men are dead. The one you know about, upstairs. The other one, out in the woods. One or both of 'em was murdered."

The stunned room was now so quiet it was as though the fire itself had ceased to crackle. Chan looked around to see if he could discern an unusual reaction: a look, a gesture—anything that might betray some guilty thought or emotion.

Expressions of shock, dismay, distress—nothing that he saw appeared helpful.

"That's why we've been keepin' you downstairs here," the sheriff went on, gesturing toward his two colleagues, "so's Doctor Manston, our coroner, could examine the body. Also, some of you have met Inspector Chan of the Hawaii police. He was on the train on his way here, and he's helping with the investigation. Mr. Chan and I will be talking to each of you, and I'm sure that—with your cooperation—we'll get to the bottom of this unfortunate—"

"Surely this can have nothing whatever to do with those of us who were actually on the train," an imperious voice declared. Chan was not surprised to see Mrs. Scanlon declaiming from the far side of the room, her gloved hand upraised with a forefinger aimed at the sheriff. "Why should we have to answer a lot of questions when none of us—obviously—could have been involved in either of these, er, gentlemen's deaths?"

The sheriff returned the woman's glare with one of his own.

"The answer to that is simple," he replied firmly. "We've only identified one of the men, and we're at the stage of this investigation where we jes' don't know what we don't know. Can't rule anybody out at this stage, and as the law in this county I'm duty bound to do as I see fit to make sure that the guilty party or parties is brought to justice.

"Again, I appreciate your patience and cooperation, and as soon as—"

Mrs. Scanlon's attempt to inflict another question on the sheriff was interrupted by the loud opening of the main door. Zachary Clemden entered and beckoned to the sheriff; the two stepped just outside the doorway.

"Since they called for Doc Manston here," the big bearded man said quietly, "I'm guessin' you might need help with—" Clemden jerked his head in the general direction of the second floor. "I've got the old truck outside, and I can draft that boy Trenville to help me."

Before the lawman could answer, Charlie Chan interjected.

"The idea is an excellent one," he agreed. "While preparations are made for removal, I suggest that sheriff and I examine the vicinity of the body's unusual resting place. The dead man," Chan pointed out, "did not land at the top of stairs without some assistance."

Sheriff Fairden nodded, and looked relieved. From his experience in the woods he knew Chan's keen eyes saw things that escaped him, and he wanted to restore the lodge and its guests to normal as soon as possible. Also, Clemden's offer was a welcome solution to an unpleasant problem. The rural county's meager budget made no provision for transporting murder victims on short notice, so volunteers were something of a necessity.

Clemden may be a little off kilter, the sheriff thought gratefully, *but he's a reliable old cuss.*

Mary Roberts worried. At school, at home, and here—in Mrs. Warren's kitchen at the lodge—she fretted most of all.

A pleasant girl with a simple nature, Mary was eager to help—but prone to error. Her tendency to do the wrong thing was the chief source of her perturbations. The occasional work she did at the lodge was her first such experience, and she wanted to do well. Even as the expected group of travelers arrived at the lodge, she was doing her best to be helpful in the kitchen.

But Mrs. Warren was not easy to please.

"Mary! For heaven's sake!" The cook's outburst was so sudden, so unexpected. "Where's the sugar I asked you for five minutes ago?" The startled girl dropped the small tin she had found in the pantry. Mrs. Warren stooped quickly and picked up the little container bearing the name of a well-known manufacturer and the words, "Mother's Best Pure Cane Sugar."

The cook's wrath departed as quickly as it had arrived.

"Silly girl—where's the open container? This one's brand-new!"

Mary appeared near tears.

"That's what took me so long," she replied through trembling lips. "The open container—the little glass jar—I couldn't find it."

"Couldn't find it?" Mrs. Warren's wrath simmered. "Why, that was the last of the confectioner's sugar from Lister's. I was keepin' it for—oh, never mind.

"Tell me, now," she continued suspiciously. "You haven't been dipping into it, have you? Such a sweet tooth you have!"

"No ma'am," the girl said emphatically. "I wouldn't think of such a thing. Shall I stir the batter?"

"Never you mind the batter," the older woman said sharply. "Leave that to me! You'd best be tendin' to—"

"Something smells good—what's for supper?"

Mrs. Warren turned toward the impertinent voice of Miss Gloria Clarkson, who was leading by the hand the girl, Clarissa.

"And how may I help you?" The cook's voice was gruff but polite; lodge guests were to be treated with every courtesy, Mr. Clemden always said.

"Well, I'm Gloria, and this is Miss Clarissa, and we've just arrived," the young woman said brightly. "Truth is," she continued, "Clarissa's—er—guardian asked me to take her away from the big room—they're talking over important matters, things a young lady doesn't need to hear."

"What things?" Clarissa inquired suspiciously. "And I'm not that young. I'm seven."

"Now, dear, you're six—"

"Seven!"

"—and whatever the adults are discussing out there is none of your concern," Miss Clarkson said firmly. "As I was saying, we were told to go to the kitchen because we might be able to help."

"Lord have mercy!" Mrs. Warren was not a praying woman, but at the thought of more youthful "help" in her kitchen, she wondered how she had offended the Deity.

"Here, Mary—this is a good job for you. Take our guests into the back room by the pantry and play find the thimble with the young miss. Go on, now!"

Mary led Miss Clarkson and Clarissa out of the big kitchen into a little hallway that accessed both the walk-in pantry and a work room. The latter served as storage for household cleaning supplies, tools, and other miscellany. In its center stood a large rectangular table for work and play—the perfect spot for staff or visitors looking to while away a rainy afternoon with a game of checkers.

With the peace of her kitchen restored, Mrs. Warren sighed. Often, the kitchen was her world, and sometimes the wider world was her kitchen—one in which she tried new recipes, variations on old themes. At present she had retreated into the relative serenity of overseeing victuals for this visiting party.

Hers had not been an easy life, but nothing could deter her for long. It was rumored that she had fallen in love as a younger woman, but the relationship had foundered more than a decade ago. Where things stood now she could not be certain, but she was determined to set things to rights, to overcome the remaining obstacles in her personal life—just as she had conquered culinary challenges, from egg custards to pie crusts.

Mrs. Warren looked up from her work and caught a glimpse of her reflection in the sterling tray mounted on the wall. She rubbed away a smudge of flour on her nose and considered. She had left behind her "first bloom of womanhood," as the novels of her youth had delicately put it. *Still and all, not a bad-looking lass—and not yet forty*, she mused. *Plenty of life left in this old girl, whatever comes.*

She wiped her hands on a dish towel absentmindedly and looked out the window for signs of Clemden. *Damn the man,* she thought impatiently, *precious little caretaking he's done for someone who's supposed to be the lodge caretaker.*

Mrs. Warren's attitude toward Clemden was apparent to anyone who spent more than five minutes at the lodge. Visitors, guests, occasional part-time workers could attest that she had no use for him.

He, in turn, avoided her and the kitchen at all costs—when he was around. Since his quarters were in a little cabin some distance from the main lodge, "*Mister* Clemden" (as Mrs. Warren scornfully called him) was able to keep well shy of the short-tempered cook.

To everyone else on the property Clemden was gruff but decent enough. Folks from Eagle Bay to Big Moose and their environs who encountered him thought him a rough-and-ready fellow—the kind of man you'd want along if you were stranded along the Seward Range, away up north in the Adirondack High Peaks.

He could talk about the woods and wilderness of the mountainous region when the mood struck, but most of the time he was silent. Mrs. Warren was one of many topics about which he said nothing, and the reasons for her dislike of the big bearded man remained unknown.

Turning her attention from the window to the comestibles she had prepared, Mrs. Warren called to her temporary help.

"Mary—Mary Roberts! Come into the kitchen and leave the young ladies to amuse themselves," the cook called. Mary came running, and Mrs. Warren pointed to two trays of small plates, and an array of locally made cheeses and the last of the season's summer sausage.

"Take one of those trays into the gathering and see if anyone's interested in a nibble," the cook directed. "Mind you, offer them a small plate from the front of the tray if they look hungry. I'll be right behind you, and we'll recruit young Master Trenville to serve up some liquid refreshment for our travelers."

Mary nodded nervously; it was her first such experience. She was worried.

Having failed twice at conversing with a young woman, Trenville glumly helped Clemden with his grim task, and the caretaker drove off to deliver the body to Doc Manston's office and makeshift morgue in Eagle Bay. Trenville retreated to the kitchen. *Perhaps*, he thought, *a quiet drink and a cigarette is what I need.*

The young man prepared to put his thoughts into action, when a sharp cry came to his ears.

"Cheater! You always cheat!"

Deducing correctly the identity of the accuser from her childish voice, Trenville approached the work room where he found Clarissa confronting Miss Clarkson over a checkerboard.

"Now, Clarissa," the young woman cautioned. "It's not ladylike to shout and call names. I'll have to tell Mrs. Scanlon about your behavior. You've won five games, and I've won two—"

"You don't play fair," the girl said accusingly. "You keep changing the rules on me. Anyway, I don't have to mind you because you're not my mother—and neither is that Mrs. Scanlon!"

Miss Clarkson remained calm; Clarissa's behavior challenged her daily.

"The other children at the home won't want to play with you if you behave like this," Miss Clarkson warned. "No one likes a sore loser."

Clarissa's face was turning beet red.

Trenville thought it might be an opportune time for him to intervene. He put his hand in his pocket, withdrew it, and tapped the little girl on the shoulder.

"Hello, Clarissa," he said cheerily. "My name's Matthew—but you may call me Matt."

"Go away," Clarissa ordered, pointing toward the doorway. "I'm not allowed to speak to strangers."

"I'm not a stranger," Trenville assured the little tyrant. "Why, I met Miss Clarkson on the train! I work here at the lodge. Say," he continued in an astonished voice, "what's that behind your ear?"

The young man reached forward and produced a coin, which he handed to the surprised little girl.

"How did you do that?" Clarissa's eyes widened for a moment as she questioned the miracle before demanding, "Do it again!"

"Only one per customer," Trenville laughed. "I tell you what, Clarissa, if you promise to play nicely with Miss Clarkson, perhaps I'll find another dime for you—maybe even a quarter."

The promise of future wealth had the desired effect.

"Miss Clarkson," Clarissa pleaded winsomely, "would you please play another game of checkers with me? I promise to be good."

The young woman eyed her opponent skeptically.

"Well . . . I don't know," she considered, raising an eyebrow. "You did call me a cheater, I believe. I'm not sure that I should reward that kind of behavior with—"

"I take it back, I take it back!" Clarissa surrendered. "You're not a cheater, and I promise to play nice—I might even let you win."

Gloria Clarkson laughed, and looked thankfully at Trenville. The young man wished for a barrel of quarters so that he could purchase more such appreciative looks.

"You mind if I stay and watch the game—that is, now that I'm not a stranger?" The question was posed to the younger player, who nodded as she placed red and black checkers on their appropriate squares.

"You're sure you aren't needed in the other room?" Miss Clarkson said innocently. "That woman you were talking to—what if she needs a snack or a drink or—"

"I'm sure that Mrs. Warren or Mrs. Glas, or Mary can take care of things," Trenville said firmly. "I'd much rather assume the duties of referee here, if you don't mind."

"Oh, I *suppose* it's all right," the young woman acquiesced with just a hint of mischief in her eyes. "It's just that you seemed to be enjoying yourself, and we certainly wouldn't want to keep you from—from . . ."

Trenville eyed the girl suspiciously, then relaxed and admitted defeat.

"Okay, okay," he laughed. "I surrender to a superior opponent on this field of verbal battle. Truce?"

"Quiet," Miss Clarkson said with a smile. "The referee should not speak to the players while they are concentrating on the game."

The sheriff and the detective made a brief but thorough investigation of the immediate area around the newel post on which the body of Walter Merriweather had been found. Blood had stained the decorative antlers that had been under the corpse.

"Fellow landed on those points almost hard enough to drive them into his chest," the lawman noted, as Chan looked closely at the antler in question with his pocket magnifying glass. "I know what Doc Manston said, but it seems to me he could've tripped and fallen onto the railing. See there, how the carpet's scuffed up in places?"

"Sheriff misses nothing, even traces left by unsteady footsteps—perhaps those of victim Merriweather," Chan said approvingly. "But please recall the doctor's certainty that the larger wound in the dead man's back was from some unknown weapon that pierced his heart. As for condition of carpet—"

The detective knelt swiftly at the top of the stairs, looking intently through his pocket lens at the area indicated by the sheriff. Chan moved quickly on his hands and knees, following a faint trail in the carpet that he was able to discern only with the aid of the magnifying glass.

"Well, I'll be a—" Fairden murmured, admiring the detective's agility and sharp vision. "What can you . . . "

Chan had made his way over to the small alcove where he and the sheriff had convened earlier. With a sharp exclamation, he stood up and pointed first to the lower shelf of the liquor cabinet and then at its top.

"Look," he said excitedly to the sheriff, "and observe what I failed to grasp when we sat here earlier."

Fairden leaned over to look at the marble top. On either side of a used ashtray he saw two faint circles, one at each end of the little liquor cabinet's tabletop.

"So?"

"Also," Chan continued, "please deign to stoop and examine the gap on the shelf, and the carpet under this chair." He pointed downward.

The sheriff sighed and bent down, genuflecting. Noting a set of cocktail glasses on the shelf, he saw where two additional tumblers had resided until very recently. Then he ran his hand over the floor covering.

"Say, it's damp!" Fairden exclaimed. "Somethin' was spilled here, and not that long ago."

"Your perceptive deduction agrees with my humble thought," Chan said generously. "I additionally suggest further possibility."

"What's that?"

The detective seated himself carefully in the chair and leaned over the table top. The dim lighting from the nearby candle sconces did him no favors, but with the aid of the pocket lens Chan found what he was looking for.

"See here," he told the sheriff, handing him the magnifier. "Two rings on the table—not yet dry—and dampened carpet, below one chair only, suggests to me that an accident occurred."

Fairden whistled. Through the lens he could see several tiny shards of glass glistening on the table top.

"What's that?" The lawman pointed to a tiny lump of green among the glass fragments and handed the lens back to Chan. The detective carefully took the little green object between his thumb and forefinger for a closer look.

"Not glass," Chan murmured, looking up at the sheriff. "Possibly left here by accident as one or both persons acts in haste." He twisted a page from his notebook into a spill and

tucked the find into it, pocketing the paper shape for safekeeping.

"So two people were here, and one of 'em broke his glass,
spilled something . . ."

The sheriff's voice faded.

"And then what?" Fairden wondered.

Chapter Fourteen

THE MAN IN THE TAN SUIT

Before Chan could answer, raised voices from below interrupted. The sheriff stood abruptly.

"Hell, I can't keep those people penned up down there any longer," he groaned. "Do you need more time here, Mr. Chan?"

The detective shook his head.

"For the present, we have seen what is necessary," he remarked, getting to his feet. "One thing only—"

"What's that?"

"If you would be so kind, please collect this robust specimen of *Nephrolepis exaltata* and bring it with us."

"That damn plant?" Fairden sputtered. "Sure, but what did you call it—was that Chinese?"

"Latin term for this green and flourishing plant," the detective said patiently, "sometimes called Boston fern, or fishbone fern.

"Also known," he added grimly, "as sword fern."

The two men descended the stairs to face the restive gathering. Sheriff Fairden raised his voice to address the much put-upon lodge guests.

"Here, now," he said loudly, his face partly obscured by the potted fern. "Folks, good news—you're free to go upstairs jes' as soon as you want. Thank you again for your cooperation—"

The rest of the lawman's speech was swept away by the small stampede of impatient travelers who brushed past him on their way up the stairs.

"I'll have some questions for all of you," the sheriff called up the stairs. "In the morning," he finished wearily, shifting the fern slightly to move its fronds from his face.

"Is there someplace special you'd like me to deposit this—this—fern, Mr. Chan?"

The detective considered.

"Perhaps in the kitchen we might explore this fine example of nature's beauty under a strong light," he suggested. "If you would please lead the way, I will follow."

The two men entered Mrs. Warren's domain just in time to see the cook and her temporary assistant preparing to depart for the night. Chan apologized for the intrusion and inquired about a well-lit place where they might examine the plant without disturbing the well-ordered kitchen.

"Just down this hall, past the pantry. Come, Mary." The cook and her helper led the way down the short corridor. Mrs. Warren indicated the entrance to the work room; then she and Mary said goodnight and exited the lodge through its side door.

"Last round, Clarissa," a familiar voice said, "and then it's bed for you."

As Chan and Fairden entered the work room, three pairs of eyes glanced up from the table—but only for a moment. Playing cards skittered one at a time across the table. Matthew Trenville was dealing, and the other players—Miss Clarkson and Clarissa—were absorbed in the game.

"Last hand, Clarissa," Miss Clarkson emphasized. She knew all too well how quickly the child's mood might change once the evening's play was concluded.

The little girl looked up curiously at the two men and the sheriff's burden.

"Why are you carrying that plant around?" Clarissa asked the sheriff quizzically. "Are you a farmer?"

Setting the big potted fern on the table with a dull thud, the county's chief law enforcement official reddened.

"No, young lady, I am most certainly not a farmer," he replied firmly. "I'm the sheriff, and isn't it way past your bed-time?"

"Miss Clarkson let me stay up and play games so that she could talk to Matt," the girl explained guilelessly. "They've been pretending to be interested in checkers and cards, but they're really more interested in—"

"That's quite enough out of you, missy," a mortified Miss Clarkson interjected. "Matt—er—Mr. Trenville, I don't have any cards to play, do you? I thought not. Clarissa, you won that hand, and now it's off to bed for us, my dear."

"I won—again!" Clarissa said gleefully. Apparently her win-ning streak was sufficient to offset any complaints about bed-time. The little girl dutifully said goodnight before she was led away by the red-faced Miss Clarkson, leaving the room to the three men.

"Gentlemen," cried Matthew Trenville. "I sense some par-ticular purpose has brought you here, and I'm happy to assist in any way needed. First, may I offer either of you something to drink from the kitchen? I think some of the coffee might still be on the hob."

Both men declined. The sheriff looked at Chan, who turned his gaze on the young lodge worker.

"Perhaps while we engage in a brief indoor gardening pro-ject you would like to observe—and maybe answer a few ques-tions from esteemed Sheriff Fairden, with whom you are no doubt already acquainted?"

"Glad to," Trenville chirped. "I have had the pleasure of meeting the sheriff before—not professionally, I hasten to add—but it's been a while since he's graced the lodge with his presence."

"Well, the way things are going," the lawman remarked, "I might as well have a room here 'for the duration,' as we used to say during the war."

"Yes," the younger man replied, his demeanor becoming more appropriately serious. "Terrible! First one—er—death, then another. You mentioned questions, Mr. Chan? I'm happy to help, but I was with you, on the train, so I don't really see how—"

"Perhaps recount to us how you came to be on the train that stopped in the forest," Chan said. "Sheriff will prompt you with thoughtful questions while I—" Chan looked among the tools stored along one wall and found a pair of leather work gloves, which he donned—"I will probe the soil beneath this silent witness."

"Well—all right," Trenville said uncertainly as the detective began removing and sifting the dirt from the pot. "I was on my way back from visiting my folks, my parents, and I usually take that train—the one on the regular schedule that gets into Big Moose Station before dark this time of year."

"Parents live far from here?" Chan inquired. The detective had uncovered something buried in the pot and was scraping the dirt away from it with a small screwdriver from the lodge tool collection.

"On a farm in a place called Marcy, where they retired recently," the young man replied, fascinated by the detective's painstaking work. "They drove me to the train at Utica, and that's where I got on for the return trip."

"But you traveled in the reserved carriage," Chan pointed out, "unavailable to the general public. How were you able to secure a ticket?"

Trenville smiled.

"Oh, they know me—the railroad men," he explained. "Since I work at the lodge they let me ride for free this time, because the—the whole train was paid for, and there was plenty of room."

Sheriff Fairden cleared his throat.

"Now, Matt—why don't you tell Inspector Chan about the lodge and its—er—well, you and Mrs. Warren, and—"

"And Mr. Clemden? Well, Mr. Chan asked me about the lay of the land, so to speak, when we were coming up on the train," Trenville said promptly. "I mean, I'm no expert; but I know generally what everybody knows about the lodge. I haven't worked here long enough to know anybody really well, I guess."

"That's fine," the sheriff said encouragingly. "Just remember that Mr. Chan is from a ways away, and it would be helpful for him to get the, you know, the general idea about the day-to-day things that happen here—and how you and the others work together. Who gets along, who doesn't."

"One moment, please," Charlie Chan interrupted. He had carefully lifted a sizable sliver of glass from its shallow grave in the pot. In a few seconds he unearthed two other pieces apparently from the same glass: one curved, which appeared to have been parted from the first sliver; the second, a thicker, round base for what must have been a short tumbler.

"Young man possesses a clean handkerchief?" the detective inquired.

"Why—yes," Trenville replied immediately. He reached into an inner pocket and produced the requested item, handing it to Chan.

"Thank you for the loan of useful cloth which I hope to return to you soon," the detective acknowledged, wrapping the handkerchief carefully around the three recovered pieces of glass. "Sheriff no doubt has better equipment elsewhere for further examination of interesting artifact," Chan said, casting a hopeful glance at the lawman. Fairden nodded.

"Sure do, but say—what happened to the second glass?" The lawman looked quizzically at the detective.

"Almost certainly it was removed from the scene by one who wished to hide his fingerprints from sheriff's gaze," Chan replied.

"To continue," the detective removed the gloves and looked to Trenville expectantly. "Please search your memory of recent days—has anything unusual occurred involving you or your fellow lodge workers?"

The young man rubbed his cheek with one hand thoughtfully.

"Well, I don't know that I'd say 'unusual,'" he began slowly, "but Ma—I mean Mrs. Warren, had words with ol' Clemden. Mrs. Glas and I were in the Great Room. I had just come in with an armload of logs and she was laying the fire when we heard loud voices coming from the kitchen. It was definitely Mrs. Warren's voice, and I'm pretty sure the man she was—er—talking to was Mr. Clemden. Couldn't hear the man's voice quite as well, but Mrs. Warren—she mostly carried the conversation, you might say. They were having a real set-to."

"Perhaps the nature of disagreeable conversation was audible also?" Chan inquired. "Some matter concerning the running of the lodge—or a personal quarrel?"

Trenville shook his head.

"Couldn't make out most of it," he admitted. "They were pretty well shouting—at least she was—but the sound was muffled. You could check with Mrs. Glas; maybe she heard more than I did.

"I guess the peculiar thing about it," Trenville went on, "is that Mr. Clemden got close enough to Mrs. Warren to even talk to her. Usually he avoids the kitchen, and she never has anything good to say about him."

"When did all this happen?" Fairden put in.

"A little more than a week ago."

"Were preparations made for the coming of guests on to-day's train?" Chan queried. "Maybe there was talk about nature of gathering, expected participants?"

"Not really," Trenville said with furrowed brow. "Leastways nobody said anything to me about the reason all these people were coming to spend the weekend.

"Except, of course," he added, "that there was money behind the whole thing—I mean, the fellow who owns the lodge must've had enough spare change to book a special train—but why bring this particular group to the lodge for a weekend?"

Charlie Chan and Sheriff Fairden exchanged glances.

"No doubt many questions will be answered in time," Chan said blandly. "Sometimes a detective's strength is his patience.

"To prepare tea properly one must wait until the water boils."

Sheriff Fairden prepared to depart, promising to return in the morning.

"I know we've got to talk to the rest of these folks," he told Chan, "but I've a feeling that none of 'em will be up early. Maybe you and I can make a flying trip while they're still asleep to see Doc Manston and find out more about his two most recent patients."

"You think coroner-doctor will already have results of interest?" Chan sounded surprised.

"I know Doc," Fairden said confidently. "Anytime he gets the itch—usually when things pile up in his lab—he'll work through the night. Probably call in the young doctor from Old Forge who hopes to run for coroner when Doc retires."

"Speedy results would be a great help to us," Chan noted. "Identity of body in woods may provide some indication that will help determine further connections to deceased Merriweather. Also, I am interested to hear what role narcotic substances may have played in his death."

Fairden agreed and took his leave.

The work room was quiet. Charlie Chan went into the kitchen, found a candle and lit it. He thought it would come in handy in finding his way upstairs, since electric lighting on the upper floor might be as scarce as on the dimly lit stairwell.

He made his way through the Great Room, pausing to experience its stillness. The silence was broken only by the subdued hissing of remaining embers in the fireplace. A faint glow emanated from it, but the detective was grateful for his candle as he approached the main staircase.

From outside the lodge a faint noise like the faroff snapping of a finger or cracking of a whip came to Chan's ears, and he stopped in his tracks.

The single sound, so faint that he wondered for a moment if he had imagined it, was followed by a profound silence. Instinct told the detective to remain where he was; experience told him that the sound he had heard was no stirring of some nocturnal animal.

Extinguishing his candle, Chan kept still—as silent and unmoving as some statue of the standing Buddha. The seconds went by. By his reckoning, more than two minutes passed before he heard the faintest of sounds from outside: footsteps on the gravel path that led to the lodge entrance.

Slowly, quietly, someone approached the massive (and always unlocked) entrance doors. Chan put his hand on the automatic in his right-hand coat pocket and waited.

The left door of the pair swung open slowly, only a crack at first—and then wide enough for the pale moonlight to reveal the figure of a man. The dark form was hatless and—despite the chill mountain night air—wore only a light-colored suit.

Invisible in the stygian darkness of the lodge, Chan had the advantage.

"Good evening, Mr. Yantzen," the detective said quietly.

"Who's there? Clemden—is that you?" William Yantzen hissed, peering uncertainly into the darkness. He opened the door wider, and his hand went into his coat pocket.

"Please come in and close the door, Mr. Yantzen. The lateness of the hour dictates that we should speak quietly while others enjoy repose," Chan directed, in a voice barely above a whisper. "Also, you will find it unnecessary to keep your hand in your pocket—the warmth of the lodge is most welcome."

Charlie Chan relit his candle as the man in the tan suit closed the door and stepped forward to get a better look at the detective.

"Who the hell—" Yantzen began, before seeing Chan's face in the glow of the flickering candle. His voice was equal parts rasp and sneer, and the words slurred with an alcoholic accent. "You're the one I saw inside earlier—the Chinese cop."

Chan nodded.

"I am Inspector Chan of Honolulu police," he acknowledged, his eyes shining like black buttons in the candlelight. "You are William Yantzen."

Yantzen took his hand out of his pocket and laughed derisively.

"You're kinda out of place here, aren't you, officer? A Chinese guy in this part of New York—and a cop to boot!"

He reached into his hip pocket and pulled out a crumpled pack of Twenty Grand. Tapping the end of the pack to jettison a cigarette, he put the butt between his lips, leaned forward and grabbed Chan's wrist to hold the candle and its flame steady.

"Thanks for the light," he said, releasing the detective and exhaling smoke in his general direction. "Why are you up so late when everybody else has hit the sack?"

Chan's demeanor betrayed nothing of his inner contempt. Ignoring the man's behavior, he gazed steadily at him. The detective's eyes narrowed, but his tone was calm.

"I might well ask you the same question, Mr. Yantzen," he retorted. "Adding a second question: Why does a man go out into the cold night without a hat and overcoat?"

Yantzen smiled uneasily. He was squeezing the empty cigarette pack, flattening it between his fingers nervously.

"Maybe I wanted some fresh air," he suggested. "Anyway, what business is it of yours? You're a long way from home, officer. You got no authority here, you have no—what do they call it?—jurisdiction."

"Two men are dead," Chan said flatly. "Cooperation from all persons here will assist Sheriff Fairden in arresting those responsible. If you choose not to respond to me, you will answer to sheriff."

"Sure, sure," Yantzen returned, his voice faintly mocking Chan's. "Always happy to cooperate with the law—the *real* law, that is."

He knelt suddenly to tie his laces, Chan thought—but the detective's keen eyes told him that both shoes were already tied. After a moment, Yantzen stood up, flushed with the effort.

"Now, if you'll lead the way," he pointed toward the stairs, "I'd like to turn in. It's been a long day."

The detective smiled politely and held out the candle.

"Courtesy dictates that the one already well acquainted with this establishment should lead the way," he responded. "With cigarette in one hand and candle in the other, you can light the way for both of us—thank you, so much."

Yantzen glared at the detective and took the candle grudgingly. And the two men made their way up the stairs.

At the top of the stairs the only signs of the recently removed body were the bloody marks on the handrail. Yantzen took a drag on his cigarette, and the candle in his other hand wavered.

"Perhaps you are acquainted with this comfortable nook?" Chan inquired casually, indicating the alcove he and the sheriff had examined earlier. The detective's voice was little more than a murmur. "It seems a place where lodge guests like you might relax and talk."

Man and candle stopped briefly, and Chan watched curiously as Yantzen looked hurriedly at the desktop—searching for something, it appeared.

The moment passed. And Yantzen looked uncertainly at the detective.

"Anytime you want to have a little chat, I'll be easy to find," he whispered. "I'm in the room next to yours, halfway down the hall on the left—the names are on the doors."

Handing the candle abruptly to Chan, Yantzen made his way down the hall with an easy familiarity, one hand brushing against the wall, and quietly opened a door. Glancing back at the detective, he stood in the doorway and took one last puff on his cigarette. Chan could see the glowing end briefly before the man in the tan suit entered the room and shut the door.

Returning to the landing, Chan sat down in the chair closest to the newel post that had served as the unfortunate Merriweather's recent resting place, set the candle on the table, and collected his thoughts. His reason for traveling to this place—how remote it now seemed! Where was this Frederick Scanlon—would he arrive soon to shed light on the situation?

If anyone knew more about this weekend gathering they had kept it to themselves. Perhaps the necessary questioning tomorrow would yield more information on both fronts. For now, Chan mused, Scanlon's fear of a would-be murderer seemed far less urgent than finding a very real murderer—a person or persons responsible for two deaths.

He sighed, and his eyes again traced the few feet between the banister and his seat, considering possible sequences of events. Had Merriweather sat here, tête-à-tête with his killer? Did they drink together before the unknown struck?

The detective thought of the broken glass and wondered.

He ran his hand carefully over the table's marble top—nothing. Getting to his feet, he carefully moved the two chairs aside and got down on one knee to examine the carpet next to and underneath the table.

The damp spot he had discovered earlier was almost dry, and he patted the carpet around it gently in an ever-widening circle until he found them: tiny bits of glass. From his coat pocket he withdrew a small envelope and carefully deposited into it all the sharp fragments he could find.

He stood up, satisfied. Such meager evidence could lead to more substantial things. Picking up the candle, he stepped quietly down the hall. The wilderness theme of the Great Room below continued here. Smaller heads of lesser beasts were mounted on both walls down the hall, as far as he could see. In between these, a few shelf tableaux depicted lesser creatures—squirrels, birds, rabbits—preserved, lifelike, by the taxidermist's art.

Chan reached the door with his name on it, and sighed.

The night was well advanced; morning would be here all too soon.

Chapter Fifteen

THE BREAKFAST GATHERING

The guest with the most complaints was the first to encounter Mrs. Warren's breakfast.

The man from the train had left his homburg hat and umbrella upstairs, but he continued to look askance at the people and things he encountered. Always an early riser when traveling, he arrived in the empty dining room in the faint light of the autumn dawn. Mrs. Warren entered, bade him good morning, and indicated a sideboard with hot dishes. He helped himself to eggs and coffee and resumed his seat.

The next to arrive was the last to retire: Charlie Chan. The detective put orange juice, coffee, and toast on a small tray and approached the little man. Chan's cheerful greeting received a noncommittal reply and a cold stare. Undeterred, he gestured toward the seat opposite.

"May I interrupt the solitude of the moment and join you for a brief conversation?" Chan asked. The man nodded indifferently, and the detective relieved the tray of its contents.

Chan sipped the hot coffee carefully and eyed his breakfast companion. The man seemed to have little appetite; his eggs lay untouched, and he stared at them as though deep in thought. The detective's calm voice brought his attention back to the present moment.

"Please allow me to introduce myself," Chan began, but the man needed no introduction.

"No need," he said in a clipped voice "You're the police detective from Hawaii, Charlie Chan. They were talking about you on the train, you know."

Chan smiled.

"The advantage, then, is yours," he replied politely. "You are—?"

"A hungry man disappointed in his eggs," came the tart reply.

"The traveler who hungers finds delight even in a crust of bread," Chan persisted. "This toasted slice is delicious."

The man smiled faintly.

"Please forgive my rudeness, Mr. Chan," he said apologetically. "A long day of travel, a night on a kind of bunk instead of a proper bed—and then this." He pushed the plate to one side and raised the steaming coffee to his lips before continuing.

With a satisfied sigh he set down the cup.

"My name is Bainie, Cecil N. Bainie," the man said primly. His short goatee did a little dance that accompanied his clipped manner of speaking. Chan looked closely at the man whose unusual hat and complementary umbrella had attracted his attention on the train. Now, he could examine him more closely.

As the detective had glimpsed earlier, Bainie favored a dandified fashion of some years previous. The goatee was accompanied by a thin mustache; both of these and his slicked-back hair were suspiciously black. Dark eyes looked intensely at the detective, and Chan noticed the occasional twitch at their corners, the tic that spoke of too little rest and too much coffee. *Or the frayed nerves of a troubled man*, the detective speculated.

Removing his pince-nez to polish its lenses with a monogrammed handkerchief, Bainie looked hesitatingly at Chan. *He is considering what version of the truth to tell me*, the detective intuited.

"I realize that a man of my appearance may seem an oddity in these rustic surroundings," Bainie said carefully, replacing the gold-rimmed eyeglasses on the bridge of his nose. "It is my first such experience—this trip so far outside the city, and so far into the—er—wilderness.

"I assume that you want to ask me about the deaths," he continued, before Chan could speak. "The *cognoscenti* last night said that you would be assisting the sheriff—or perhaps the other way around," Bainie said with a straight face.

"Sometimes, as the ancient philosopher Laozi wrote, 'Those who speak do not know,'" Chan retorted. "Sheriff Fairden has kindly accepted my offer of assistance, but the investigation is his to conduct.

"You are not the only one who might appear strangely out of place," the detective assured him in a more measured tone. "Thousands of miles from familiar surroundings, I, too, stand out in this wooded mountain lodge—like a duck in the desert."

Bainie's mustache twitched in what might have been the beginnings of a smile.

"Before you pose your questions, I want to make you aware of the reason for my presence here," he declared. "No doubt you already suspect that I am not here by chance?"

Chan nodded. He was not surprised by what came next.

"I am an accountant by profession, and for some years I have been acquainted with a Frederick Scanlon. My firm in New York has undertaken various tasks pertaining to his business interests, and Mr. Scanlon and I have come to know each other."

Bainie paused and took another sip of coffee.

"Imagine my surprise some weeks ago when I received some rather peculiar correspondence," he went on, pulling an envelope from an inside breast pocket and pushing it across the table to the detective. "Please feel free to read it yourself; he said that he valued my professional expertise, and that he wanted me to undertake a commission that would require some travel. All expenses paid—a handsome fee for my time and trouble, and he would brook no refusal."

Charlie Chan pulled the letter from the envelope and digested its contents. In form, substance, and style, it was nearly identical to the one he had received. Only the nature of Bainie's "commission" differed.

"For reasons he did not disclose in the letter, he suspected some incidents of defalcation—perhaps embezzlement—had taken place in one or more of his interests," Bainie continued. "He preferred to disclose the details to me in person, and the only concrete information he committed to writing was the name of the man he suspected."

As Bainie uttered the name of Scanlon's suspect, Chan read it:

"Walter Merriweather."

"Apparently this Merriweather has had a position of trust in Scanlon's business empire for some time, but he—" Bainie stopped abruptly when he saw the detective slowly shaking his head. "What is it, Mr. Chan? Something in the letter?"

Chan replaced the missive in its envelope and returned it to the accountant.

"This Merriweather's misdeeds, whatever they were, are over," he informed Bainie. "The sheriff spoke last night of two deaths, one here and one in the woods."

The detective watched the accountant carefully for his reaction.

"On the second floor of this lodge Mr. Merriweather was found dead—murdered," Chan said matter-of-factly.

"Good lord," Bainie said softly. "But why would anyone kill *him*?" The accountant's face betrayed no great surprise, no emotion of any kind, Chan thought.

"Well, then," Bainie continued dismissively, "I consider my commission for Mr. Scanlon discharged. Money went missing, a certain man was suspected, and now that man is dead. I can return to the city and make my report."

"Question remains," Chan reminded him, "as to the identity of Merriweather's killer. Your financial investigation may bear on the motive for murder, so Sheriff Fairden will welcome your continued presence at this lodge while he searches for guilty party."

"You put it so eloquently, Mr. Chan," Bainie replied. "I'm to remain here with the other guests until your—that is, the sheriff's—investigation is concluded."

Chan smiled and nodded.

"However," Bainie rejoined, "There's no reason why—"

"Good morning to you both!"

The accountant's objection was cut short by the arrival of the Bryants, her cheery greeting as she entered the room contrasting comically with her husband's sleepy demeanor. "You'll have to make allowances for Daniel," she apologized. "I'm afraid he's not at his best this time of day. However, coffee will improve him."

Mrs. Warren, hearing the new voices from the kitchen, brought two fresh pots of the necessary beverage, placed one on the sideboard and fulfilled the needs of all present with the other.

"Dr. Collins should be joining us shortly," said Muriel Bryant to no one in particular. "He was just down the hall—oh, there you are, Doctor!"

The physician entered the dining room, exchanging greetings with all present.

"I was just admiring the taxidermy work on display upstairs and down," he explained. "Really quite—hmm—remarkable."

A murmur of conversation from outside the room presaged the arrival of Mrs. Scanlon and Monsignor Plevna. The two appeared to be engaged in a spirited theological debate concerning the sanctity of marriage. The new arrivals made their way past the sideboard with varying degrees of interest, and in a few minutes all were seated around the long table. General introductions and the flow of small talk gave way to the consumption of Mrs. Warren's cooking. Since none of the late arrivals had heard Bainie's dyspeptic dismissal, there was a general enjoyment of the eggs, as well as bacon, ham, biscuits, and a great deal more.

Chan noted that the breakfast gathering now comprised all those on Frederick Scanlon's list except for his former business partner Alexander Creighton and William Yantzen, who—the detective suspected—was not an early riser.

The time had come.

"Ladies, gentlemen, if you would be so kind," Charlie Chan intoned, rising to his feet. "An urgent matter compels me to interrupt your breakfast conversation—"

"Tea, not coffee," chided Mrs. Scanlon. "I despise coffee."

Mrs. Warren's gaze was far from servile, but she seldom lost her temper with guests. "Yes, ma'am, right away," she replied in a low voice, and returned to the kitchen to put the kettle on.

"Mrs. Scanlon," Chan said evenly. "How fortunate that you are here since some of what I have to discuss with these persons pertains to you. Thank you for your willingness to speak your mind even on issues of lesser gravity—I will call on you shortly."

This perceived impertinence left the redoubtable Scanlon woman speechless for a moment. Chan forged ahead before she could completely recover the use of her sharp tongue.

"I promise to keep you no longer than is necessary, but please be reminded that serious business concerns us all—the deaths of two men. One, perhaps both, murdered. Sheriff Fairden has authority over criminal matters in this area of New York, this county, and he has kindly agreed to tolerate my participation in his work. Later, he will also speak with all of you, perhaps one at a time.

"First, let us consider another matter," the detective continued, looking around the room carefully at the names on Frederick Scanlon's list—except for two—in the flesh. "The reasons we are here.

"Already one of you has revealed to me the receipt of a most curious invitation—a letter quite similar to one I received. This person and I were invited by Mr. Scanlon to attend this weekend gathering to conduct investigations."

Chan paused for a moment. All eyes were on him.

"Frederick Scanlon wrote to one person at this table that he suspected someone of financial wrongdoing at his company. With me, Mr. Scanlon shared that he feared death—death at the hands of one of the people on a list he provided to me."

Mrs. Scanlon started to speak but thought better of it. Bainie looked on with interest; the rest of Chan's small audience sat transfixed.

"One of those on the list lies slumbering upstairs. Another, Alexander Creighton, has yet to arrive here. A third party suspected by Mr. Scanlon is dead.

"The rest of those enumerated by Mr. Scanlon," the detective said solemnly, "are seated at this table."

A moment of silence, hardly more than a second, followed Chan's revelation before several of his listeners spoke at once. The detective raised both hands, and the commotion died away.

Mrs. Warren entered to refill the sideboard's pots of coffee and to see if she might clear away, but the room's tense atmosphere told her that whatever needed doing in the room could wait.

She departed for the calm of the kitchen.

Once the cook had left the room several voices began anew, but Mrs. Scanlon drowned out the rest and took control of the floor.

"This is outrageous," she began icily, with an anger that seemed to grow with the rising sound of her voice. "My former husband has faults, but he is not completely mad. If we are to believe what you say—and I have my doubts—then we are all suspected of wanting to do away with him? The whole thing is monstrous.

"And where *is* Fred? From the letter I received, I assumed that I and a few others were to be his guests for a pleasant weekend at this—this—"

Mrs. Scanlon's face was scarlet, but her descriptive powers had failed only temporarily.

"This ramshackle excuse for a hotel," she went on hotly. "And after all this folderol, you have the temerity to make these ridiculous assertions. You! A—a foreigner! Why, I—"

Chan's eyes narrowed, but his reply was almost gentle in its reproach.

"So sorry to disagree with one so distressed by the embarrassment of the moment," the detective murmured, "but I am happy to set your mind at ease in one respect. Citizenship comes even to unworthy persons like myself, born elsewhere but resident of this country for many decades.

"As for 'ridiculous assertions,'" he continued, "all blame or credit for same must be assigned to Frederick Scanlon, writer of epistles—letters you all received, I believe?"

Dr. Collins cleared his throat preparatory to speaking.

"I got one," he offered. The doctor's second cup of coffee had been reinforced by a dollop of something from his pocket flask, and he appeared to be enjoying the breakfast drama. "Nothing startling in it, just a passing reference to the vicissitudes"—the word required two attempts—"the ups and downs, of life and friendship, and so on."

"Daniel received just such an invitation," Muriel Bryant said brightly. "That is, it was addressed to Daniel—and I never read his correspondence—but I believe I was mentioned in it, wasn't I, dear?"

Awakened by two cups of coffee and the discussion of the last several minutes, Mr. Bryant nodded.

"Fred did send me a note out of the blue, mentioning our past disagreements and hinting that we might move beyond them—that if I were to come for the weekend I might, 'hear something of great interest,' I think is how he put it. And, yes, he made it clear that Muriel and I were both welcome to come to this—this conclave."

"An apt way to describe this meeting," Monsignor Plevna put it. The priest had lit a cigarette earlier and was tapping it frequently and unnecessarily into a cut-glass ashtray. "I, too, received an unexpected invitation from Frederick. Somewhat vague, but I took it as a kind of olive branch—an effort to mend whatever disagreements we might have had once."

Chan looked around the table.

"In letters received by all of you did Mr. Scanlon indicate his planned attendance here—or imply that he would act as your host?"

This question yielded mixed results. It seemed that all except Bainie had either discarded their letters or left them at home. Mrs. Scanlon's view appeared to be that of the majority:

"I don't recall exactly what the letter said, but of course my former husband intended to be here," she insisted. "He is a determined man in charge of every situation, and he would not assemble a group of people, accuse them of—of—what we've been told—and then absent himself."

A nodding of heads and murmured agreement greeted Mrs. Scanlon's statement. Chan looked at his wristwatch; the sheriff would arrive soon, and they would need to depart for the doctor-coroner's office.

A veritable hammering at the lodge's main entrance brought further conversation to a halt, and the dining room fell silent. Mrs. Warren's footsteps came and went, and the faint sounds of a brief conversation at the door followed.

"Mr. Chan?" The cook's voice called from the lodge entrance. "Would you come here, please?"

The detective moved with surprising alacrity, given his normally calm pace. In a moment he was at the lodge entrance, where Mrs. Warren was speaking to a roughly dressed man who stood in the open doorway with an envelope in his hand.

"This is Norman Boesch, from the post office," the cook explained. "Says he has something that has to be delivered to you in person."

"Inspector Charlie Chan of Honolulu, temporarily residing at this address?" Boesch inquired. Chan acknowledged his identity, showing the mailman his badge.

"Special delivery," the man said, handing the detective the envelope. "Good day to you, and to you, Mrs. Warren."

Chan thanked the departing mailman and examined the envelope, which was addressed to him "in care of The Great Lodge at Big Moose Lake." The smudged Manhattan postmark was dated three days ago. Chan opened the envelope and removed its enclosure.

It was a letter from Frederick Scanlon.

> *Dear Inspector Chan:*
>
> *By now, I trust that you and I have already met at the lodge—in which case you may ignore this letter. If, on the other hand, pressing business or some travel setback detains me, please be assured that I will join you and the other guests by Saturday noon at the latest.*
>
> *I have received responses from those persons invited to the gathering with the exception of my former wife, Edna (whose willful inattention to such social protocol is all too familiar to me), Alexander Creighton, and Edna's brother, William Yantzen.*
>
> *Until my arrival and further consultation, you will proceed as you think best.*

Please enjoy the hospitality of the lodge, a truly remarkable place in a region filled with natural wonders.

Sincerely,
Frederick Scanlon

Chapter Sixteen
ITEMS OF LOCAL INTEREST

Chan had just finished reading the letter when another caller came knocking at the entrance. Knowing that Mrs. Warren had returned to the kitchen, the detective opened the door. The county's chief lawman was on the porch. Chan stepped outside to join him, closing the door.

"Good morning, Inspector," Sheriff Fairden exclaimed. "Didn't expect to see you on door duty."

"First job as a boy in Honolulu required such skills, and I have not forgotten them," Chan grinned. "Truth of the matter is—I was called to the door to receive this interesting letter from still-absent Frederick Scanlon."

"I wondered what Norm Boesch was doing out this way this time of day," the sheriff said absently, scanning the contents of Scanlon's latest communication.

"Hello, there—good morning!"

Matthew Trenville approached. As he always did, the lodge worker had parked his flivver some distance from the entrance in deference to guests and visitors like the sheriff, whose truck was less than a stone's throw from the front door.

"Morning, Matt," Fairden replied. "Say, you might still have a guest or two show up to join the folks that are already here."

"Really? I've been wondering if this was the whole crop," Trenvill replied.

The sheriff nodded, pointing to Chan.

"The Inspector here got a letter this morning that says the big businessman, Scanlon, will be here pretty soon," the lawman informed him. "Heck, you tell him, Mr. Chan, it's your letter, after all."

"Sheriff has delivered the most important tidbit of news," the detective summarized. "Mr. Scanlon writes to inform me that if circumstances delay him he will arrive nonetheless by noon today.

"Also possible," he continued, "that another of his invited guests may or may not attend, but such uncertainties must be familiar to one such as you—keeper of visitors who come and go unexpectedly."

Trenville laughed appreciatively.

"Such things have been known to happen," he admitted. "Well, thanks for the 'tidbit'—I must be running along now, to tend to current guests and prepare for the One Who Comes Soon."

The young man smiled and entered the lodge, leaving Chan and the sheriff on the expansive porch.

"I hope I'm not too early, Mr. Chan, but I figured we'd best get over to Eagle Bay to see Doc Manston before the day gets any older," Fairden said briskly.

"I am glad for the opportunity to accompany you to the coroner's office," Chan said eagerly. "Have already had breakfast—one moment, please, while I retrieve hat and coat."

"That's fine—we can have a little talk about things on the way," the sheriff replied.

When the detective emerged suitably clad for the chill morning, he was struck for the first time by the beauty of Big Moose Lake. Arriving after dark, he had not realized how close the lodge was to the lakeshore. The shining body of water lay like glass, reflecting the surrounding trees—a dense evergreen forest with a sprinkling of fading maple tree foliage. Far off on the lake a faint mist seemed to join with a low-hanging cloud.

Chan was impressed. Used to the tropical scenes of his beloved islands, he found a particular and breathtaking grandeur in this view of a cold mountain lake in autumn.

The noise of the sheriff's truck brought him back to more mundane matters, and he committed his first full view of an Adirondack lake to memory.

In a few minutes the two men were on their way, speeding along a rough road dappled by the morning sunlight flickering through the trees. Fairden pointed out items of local interest along the way, starting with a small log house set back from the road, about a quarter-mile from the lodge.

"Caretaker's cabin," he said, with a wave of his hand. "Clemden built that himself, though where he found the time is beyond me."

"My only meeting so far with this Clemden was on the train," Chan reminded the sheriff, "but he seems like a man of enterprise. Does he have many demands on his time?"

"Well, folks say he spends his days—sometimes weeks—in the woods, away from the lodge," the sheriff said carelessly. "I'm sure I don't know—I've got better things to do than worry about Clemden and his doings. I'm more interested in some of the characters staying at the lodge."

Chan apprised the sheriff of his late-night encounter with William Yantzen and the early morning sessions with Cecil Bainie and most of Scanlon's listed suspects.

"That Yantzen fellow," Fairden grunted. "He looks like a bad apple, and that's a fact. The rest of 'em all seem okay to me—some of 'em look like they stepped out of a moving picture."

"Appearances sometimes are big liars," Chan raised his voice to compete with the truck's noisy engine. "Fine feathers do not make a fine bird,"

"That's a good one," the sheriff chuckled appreciatively. "Who said that—Shakespeare?"

"K'ung Fu-tzu," Chan grinned. "Or, as some in the West would say, 'Confucius.'"

A rough spot in the mountain road jolted the two men thoroughly, Fairden suddenly snapped his fingers emphatically. His other hand gripped the steering wheel, swerving the truck to avoid an opossum scuttling across their path.

The sheriff was familiar with the road; Chan tightened his grip on the edge of his seat.

"Say!" Faiden exclaimed. "Haven't had time to ask till now—what do you make of the things we found on the bodies?"

Inwardly, Chan smiled at the "we" as he responded carefully.

"Strange assortment of items, like broken weather vane, points in uncertain directions," he admitted. "Should we attach importance to the presence of black feathers, one on each body? Some connection seems indicated, but —who can say?"

Sheriff Fairden snorted.

"Feathers," he muttered. "I'll be a—"

Chan went on hurriedly as the truck lurched again.

"Another common feature—no doubt you noticed it—was the unusual symbol found on a ring in one man's pocket and also on the watch fob of Merriweather. The thought has occurred to me that your Dr. Manston, who is both physician and coroner, may help us identify it."

"Ol' Doc is better educated than just about anybody who lives around here," the sheriff declared. "He's a man of many interests, as you'll see when we get to his place.

"What about the empty wallet?" Fairden went on. "Was that fellow under the train robbed before or after he was killed?"

Chan considered the sheriff's question carefully before replying.

"You are correct that a billfold without bills often points to robbery," he said slowly, "but only a very energetic and desperate robber would ply his trade in the middle of the woods—and dispose of his robbery victim with a train. A tremendous undertaking for what a man's wallet usually holds.

"Unless," he added, "the man's pocketbook contained some item of immense value—beyond the mere currency suitable for a traveler."

Sheriff Fairden was silent for a moment.

"Well, I sure hope ol' Doc has something to tell us," he declared. "Eagle Bay is just a little ways ahead, and Doc's is on the other side of the village."

The doctor and coroner lived and worked in a big house with an attached laboratory-workroom-storeroom, a space sufficient to house the trappings of his profession and the equipage necessary for his hobbies and interests.

"No need to try the front door," Sheriff Fairden told Chan, and the lawman led the way to the back of the property. Manston's catchall addition looked like a small barn that had embraced the back of the house, and its entrance was a genuine barn door, which was slightly ajar.

"Hello in there!" Fairden called. "Doc? It's Farley Fairden."

The sheriff pushed the big door open far enough for the two men to enter.

A full-grown moose stood facing the two men, and Charlie Chan blinked.

The sheriff noted his reaction and laughed.

"I forgot to mention that one of Doc's hobbies is taxidermy," he said with a grin. "Sorry I didn't prepare you for this fellow. You get used to the stuffed critters after a while, 'specially when they're hangin' on the wall, but Big Bull here—that's what Doc calls him—he makes quite an impression."

Chan was fascinated by the lifelike appearance of the majestic—but long dead—creature.

"Good morning to you both!" Manston appeared from behind Big Bull, clad in an apron stained with the evidence of his morbid work. "I hope you had a more restful night than we did."

He turned and gestured toward a similarly dressed younger man who smiled politely despite his bleary-eyed appearance.

"This is Dr. Strickler," the coroner told them, "and he was kind enough to forgo a night's sleep in the interests of science and public duty.

"Therefore," Manston said as he walked toward the other side of the huge workroom, "we have some preliminary findings on the two bodies that may be of interest."

"Now you're talkin'," the sheriff said encouragingly. "We're all ears."

"Which is more than I can say for our first client," the coroner deadpanned. "'No ears' would be more like it.

"Now, I could give you chapter and verse and impress you with all the medical words that I know," he began, "but maybe it's best if I give you a few conclusions first. This man—" he pointed to a figure under a sheet "—was dead several hours before the train came along. The cause of death—well, the condition of his head makes a definitive determination difficult, but I can tell you that he was certainly given a drug, one of the barbiturates. Probably barbitol."

"Is that what killed him—too much of the drug?" Fairden cut in.

"Well, he sure had enough of it in him to render him unconscious—maybe put him in a coma. A blow to the head or some other trauma of sufficient force could have done it.

"Hell," Manston threw up his hands, "you both saw what the train did to him. There were no injuries of any kind to the rest of his body, so either he died from the drug or some unknown injury to his head before the train struck him.

"Which, by the way, reminds me that the person who did this was keen to conceal the actual cause of death. Hence the train. This is probably something you've already thought of," the coroner went on, "but considering the state of the victim prior to his encounter with the train I'd say you're looking for two people. It would be quite a chore to get an inert body into the woods and onto the tracks."

Chan nodded. The coroner's findings confirmed what the detective's preliminary examination had revealed. The sheriff appeared to be rethinking some earlier theory, adding a hypothetical accomplice to it.

"Jes' when I was hopin' to make one arrest, now you say I've got to make two," he grumbled. "I suppose you're right, though it would be a lot easier if you told us this fellow walked into the woods on his own two legs."

"Question, please," Charlie Chan addressed the coroner. "Apart from evidence of cyanosis in the fingernails due to drug, did you observe other signs on fingers of dead man?"

Dr. Manston looked at Chan with rising respect.

"You mean the erythema present just above the Metacarpophalangeal Joints?" The coroner rattled off the term easily. The sheriff snorted, and Manston's assistant, Dr. Strickler, smiled wearily.

"Damned jawbreaker words," the lawman grunted. "Sometimes I think doctors make 'em up on the spur of the moment. Again, in English, please?"

Chan grinned.

"Learned doctor describes the reddening of skin above the deceased's big knuckles—something I noticed when examining body in the woods," he explained. "Tell me, Dr. Manston, is it possible to know the cause of these marks—and whether it happened while the victim was still alive?"

"The cause?" Manston reflected. "Any number of things can make the skin red, temporarily. I'm sure you both are familiar with handcuffs. Think of what happens when they're too tight, or the person you've put the cuffs on tries to wriggle out of them. Some similar friction occurred here.

"Now, it surely happened before death," the doctor-coroner added, "and the victim could have been conscious or unconscious."

"Your expertise and years of experience serve you well," Chan remarked. "Sheriff of this county is lucky to have such a capable colleague."

"Very kind of you to say so, Mr. Chan," Manston replied. "See there, Fairden? Maybe I'm not such a burden to the taxpayers after all."

General laughter greeted this assessment. Chan looked around the room, amazed by displays of the coroner's avocation. Every wall featured several mounted specimens—mostly deer and the occasional moose. At least one bobcat in toto stood in his own mock den, situated behind Big Bull the moose.

While the coroner and sheriff bandied back and forth, the detective walked to the nearest wall to admire a twenty-foot-long wilderness diorama with several species represented in wilderness scenes. Raccoons, opossums, squirrels, birds, chipmunks—even a beaver and dam—many of the region's smaller creatures were frozen eerily in place.

"Are you a connoisseur of preserved wildlife, Mr. Chan?" Dr. Manston said pleasantly in the rhetorical tone of a museum tour guide. The coroner approached the display, pointing out some of its permanent residents and explaining their place in the Adirondack hierarchy.

"Doc!" Fairden called from the vicinity of the sheeted table. "Don't take up the Inspector's time with your tomfoolery. We need to get back to—"

"Keep your shirt on," the coroner rejoined. "How often do I get to show off my collections to somebody who might appreciate them?

"Just one more thing you must see—quite remarkable—before we take a look at my second patient," Manston said, leading Chan to a waist-high display cabinet that contained a number of rocks of varying sizes, all of them greenish-dark gray in color—some almost black. Embedded in each was one or more dark reddish-brown stones.

"Garnets in their natural state," the coroner intoned. "The hardest and largest gemstones of this kind come from the Adirondacks, not far from here. What you see here is what the miners find from time to time—the dark-colored rock is called amphibolite, and the gemstones show up like raisins in sweetbread."

Chan looked with interest at the collection.

"Precious stones appear even more brilliant when extracted from their surroundings—and polished?"

"Sure." Manston pointed at the end of the display case. "There's one."

A pebble-sized gem sparkled in the laboratory lights; it was still deep red, but lighter in color than its unpolished siblings nearby.

"Some garnets can be worth quite a lot, as jewelry," Manston continued. "But the kind that comes from around here—over close to Gore Mountain, to be precise—they're mostly used for industrial purposes.

"Now where did I put that . . ." Manston had turned to a long table adjacent to his display case and was rummaging in a pile of books and papers. "Ah! Here it is—please feel free to look through this little volume while you're staying at the lodge. It's a kind of overview of the Adirondack region and its finer points."

Opening the well-thumbed reference work, he pointed to a chapter heading.

"See here—garnets galore in our own backyard," he crowed. Chan accepted the book with a smile, and skimmed the indicated chapter on gemstone mining.

"Yes, indeed, most folks don't know about the region's mining history," Manston said regretfully. "Then again, most folks can't be bothered to learn anything about their own backyard. Take it for granted, they do."

"Most interesting," Chan remarked. "Writer of this book says Gore Mountain area holds rich deposits of red industrial-type garnet stones, but he also notes that, 'Miners are always on the lookout for demantoids, the rarest of garnets. Such green gemstones, with their characteristic horse-tail inclusions, are greatly prized by jewelers and collectors.'"

The detective closed the book thoughtfully and turned to the coroner.

"What is an 'inclusion'?" Chan queried.

"Ah!" Manston showed signs of warming to one of his favorite topics. "It's a fancy word for what might look like a flaw in the stone, like a little bubble or crystal. In the case the author's describing, the green-colored garnet has a yellowish inclusion that's shaped a bit like a horse's tail.

"Saw one one of those green garnets once, in a museum," the coroner went on, "but nobody's ever found any in this part of the country."

"One moment, please," Charlie Chan pulled from his pocket the paper spill he had tucked away earlier. Untwisting it, he shook onto the palm of his hand the little green crystal and held it up for Manston to examine.

The coroner let out a long, low whistle.

"Doc," Fairden's voice had a pleading quality. "This body over here—"

"Sheriff," the coroner replied, "Mr. Chan here has something you ought to see."

Manston pulled a large magnifying lens from a desk drawer and looked closely at the object in Chan's hand.

"It sure looks like the genuine article," he muttered excitedly. "But I'm no expert."

Fairden was unimpressed.

"Mr. Chan found that when we were—we were lookin' for somethin' else," he explained. "But I don't see—"

"Farley," the coroner exclaimed. "If this is what I think it is—the rarest of garnet gemstones—it could be worth what the county pays you in a month of Sundays."

The sheriff now looked suitably impressed.

"And the thing is," Manston continued, "where there's one, there will be others."

He eyed Charlie Chan curiously. The detective's eyes had a distracted look as though his thoughts were elsewhere.

"All right, sheriff," the coroner turned to Fairden. "You two found it—found it where? You see the point, don't you? Garnet mining is well known in this part of the country, as it says in that book, but they've never found anything as rare as a demantoid. If somebody dug this out of the ground—maybe over by Gore Mountain—"

"Now, let's not get ahead of ourselves," the sheriff cautioned. "We don't want to get folks all worked up—least of all in the middle of a murder investigation. Let's jes' keep this to ourselves for the time being, and I'll make sure this bit of trouble gets to somebody who can tell us for sure exactly what it is."

The lawman took charge of the green stone and reminded the coroner why they had come.

"All right, all right," Manston surrendered, and he led Chan away from the amateur museum displays. The detective's expression was thoughtful.

"Your expertise in taxidermy, Doctor," Chan queried, returning his attention to matters at hand. "Was it responsible for the many fine works displayed in the lodge?"

"Indirectly," Manston replied, leading the two men to the second sheeted figure. "I taught Clemden, and he's responsible for most of those specimens at the lodge. He's one of the few people hereabouts that can talk intelligently about the Adirondacks—I mean, beyond 'fishin'' and 'huntin'' for their own sake. Intelligent fellow. Appreciates both my humble artistry in taxidermy *and* my pitiful rock collection."

"Hurray for you," the sheriff chaffed. "Now, what about our Mr. Merriweather?"

Returning to business, the coroner gestured at the second body.

"Something a little less perplexing, this one," Dr. Manston said, pulling the sheet off the body. "Dr. Strickler, would you be so kind—"

The two men grasped the corpse expertly and turned it over to reveal the ugly round wound between the shoulder blades.

"No great mystery here," the coroner told them. "As I said at the lodge, some kind of sharp-ended weapon or tool caused this single wound, and the cause of death was massive internal bleeding.

"So much so," Dr. Manston went on, "that when he landed on the prickly railing of those stairs, he didn't bleed much from the minor wounds received."

"Any idea what kind of weapon—size, shape, anything?" Fairden put in hopefully.

"Something like a garden stake—the ones the old timers whittle down to a point," the coroner speculated. "It could have been wood or metal—anything with a fairly sharp tip—and it was driven into him with some force.

"Another thing," the coroner continued. "Unlike our railroad friend, this man died not long before I examined him—only a few hours prior, very likely."

"That means someone from your group could have killed him, Mr. Chan," the sheriff speculated. "Those folks that Clemden took from the train to the lodge—and the man himself, by gad—why, any of 'em could have done it."

Dr. Manston nodded to his assistant, and Dr. Strickler replaced the sheet.

"Best wheel both of them back to the icehouse, if you please," the coroner told Strickler. "That's what we call the makeshift morgue," Dr. Manston explained to his visitors. "It's been quite a while since I had two—er—guests at once, and so Dr. Strickler and I rigged up temporary quarters—and the undertaker will be along just as soon as we're done.

"Oh"—the coroner exclaimed. "One last thing. Just because of the other fellow's bloodwork results, I thought it would do no harm to look for something similar with the second one—and I found it."

"He was drugged, too?" Fairden asked.

Manston nodded.

"Significant presence of the same barbiturate or one very similar to the drug found in the other body," he confirmed. "Only difference is, it appears that death came not long after the barbital was ingested."

Sheriff Fairden cleared his throat.

"Maybe the person we're looking for decided that dosing a man would make him easier to deal with," he asserted. "Even a woman could have done for both of 'em—but she would have needed some help getting the headless fellow into the woods."

"Woman, man, somebody was not fond of these two," Dr. Manston concluded. "I wish you luck in your hunt."

The sun had disappeared by the time the two men left the coroner's headquarters, and the late morning sky was gray, with thickening clouds.

"Change in the weather," the sheriff remarked as the truck pulled away from Dr. Manston's curious workshop-cum-museum. "Never know what you might get this time of year in these mountains—anything from a warm, sunny day to a blizzard.

"Here's Eagle Bay," Chan's tour guide continued. "Thirty, maybe forty years ago a lot of the land here was owned by a man named Webb—they named the town after him."

"Town of Eagle Bay takes its name from a man called Webb?" Chan questioned.

"No, no," the sheriff hastened to explain. "The whole town—a much bigger area—that's what they named after him. Eagle Bay isn't a town in the legal sense of the word."

"Village?" Chan hazarded a guess. "The English word used to describe smaller communities, I think."

Sheriff Fairden laughed shortly.

"Maybe if a few more folks move in, they'll go to Albany and ask for permission to incorporate—to become a village," he clarified. "But for now, according to the lawmakers and the lawyers, Eagle Bay is what's known as a 'hamlet.'"

"Name of famous work by Englishman William Shakespeare," Chan recited, as though from some reference book he had consulted. "I have never seen the play performed, but I believe it is one with many murders."

He was silent for a moment.

"Place called Big Moose, site of the lodge on the lake," he mused, "this small settlement is also a 'hamlet'?"

Fairden glanced at the detective and nodded. Charlie Chan looked out the window at the thickening clouds.

"Most appropriate," he said.

Chapter Seventeen

A STRANGE CONTRAPTION

The return trip continued for a time with both men seemingly lost in their thoughts. Each was interpreting the coroner's findings. Finally, Chan broke the silence.

"Did you find Dr. Manston's report enlightening?"

The lawman shrugged.

"He told us mostly what we already knew—or, I should say, 'What you already knew,'" he admitted. "Ol' Doc knows his business, but he's no magician. He couldn't tell us who that fellow under the train was, and in the end both of these deaths come down to, 'caused by person or persons unknown,'" he grumbled.

"Perhaps," Chan acknowledged. "But we did learn something that we did not know before."

"What's that?" Fairden said curiously.

"Coroner and caretaker's common interests," Chan said cryptically. "Maybe on our way back to the lodge we might pay a call on Mr. Clemden?"

"Fine by me," the sheriff said agreeably. "We're almost there now."

"A brief conversation with this caretaker will not keep us from arriving at the lodge well before noon," Chan said after consulting his wristwatch.

"You in a hurry to get back?"

"Hour of noon, you will recall, is the deadline by which Frederick Scanlon has indicated that he will arrive," the detective reminded the lawman. "From this Scanlon we may learn many things—very important that we talk to him at the earliest possible opportunity."

"Before somebody kills him, too," the sheriff muttered under his breath.

The truck pulled into the turnoff that led to the caretaker's cabin. The two men got out and approached the little dwelling.

"Smoke's comin' out of the chimney," the sheriff noted. "So he's either here or was here not long ago."

Chan was looking in amazement at a strange contraption that sat near the side of the cabin. He recognized parts of it, but in its entirety it seemed to him like some mad scientist's mechanical dream turned nightmare.

"You must surely know," he asked the sheriff, "what manner of machine is this?"

Fairden laughed till his face reddened.

"I guess you probably wouldn't see one of these making its way down Main Street in Honolulu," he chortled. "This is something that comes in handy during the winter months—it's called a 'snowmobile.'"

Chan looked skeptically at the vehicle. Upon closer examination he realized that part of it had once been a Ford automobile, but the rest? The front end featured a pair of large wooden skis, and the rear wheels had been replaced by something resembling the tank treads that had made the fearsome weapons of the war nearly unstoppable.

"Fellow in New Hampshire had the bright idea some years back that he could take a Model-T and turn it into something that would make it through the snow a lot better than a Tin Lizzy with rubber tires," the sheriff explained. "He started making and selling kits for folks to turn their cars into what he decided to call snowmobiles. A lot of 'em did, in places like this. I think Clemden has had this thing for more than ten years now."

The front door of the cabin slammed shut behind the owner of the snowmobile, who had just stepped outside.

"I heard somebody—sounded like you, Sheriff—laughing," he said, smiling through his tremendous beard. "Just remember that the funny-looking piece of machinery you're finding so amusing sure comes in handy in December and January—"

"I was explaining to Mr. Chan how such a thing came to be," Fairden replied goodnaturedly. "First time he's ever seen a snowmobile."

"Most interesting," Chan assured the caretaker. "Sad to say, I have no camera to capture an image of this snow-vehicle—proof for skeptical family members that I truly encountered same during this visit to New York."

"Sorry I can't offer you a ride in it," Clemden said regretfully. "Unless the weather really takes a turn, that is."

"I don't know, Zach," Sheriff Fairden, looking up. "Seems as though we get snow earlier and earlier each year."

"Well, it may not be snowing right now," the caretaker said, opening the cabin door, "but it's beginning to feel cold enough for it. Why don't you two gents step inside where it's warmer?"

The three entered Clemden's cabin, a one-room affair that reflected the sole resident's personality and interests. Chan took a moment to admire the snug interior.

A squat, cast-iron stove stood in one corner of the room, and an array of tools and utensils hung on the walls to its left and right. The skin of a black bear lay on the floor, and the few pieces of furniture—a sturdy desk and chair and a long couch—looked handmade. Animal furs of various colors and shades provided comfort. On one wall the head of an antlered deer hung, seeming to stare endlessly at a large framed map of the Adirondack region that adorned the opposite wall.

The sheriff and Chan sat down on the sofa and their host pulled his only chair away from the desk. Seating himself opposite the two men, he looked first at the sheriff, then at Chan.

"I'm not in the habit of entertaining guests," the bearded man said gruffly, "but I reckon you've come to talk about the goings-on of late."

"Guess you could put it that way, Zach Clemden," the sheriff retorted. "But 'goings-on' is an awful poor way to describe two dead men in one day. And both of 'em murdered," he added for emphasis.

"Beg pardon," Clemden grunted. "Guess I wasn't thinkin' about the—er—seriousness of the situation, particularly from your perspective, Fairden—I mean, you havin' a job to do and all. It's jes' that I didn't know either of 'em, so—"

"Pardon, please, this interruption," Chan cut in. "How can you be sure the man found dead in the woods was unknown to you?"

Sheriff Fairden stared at the caretaker.

"Say . . . we're still tryin' to identify that body," he declared. "You know somethin' you're not tellin' us?"

A rumbling laugh escaped from the beard as Clemden got up and added a small log to the fire in the stove. He closed the iron door with a clang and turned toward the two men.

"I'll bet I know lots of things you don't," he mused, "and vicey versey, if it comes to that. All I know about the matter at hand is this: Nobody *I* know is dead, so I figure these two fellows are strangers to me. Probably strangers to everybody else around here, too, by all accounts."

"Not strange to everyone here," Chan countered softly. "Some person or persons knew them well enough—to kill."

Clemden sat down slowly and looked at both men steadily.

"Well, whoever that was that killed 'em is a mystery to me," the caretaker said emphatically. "That's one thing I know for sure. And it sure as hell wasn't me, since I was on the train with you, Inspector."

Chan nodded.

"Thank you for reminding me that your presence provided timely assistance to passengers," he noted. "The fact that you volunteered to guide them to the lodge—that was a great kindness."

Clemden grunted.

"Seemed like the thing to do," he muttered. "I wasn't any too keen to sit on that train any longer than I had to."

"You are frequent passenger on the line, perhaps? What was the nature of your journey this time?"

"I wouldn't say frequent," Clemden countered. "Maybe several times a year I have to make a trip for this or that. Had to go to Utica a few days ago to get a part for the big boiler at the lodge—what with winter comin' on—so I left that morning, hitched a ride down to Thendara to catch the early train.

"But the city fellow didn't have the part, blast the luck. So I took that afternoon train back."

"And then you helpfully volunteered to lead passengers from one car only—those bound for the big lodge—to their destination," Chan said thoughtfully.

"That's right," Clemden said, looking warily at the detective. "It seemed to me that there was no sense—"

"How did you know of the reserved carriage and the destination of those traveling in it?" Chan cut in.

Clemden stared at the detective for a moment.

"Heard the conductor mention it, and then I remembered," the bearded man explained. "Mrs. Warren at the lodge, she had said somethin' a while back about a big to-do at the lodge—but all this time, I was thinkin' it was next weekend.

"When I heard the railroad man say something about a special car of folks headed for the lodge at Big Moose, and then—"

"Then the train stopped, and you decided to serve as unofficial guide," Chan finished.

"That's about the size of it," Clemden rumbled.

The sheriff consulted his watch and got to his feet.

"Unless you've got more questions, Mr. Chan, I think we'd best be on our way." He looked meaningfully at the detective.

"It's gettin' on toward noon—the morning jes' got away from us."

"Anything else you need while you're at the lodge," Clemden offered, "jes' let me know. That young fellow Trenville will be in charge today and most of tomorrow—I have to head over to Raquette Lake to see to some business there."

Thanking Clemden for his time, the two men followed the caretaker to the door.

Like the cabin's other features, the door and its frame were artistic creations. The door itself was a great, thick slab formed by two layers of planking. Its interior side was smooth and unadorned, but outside a formidable black metal knocker greeted Clemden's visitors. The doorknocker consisted of a three-inch ring coupled with a combined base and strike plate at least a foot high—ironware more suited to a castle than a one-room cabin.

While the sheriff started up the truck Chan paused in the doorway and ran his hands over the box-like strike plate, rapping on it with his knuckles, and complimenting the caretaker on his handiwork.

"Caretaking job allows time for you to explore many interests," he commented. "Dr. Manston said you are both very fond of preserving deceased wild animals."

Clemden chuckled.

"Ol' Doc—he missed his calling. Should've been a taxidermist instead of a sawbones! But he's done quite a fair amount of work—some of those heads at the lodge and Big Bull, too, of course. Fine pieces of work, all of 'em."

Chan smiled guilelessly.

"Coroner also showed us his display of rocks with famous Adirondack gemstones," he said casually. "Most interesting."

"Gemstones," Clemden looked puzzled. "What kind of—oh! Of course," he exclaimed. "Ol' Doc has a liking for garnets. He has a nice little collection of 'em in their natural state. Not much value to be had from 'em, but they're nice to look at."

Chan smiled and took his leave.

"Well," the sheriff said as they drove away from the cabin, "what do you think of Clemden now that you've had a good look at him?"

"True wilderness man in many ways," Chan replied. "In dress, in occupation—living quarters, interests. All these speak of a man who is rough, rugged—like his mountain surroundings."

"That pretty much sums him up," Fairden agreed. "I jes' can't see that he'd have any reason for tangling with people from the city, visitors to the lodge—those folks are hardly his cup of tea."

Charlie Chan was silent, his face an expressionless mask.

"Anyway," the sheriff went on, "I'm anxious to meet this fellow from the city, this Scanlon. And it's jes' now noon."

The truck pulled into a spot near the back entrance to the lodge, and the two men presented themselves to Mrs. Warren. "Good day to you," the sheriff said heartily to the woman as she ushered them through the doorway. "Mr. Chan and I are hoping that a caller has come looking for us—a fellow from New York."

"A Mr. Frederick Scanlon," Chan added, looking at the cook carefully. He thought a look of—Unease? Uncertainty?—had flashed across her face.

"Heavens!" Mrs. Warren blurted. "The cake!"

She turned and hurried to remedy the situation. The two men noticed a faint smell of baking as they followed her into the warm kitchen. Mrs. Warren pulled two cake pans from the oven and put them aside to cool.

"You'll pardon me, gentlemen, but some things won't wait," the woman declared, her face flushed from the heat of the oven.

"The kettle's on the boil, and I was just about to have a cup of tea if you'd like to join me. No? Well, don't mind me."

Mrs. Warren poured the steaming water into a stoneware mug and gestured toward two wooden chairs normally reserved for the help, and her guests took their seats.

"Now, you were asking about a caller. No one has come to the lodge all morning," she said emphatically. "I haven't heard so much as a knock on the door till you two came and nearly spoiled my layer cake."

"So sorry to disturb the lady of lodge," Chan said contritely. "The wise man treats his cook like a queen—the fool who does otherwise goes hungry."

"No danger of that in this house," Mrs. Warren said promptly. "We make sure everyone's well fed, whether he's a fool or not."

The sheriff eyed the cake, and the cook's preparations—he assumed—for frosting, and all the makings of his favorite dessert: any kind of cake, with any kind of frosting.

"Sure smells good," Fairden said hopefully. "Mrs. Warren bakes the best cakes in the whole county, Mr. Chan. You being a lodge guest and all—why, you're a lucky man."

"Now, Farley Fairden," the cook ordered, "You take yourself and your flattery out of my kitchen. I've work to do, and—"

"Mrs. Warren, that jar of sugar that went missing—I found it! Will it do for the icing?"

Mary Roberts appeared from the pantry with a small glass jar in hand and a hopeful look on her face. She had already provoked Mrs. Warren's ire once today.

"Mercy, child!" Mrs. Warren's face was puzzled. "No, that's not it—I don't recall seeing that before. It must be left over from some—well, no matter. Give it to me."

The girl handed over the container, which the cook opened absently with a twist of its lid.

"There should be a full bag that hasn't even been opened," Mrs. Warren said irritably. "Now, you go look for a label that says 'Imperial Confectioner's Sugar,' and bring that bag to me."

Redfaced and near tears, the girl returned to the pantry. Mrs. Warren's audience of two looked on silently, and the cook apologized for what they had witnessed.

"Begging your pardon, gentlemen," she whispered. "Mary has been something of a trial to me—"

"One moment, please!"

Charlie Chan extended a warning hand as the woman prepared to spoon some of the jar's contents into her steaming tea.

"In light of recent events," the detective cautioned, "it is best to view unfamiliar substances with caution—even in the kitchen."

"Why, I'm sure I don't know—there's surely nothing in that pantry that I didn't put there my own self," Mrs. Warren protested. "Or one of the other staff here."

"Yet you did not recognize this particular container," Chan reminded her, gently returning the spoonful of the white substance into the jar.

"What are you thinkin', Mr. Chan?" Sheriff Fairden put in.

"More intuition than thought, in this case," the detective replied. "As cousin Willie Chan would say, I am 'playing hunch.'"

Chan inserted a fingertip into the jar and tasted a minute amount of its contents.

"Crystalline powder resembles sugar," he remarked, holding the jar up to the light. "But bitter taste indicates this substance is likely barbital—the drug sold to many as a sleeping aid.

"In a small dose it brings sleep," Chan went on, replacing the lid and handing the jar to the sheriff. "In larger quantities, this drug results in unconscious state—even death."

Mrs. Warren blanched.

"But who—"

"That's what we aim to find out, ma'am," the sheriff reassured her. "Mr. Chan, I can have Doc Manston confirm your hunch. Personally, I think you're on the right track, but—"

"Here you are, ma'am." Mary had returned with the requested item, which she set on the counter.

"Ah! That's just what we need," the woman declared. "Now, let me show you how this is done—properly, mind you—and we'll have something that will please the guests tonight."

"I have a great favor to ask," Chan said to the sheriff, after the two men had exited Mrs. Warren's domain. The sounds of Miss Clarkson and Clarissa mingled with the barking of Mischief the dog came faintly to their ears as they stood outside the back door.

"Ask away," the sheriff responded.

"The man Clemden told us that he would travel to a lake—"

"Raquette Lake, he said," the sheriff supplied. "What are you thinkin'?"

"My thought is that you might follow him to this place, if you would be so kind—discreetly, so that he is unaware he is observed—and see what he does there."

"Good lord," Fairden exclaimed. "You think—"

"For the moment, my thoughts are many," Chan cut in, "but we must begin to narrow our search—to rule out certain persons, while examining others more closely.

"Consider," he began, ticking off points on the finger of one hand as the sheriff listened intently. "Passengers on train—should we consider them innocent of the deaths, since murders both occurred while they were traveling to the lodge?"

"I would say so, yes," Fairden agreed. "But that leaves us with what, exactly—'person or persons unknown'?"

"The point is an excellent one," Chan replied. "Involvement of someone on the train is still possible—if they conspired with an accomplice who actually committed one or both crimes. This person, possibly, remains to be identified."

"Speaking of which," the sheriff pointed out, "how in the Sam Hill are we ever goin' to figure out who the dead man under the train was? I even thought of taking his fingerprints, but what's the point?"

"Correct," Charlie Chan said. "Fingerprints of an unknown man must be compared with some existing record—a tall order, in this case.

"Still," he reminded the sheriff, "one possibility has occurred to me—possibly to you, also?"

"What's that?" Fairden demanded.

"Failure of Frederick Scanlon to arrive here by his guaranteed deadline of noon—what could have prevented his arrival?"

The sheriff snorted skeptically.

"Heck, a dozen reasons! Maybe his train was late, or some big business deal came up unexpectedly, or . . ."

"Or maybe," Chan said thoughtfully, "his body now lies in your coroner's makeshift morgue."

Sheriff Fairden had just settled a fresh wad of chewing tobacco between his cheek and gum. The idea that a business tycoon of Scanlon's stature might have met his end in Big Moose nearly choked him, but the sheriff recovered quickly—even if some of his tobacco did not.

"You think," he said, hoarsely—a few shreds of Red Man were struggling to escape from his throat— "I mean to say: You think that Scanlon, the fellow who hired you to figure out who was trying to kill him; Scanlon, the big businessman from New York—"

"—could be the unfortunate victim of the person or persons he suspected," Chan finished. "Killer then demonstrates his contempt for Scanlon—and for police who will investigate his murder—by erasing his features under the wheels of a train. A crude but effective method."

With the wad of tobacco in one cheek, Sheriff Fairden looked like a puzzled squirrel. The thought of some well-known titan of Wall Street murdered at Big Moose—it would be a nine days' wonder like that Gillette case thirty-odd years ago.

"In the case of the second murder," Chan went on, "train passengers are ruled out, of course, but some guests were already present at the lodge. The monsignor, I think, was one. Also Scanlon's former brother-in-law, William Yantzen. You may recall the name of Alexander Creighton from Scanlon's letters to me: Is he truly absent, or has he been responsible for one or both killings? Also we must not forget those who work at or visit the lodge regularly—even the postman."

The sheriff's thoughts returned to the present day.

"Well, my money's on Yantzen, a shifty looking no-good. As for people who work at the lodge—Mrs. Warren and that young fellow, Trenville? And the mailman?" Fairden scoffed. "One thing's for sure—there's no way a priest could be responsible for what's happened here," he declared confidently.

The detective smiled faintly.

"History tells us that priests are also men," he pointed out, "and men are capable of many things. Experience has taught me to consider all possible suspects equally. For this reason, while you travel to Raquette Lake, I will engage in conversation with both men—separately.

"Who knows?" Chan said with a grim smile. "Maybe one of us will discover a murderer."

Chapter Eighteen

A GRIM DIORAMA

The sheriff departed to shadow Clemden, promising to report what he discovered about the caretaker's doings. Charlie Chan walked around the lodge, admiring the lake and its surroundings, toward the front entrance. Clarissa was playing in the grass with Mrs. Warren's dog, Mischief, under the watchful eye of Miss Clarkson, who was dividing her attention between the little girl and a beaming Matthew Trenville.

"Greetings, Mr. Chan," the young man said cheerily. "Fine day for viewing the lake or strolling through the woods! How goes your investigation?"

"Investigation develops like nearby trees called 'spruce,' the detective grinned. "The progress is not visible at first, but eventually all will see the results."

The two young people laughed.

"I'm sure you'll get there," said Miss Clarkson encouragingly.

"Thank you for your confidence," the detective replied. "May I take some few minutes to ask you a small number of questions?"

"Me?" Gloria Clarkson laughed nervously. "Why, certainly! But Clarissa—"

"I'll take care of your shadow for you," Trenville said gaily. "Clarissa! Let's see if Mischief knows how to fetch."

The two ran toward the dog, leaving Chan and the girl to their tête-à-tête.

"How fortunate for Mrs. Scanlon," Chan began tentatively, "that she can rely on you to help care for such an energetic daughter. Have you held this position for long?"

"Oh! Clarissa isn't Mrs. Scanlon's child, Mr. Chan," the young woman said quickly. "At least, not yet."

The detective paused, his eyebrows raised.

"She is, then, a foster parent?"

"Temporarily, yes," Gloria Clarkson said slowly. She sighed. "You see, Clarissa has been at St. Michael's Home since her parents were—well, ever since she was orphaned as a baby."

The young woman paused for a moment.

"I've been working at the home for nearly three years now," she went on. "Mrs. Scanlon was a donor for quite some time—or so I've been told—before she began to consider adopting a child.

"For the past month Clarissa has lived in the Scanlon home, and I have been assigned to provide support and companionship for her," she explained. "By next week, Mrs. Scanlon is supposed to decide whether or not she'll adopt Clarissa."

"Excuse this interruption, please," Chan put in. "Possibly Mrs. Scanlon's financial support helped bring about this arrangement?"

Miss Clarkson smiled faintly.

"It's not for me to judge, but donors—especially donors like Mrs. Scanlon—are important to St. Michael's. *Very* important."

Mischief barked in the distance, and the dog's playmates could be heard laughing at his antics.

"Mrs. Scanlon's behavior in recent weeks—how would you describe it?" Chan inquired.

"She's very much the same as I've always found her," Miss Clarkson replied promptly. "A very respectable woman, a no-nonsense person—very serious. Even with the child."

Her expression softened.

"Sometimes," she said quietly. "Sometimes, I wish . . ."

Chan waited, but there was no more.

Gloria Clarkson cleared her throat.

"Even the—the events here this weekend don't seem to have upset her," she concluded, looking from the playful scene across the lawn back to the detective. "Is there anything else?"

"You have been most helpful," Chan nodded, smiling. "Thank you for your assistance."

Trenville and the girl, pursued by Mischief, were running in circles nearby. Gloria Clarkson left Chan to rejoin her charge, and Trenville walked back to the detective's side.

"Quite a girl, isn't she, Mr. Chan," Trenville confided. "Too bad she's going back to the city soon—after this is all over, I mean."

The detective looked knowingly at Matthew Trenville.

"One does not need to be a detective to see there is great affection between you two," Chan observed. "The looks you exchange recall to me a young man and woman gazing at each other in similar fashion—many years ago. Like you, they saw obstacles to happiness in their path."

Trenville was silent for a moment. He looked at the detective from a far-off place—so strange a man, but so human. A remarkable person.

"And how did that couple make out?"

Chan had a faraway look in *his* eyes.

"Their determination overcame many obstacles," he said dreamily. "The gods smiled on them. Eleven children, some now grown, joined them in their bungalow over the years—eventually, there was a grandchild. And the couple still live in their little house on a hillside, spending quiet evenings together—"

Chan turned and regarded the younger man encouragingly.

"—except when the husband travels on business," he concluded with a look of regret.

"That sure is some story," Trenville said nonchalantly, but there was a gleam in his eye.

"Your story, when one day you tell it to a younger man, will be even more remarkable," Chan assured him. "Now—to business. You can, perhaps, tell me the location of one Yantzen, first name William?"

"In a sorry state, when last I saw him," chirped Trenville, sounding thoroughly unsympathetic. "Keeps late hours and, I assume, has only recently risen."

He led Chan toward the entrance and opened one of the big wooden doors for the detective.

"I think he may still be taking coffee in the dining room," the young man remarked.

As the detective stepped silently down the hallway that led to the dining room and kitchen, the sound of voices in urgent conversation arrested his progress. He grimaced—the professional obligation of a detective to listen at doors clashed with his natural inclinations—and paused by the doorway. He could hear three voices, those of two women and a man.

"I don't see that it's any of your business, Daniel Bryant." The cold delivery of Mrs. Scanlon's message to a lesser mortal was all too familiar to the detective. "In Frederick's absence it falls to me to defend him, and I tell you that he would have nothing to do with this—this—"

"I'm not saying that he's involved in the deaths of those two men," Bryant said sharply. "My only point is that we shouldn't hold anything back from the police. And Fred's state of mind for some time—"

"—has been utterly normal. There's absolutely no evidence that would support your monstrous insinuations," Mrs. Scanlon replied emphatically. "It would be folly to share such uninformed speculation with the police—not to mention it would amount to a very grave slander."

Chan's keen hearing was aided by the old wooden door's imperfect fit in its frame. The speakers kept their voices low, but the detective could hear every word.

A second woman addressed Mrs. Scanlon, and Chan recognized Muriel Bryant.

"Really, Edna, we've been friends for I don't know how many years, and you should know that Daniel and I have your best interests in mind," Mrs. Bryant said brightly. "After all, I don't see why you persist in this loyalty to a man who treated you so poorly. After all—"

Mrs. Scanlon's voice went from chilly to glacial as she interrupted her longtime friend.

"Muriel Bryant, our friendship does not give you the right to pry into my most intimate affairs," she seethed. "There is no room for debate and no need for further discussion.

"I know what course of action I will undertake," she declared. "You two, of course, will do as you see fit. But be warned—" Mrs. Scanlon's voice was quiet but harsh. "—be warned, I tell you, there will be consequences. Of that you may be sure."

Sensing that the conversation had come to an end, Chan stepped back. The door jerked open abruptly, and Mrs. Scanlon stalked out and down the hallway toward the main staircase.

Charlie Chan knocked gently on the open door and entered.

"Pardon this intrusion," he said simply. "I must confess that some part of your conversation escaped the confines of this room, but no apologies can be offered by one who seeks a murderer."

The Bryants stood in the room, a small parlor with much the same decor as the rest of the lodge—only its wildlife exhibits were of the smaller kind. A few heads hung on the walls, and a grim diorama on a side table depicted a crow pecking at the remains of some small animal. The lifelike scene startled most first-time visitors, but Charlie Chan's keen eyes swept the macabre tabletop tableau, and his face betrayed nothing. He closed the door behind him and continued.

"Duty compels me to probe further the nature of your talk with Mrs. Scanlon," Chan said, politely but firmly. "The subject, I believe, was information concerning the absent Mr. Scanlon—information you proposed to communicate to the authorities."

Husband and wife looked at the detective, then at each other. Mrs. Bryant parted her lips to speak, thought better of it, and closed her mouth. Daniel Bryant frowned and cleared his throat.

"You're quite correct, Mr. Chan, and whatever social niceties would have kept us from speaking must be discarded," he said firmly. "Not that we believe for a minute that my once-close friend Fred would have—could have—" Bryant paused for a moment, then continued.

"No," he said forcefully. "Frederick Scanlon is not a murderer. The matter we were discussing with Mrs. Scanlon . . ." Bryant hesitated, nodding at his wife, then went on.

"In recent years, we have not seen him—ever since he cut ties with me—although Muriel and Edna have kept in touch."

"What was the reason for the cutting of ties between good friends?" Chan put in, thinking of Scanlon's version of the schism. "Some business disagreement, perhaps?"

"Well-l-l," Bryant said slowly, "I guess you could put it that way. Truth of the matter is, there wasn't any business dealing between us—just this one time that he mentioned some tremendous, fantastic opportunity that had just fallen into his lap.

"Naturally, I expressed some interest in the whole thing—to be polite, really," he continued, "and he immediately clammed up, as though he sensed my insincerity, and changed the topic of our conversation. Never referred to the whole thing again, and of course I never did either."

A look of regret passed across Daniel Bryant's face.

"Not that either of us had much chance of mentioning the subject, since from that day he—as I said—abandoned what had been a close friendship. I was looking forward to seeing him here; thought I could make another attempt to set things aright. Now . . ."

His voice trailed off uncertainly. Muriel Bryant cast a sympathetic eye on her husband but remained silent.

"Unfortunately," Chan said solemnly, "it may be impossible for you to make amends with Frederick Scanlon." He paused and watched both Bryants carefully.

"Why, whatever do you mean?" Mrs. Bryant blurted. "Has something . . . happened?"

The couple gazed at the detective intently. Her eyes were bright, his were dull.

"Sheriff is considering the possibility that the body of murdered man found under the train that brought us here is that of our absent host," Chan said blandly. He waited for some reaction from either of the Bryants, but each looked suitably shocked.

"Poppycock," Daniel Bryant croaked, breaking the brief silence. "I can't believe it."

"Surely you don't believe such a thing is possible, do you Mr. Chan?" Muriel Bryant seemed to be having difficulty absorbing the idea; her voice was troubled. "It just seems so unreal that someone like Fred—so vital, so alive—could be . . . ."

Her voice quavered.

"Besides," she resumed, reining in her emotions. "Who would want to murder Frederick Scanlon? It just seems preposterous."

Chan's face was impassive. His eyes darted from husband to wife and back again.

"Chinese philosophy says we should see unity in life and death," the detective noted, "but the wicked who traffic in murder—they must be brought to justice. Different than behavior of animals in nature," he gestured toward the diorama, "but some humans behave like beasts—feeding on what remains of the dead, and—"

Chan's eyes shone brightly. The carrion bird's plumage appeared full on one side, less so on the other side.

The Bryants realized that the detective was deep in thought. They looked at the diorama and saw only another example of the taxidermist's art, one of many they had seen in the lodge.

Disgusting scene, Muriel Bryant thought. Her husband was more interested in what had captured Charlie Chan's attention. *This fellow's sharp*, he mused. *Far brighter than that sheriff.*

Chan found Yantzen as described—blearily sipping coffee from a large mug and slumped in a chair at the long table. To the detective's eye the man showed signs of dissipation older than the previous evening's debauchery. From his bloodshot eyes to the noticeable tremor in both hands, Yantzen's appearance was that of a man in thrall to grape, grain, or both.

"Good afternoon," Chan said by way of announcing his presence in the room. Yantzen had been so focused on the hot drink before him that he was unaware of much else. "May I join you?"

"Suit yourself," Yantzen grunted. "Plenty of furniture here, as you can see."

"Thank you." Chan seated himself across the table and gazed steadily at the bleary-eyed man, who found the silent scrutiny unnerving.

After a minute or more of silence, Yantzen tabled his half-empty mug with a bang.

"Is there something I can do for the only Chinese man in this part of the country?" The question was more sneer than query. "The only Chinese cop, I should say."

The detective's silent scrutiny continued for several seconds. Yantzen returned to his coffee. His words were bold, but his manner was uneasy.

Finally, Chan spoke.

"Did you enjoy walking in the darkness last night?"

Yantzen looked hard at the detective, but Chan's face was innocent of all expression.

"Surely you didn't come in here to ask me about my late-night habits?" Yantzen taunted. "Cops usually have more important things on their mind. But maybe you're new to police work—after your career in laundry—"

"Where were you when the man Merriweather was slain?"

Chan's face was impassive, but his voice cut through the other man's insults with an intensity that brought Yantzen up short.

"Perhaps," Chan continued, "you would be so kind as to describe where you were—and what you did there?"

Yantzen's face had lost some of its befogged expression, but his voice retained most of its combative quality.

"I would be happy to answer those questions," he said sarcastically, "if you can tell me exactly when this—Merriweather, was it?—when the late Mr. Merriweather was 'slain,' as you put it."

"Let us say, then, the moment when you heard a woman scream to indicate the discovery of the dead man's presence at the top of the stairs—perhaps you recall what occupied you then?"

"Dear me, dear me," Yantzen said mockingly. "I believe I was in the bath, if you must know. At the far end of the hall, far from the stairwell." He aimed an insolent look at the detective. "In answer to your next question, it was quite a long bath."

"And before you decided to devote extensive time to personal cleanliness—how did you occupy your time then, please?"

Yantzen tilted his head back as though reading the answer from the dining room ceiling.

"Let me see—oh, yes! I recall now," he replied. "I was outside for some little time—enjoying nature, you know—and then I pestered that Mrs. Warren in the kitchen for something to eat. Damn the woman! She said she was too busy to tend to the needs of one man when she was trying to feed the masses, the soon-to-arrive passengers from the late train. Of which you were one, I believe."

Yantzen cocked an eye at the detective.

"Then, failing to satisfy my hunger, I took myself upstairs to the bath—hoping that Mrs. Warren's victuals would be ready after I had washed away the dust of the previous day's travel."

Yantzen slammed the now-empty mug onto the table and glared at Chan.

"And I can assure you," he concluded icily, "that all was well when I mounted the stairs from first floor to second. Furthermore, I've never seen or met this Merriweather."

"Most informative, thank you," Chan said blandly. "One question more, please."

"Only one?" Yantzen raised both eyebrows in mock concern. "I fear my customary charm is in short supply today. I was certain that you would subject me to a much longer interrogation."

"Time enough for that, later," the detective retorted evenly. "The sheriff will enjoy a discussion with you when circumstances require it. Meanwhile, please answer me this:

"When did you last speak with Frederick Scanlon, your former brother-in-law?"

Again, Chan thought, a hint of unease flashed across the man's face.

"Frederick the Great?" Yantzen said mockingly. "Not for some years—he's never really loved me like a brother, you know. Then again, he treated my sister badly, so—"

"You have not seen him recently—here, in this lodge?" Chan persisted. "You came at his invitation after receiving a letter from him."

"A letter? From Fred? Oh, I hardly think so." Yantzen leered suggestively. "You see, I have a heavy correspondence—but very few letters from men."

"If you received no invitation to visit this lodge," Chan countered, "then why are you here?"

"My dear Mr. Chan, I didn't say I had no invitation to this lovely spot," Yantzen rejoined. "I was invited to come here by my dear sister, Mrs. Scanlon."

"Perhaps she explained the nature of this weekend gathering?"

"No, she simply invited me to meet her and her little entourage here for a few days' relaxation," Yantzen asserted. "My sister and I are close, as you no doubt already know, and I was pleased to accept her kind offer."

"You were unaware, then, that your former brother-in-law had reserved the lodge for the weekend—and paid for all guests to travel here?"

"Frankly, I left all such things to my sister, since she was kind enough to invite me," Yantzen's face assumed a puzzled expression. "What you're suggesting seems very unlikely—"

"Even unlikely things can happen," Chan noted. "Just as the truthful man may one day tell a lie, the liar can sometimes speak the truth."

Yantzen flushed angrily. "Look here, if you're suggesting that I—"

"So sorry," Chan said blandly. "I was merely quoting an ancient proverb of my people."

As the detective got up to leave, Mrs. Warren appeared from the kitchen.

"Will there be anything else, Mr. Yantzen?" The woman's face was drawn, her eyes tired.

"More coffee," the man said rudely. "I don't believe Mr. Chan wants anything— he was just leaving."

"I want only to ask a question of this talented cook and baker," Chan put in. "About last night's disturbance."

"What in particular, Mr. Chan?"

"I have been told," Chan explained, "that it was the cry of Mrs. Glas from the stairs that told all that something unfortunate had happened."

"Oh, my—yes, indeed. Fairly screamed the house down," Mrs. Warren affirmed.

"You were at work in the kitchen when the lady was heard throughout the house?"

"Oh, yes. I'd been told to expect the people from the train—the weekend party, you know."

"Please recall the time before Mrs. Glas cried for help—you had a visitor in the kitchen, perhaps?"

"This gentleman, Mr. Yantzen," she nodded in his general direction. "He wanted something to eat, but I told him to be off—that he could eat when the others arrived. Away he went, grumbling to himself, and that was the last I saw of him."

"How much time, please, between Mr. Yantzen's departure from the kitchen and the cry of Mrs. Glas?"

Mrs. Warren looked from Chan to Yantzen and back again, her face a wan, waxen mask.

"It was quite some time," she said listlessly. "Quite some time, indeed—I don't recall, exactly—I was busy just then."

"Precisely," Yantzen interjected. "As I told you, Mr. Chan, I went off to have a bath. Thank you, Mrs. Warren—coffee, please?"

The woman turned to the detective.

"I'm sorry, sir, but I can't be more precise than that—will that be all?"

Chan nodded.

"Thank you so much," he said graciously. His placid manner cloaked any disappointment he might have felt at Mrs. Warren's incomplete recall. "I have no more questions for you."

Chapter Nineteen
THE BARKING OF THE DOG

Making his way into the great room, Chan was pleased to see the two men he was looking for, Monsignor Plevna and Dr. Collins. The priest and doctor appeared to be in earnest conversation by the fire.

"Just the man we need," Dr. Collins said heartily. "Please, Mr. Chan—draw up a chair and join us."

"We've been struggling," Plevna explained, "struggling with a kind of dilemma, because of the commitment to confidentiality our two callings require of us."

"But we're increasingly concerned," Dr. Collins interjected, "about the absence of Fred—Mr. Scanlon, and since your presence here must be at his behest—"

Chan nodded noncommittally.

"—we have decided to consult you, and confidentiality be damned. Beg pardon, Monsignor."

Plevna smiled and addressed the detective.

"As you no doubt already know, Mr. Chan, Frederick Scanlon and I were great friends years ago. I suppose he considered me something more than a mere friend, though. Perhaps 'confidant and spiritual adviser' expresses it more accurately.

"I won't give you many details because he didn't tell me all, but there came a time when he shared with me that he was entangled with a young woman but had no intention of marrying her," the priest said solemnly. "With such a man, the accumulation of wealth and his future career came first; and he turned away from his obligations—against my advice.

"Our friendship deteriorated from then on, and I learned of his marriage through the newspaper gossip columns." The cleric's nose wrinkled; the whiff of unseemly journalism was distasteful. "His wife's family wealth was said to be vast, and Fred supposedly needed capital to either stave off financial ruin or to advance his goals."

"Curiosity compels me to rudely interrupt," Chan said apologetically. "What became of the young woman?"

Monsignor Plevna hesitated before replying.

"I posed that same question to Frederick Scanlon when last we met," the priest recalled. "He refused to answer me, said the matter was none of my—none of my business.

"Fred that day was not the man I knew," he said sadly. "Something about him had changed—and not for the better. He seemed hard. Cruel, even.

"That was the last time we spoke."

The priest extended an open hand toward the doctor, and Collins took up the tale.

"Throughout the time Monsignor has described, I was aware that Fred was involved with a young woman," Dr. Collins began, "but I knew nothing further.

"However, it seemed to me," he continued, "that he was under a great strain—and that worried me. About that time, my practice was thriving. I was quite busy, professionally, but still attempted to maintain our friendship."

He smiled regretfully.

"I say 'attempted' because my efforts were unsuccessful, and Fred's marriage to Edna was followed by a tremendous growth in his business—so he said, when I spoke to him the last time.

"Monsignor described a change in his temperament," the doctor continued. "I'll go further than that. In my medical judgement, Fred Scanlon had suffered a kind of nervous breakdown from which he had not recovered. Apart from that, he had acquired grandiose ideas as to his 'destiny,' as he termed it.

"I thought that he showed signs of what Jung called 'hypomania,'" Dr. Collins said thoughtfully. "There were elements of manic behavior—I found his demeanor disturbing."

The other two men sat in silence. A log sizzled and popped a glowing ember onto the stone hearth.

"There's very little more to tell," Dr. Collins concluded. "I advised him—as a medical man, as a friend—to see a specialist. He was—well, he did not accept my advice.

"In fact, he flew into a rage—a kind of fit characteristic of his troubled, perhaps diseased, mental state, in my opinion." He smiled sadly. "Even accused me of conspiring against him, or being one of his enemies. We were all in league against him, he said.

"That was his last word to me—until the letter that came to invite me here."

Chan nodded thoughtfully.

"This mental condition—it caused the Scanlons to go their separate ways?"

The priest and doctor exchanged glances.

"I would say so," Dr. Collins agreed. "The way I read the situation, Fred's so-called vision was that of a lone man against the world. His erratic behavior, his outbursts . . . I think she was relieved to see him go."

He smiled.

"She would never admit that, of course," the doctor continued. "She's a very determined person in her own right. Publicly, she's always played the part of the wronged woman—abandoned by her headstrong husband."

"Perhaps in present circumstances she will express her true feelings," Chan mused. "Local authorities believe they can explain the absence of Frederick Scanlon from this lodge gathering that he organized."

"How so?" Dr. Collins demanded.

"The body found on the train's track in the woods could not be identified by its facial features," Chan said carefully. "Very few possessions found in dead man's pockets, but one item of interest was a ring with some curious symbol—like a Greek letter—"

The detective pulled out his notebook and pen and sketched the ring's crescent, like a reversed letter "c" with a short, curved tail.

The priest smiled; he recognized the symbol. Dr. Collins was mystified for a moment. Then light dawned.

"Of course, by gad! A signet ring—may I borrow your pencil?"

The physician carefully set down a mirror image of Chan's drawing, producing something very like the letter "c" with a little tail: ς.

"You were on the right track, Mr. Chan," said Collins. "The ring's design was the opposite of the letter, of course, to produce the correct image in sealing wax. A Greek letter—just one you don't see very often. It's called 'final sigma'—"

"The ancient Greeks used this lower-case letter at the end of a word in lower-case script to signify the end of a sentence," Monsignor Plevna put in.

"Indeed," Dr. Collins acknowledged the priest's contribution. "All I know for a fact is that it represents membership in a university fraternal organization."

Chan's eyes widened.

"Location of the college club that uses this symbol, please?"

"The only one I know of is at Albany," the doctor said thoughtfully. "Whoever wore this ring must have been a member."

The detective reflected.

"Please pardon what may seem like an impertinent question," Chan said apologetically, "but how do you know of this Greek group?"

Dr. Collins shifted one side of his jacket to reveal a gold pin with the Greek letter ς on his vest. "I was at the college in Albany, too," he remarked. "This signet ring you're describing—you say it was found on the body in the woods?"

Chan nodded.

"Fred Scanlon joined the same year I did," the physician murmured. "You think—"

"Possibility has been discussed with sheriff that the body under train could be that of Mr. Scanlon," Chan admitted. "Possession of a ring bearing symbol of college group could provide further evidence.

"Something you said about the particular kind of ring," said Chan, "and its peculiar nature . . . " The detective's voice trailed off, and his face assumed a far-off expression.

The priest and the doctor looked at each other, puzzled by the detective's dreamy expression.

"Er—I said that it was a signet ring," Dr. Collins repeated. "I believe I mentioned that the character was purposely reversed—to produce its opposite in wax, whenever the wearer wanted to seal the flap of an envelope, for example."

Chan's eyes gleamed. He pocketed pencil, notebook, and the loose page.

"I find that men of great learning provide answers to many questions," the detective said cheerfully. "Like a lighthouse gives safe guidance to ships, their knowledge enlightens dim policeman."

Monsignor Plevna looked thoughtfully at Chan.

"You must possess some quality, some intuition, that enables you to interpret meanings that remain hidden to others," the priest reasoned. "I fail to see—"

"Please forgive my interruption," Chan grinned, "but you may have heard that some individuals claim to possess extraordinary powers of the mind. I make no such claim, but my belief is that all Chinese are psychic people. Something happens—a word, a gesture—and an impression is created, like camera film exposed to light.

"For now," he said, his hand on the doorknob, "I must do as son Henry sometimes says, 'Take the ball and run with it.'"

Finding the kitchen empty, Charlie Chan stepped outside the back door where he encountered Mrs. Warren's temporary helper, Mary Roberts.

"If you're looking for Mrs. Warren, she's trying to convince Mischief to come into the lodge," the girl explained. "They're over there—in the trees."

A woman's voice and the barking of the dog could be heard faintly. Chan turned his attention to the girl.

"Thank you," the detective said politely, "but I was looking for you."

"Me? Whatever for?" Mary's face registered worry—fear of the unknown. "I don't know anything about—about—"

"No need for concern," Chan assured her. "Merely wish to ask you about your work in the kitchen—and those you have met at this lodge.

"Tell me about Mrs. Warren—do you enjoy your work with her? She seems like a kind woman, one who is skilled at preparing food for lodge guests."

This was safe territory for the perpetually worried Mary. She regaled Chan with a thorough summary of her kitchen duties, the gruff kindness of Mrs. Warren, and how recent events seemed to have disrupted their routine.

"She seems quite upset for some reason—I suppose it's all because of the dead man at the top of the stairs," Mary said in a hushed voice. "This morning I was helping that nice Miss Clarkson play with the little girl, and she fairly screamed the house down—she was that put out! And yesterday she nearly took my head off when I couldn't find the leftover sugar—and then, later, it turned up after all!"

The girl looked miffed; Chan's quizzical look prompted a further explanation.

"You see, whether it's flour or sugar—or powdered sugar—Mrs. Warren's very particular about keeping things fresh," she explained. "I'm always to put the 'remains,' as she calls them—what's left from the box or tin that's just been opened into a glass jar. Pop a lid onto it and it'll be as good as new, she says.

"Keeps the remains next to the new package of whatever-it-is. I don't know what upset her more—when I couldn't find it, or when I did. I've never seen such a fuss."

Chan had witnessed the second incident; he thought the girl's account was accurate.

"Mrs. Warren avoids displays of emotion—does not show anger or reveal that she is upset?"

"Never!" Mary said emphatically. "That's why yesterday took me by surprise.

"Although," she hesitated. "I don't know whether I should mention it or not, but—"

"Anything you have seen or heard, no matter how small it may seem, could be helpful," the detective said encouragingly.

"It's not that it was a small thing—or a large thing, if it comes to that," Mary said cryptically. "It was just that—Mrs. Warren and Mr. Clemden were talking. Arguing, I suppose."

She frowned.

"They reminded me of my parents, when they go back and forth about something, I don't like it—hearing two people bicker like that.

"Anyway, it was last week—or maybe the week before—and I was coming down the hall when I heard two people practically shouting at each other. When I got to the kitchen, I realized it was Mrs. Warren and Mr. Clemden in the workroom. The door was shut, but they were that loud—I could hear them."

"You recall, please, the nature of the argument?"

"Not really," Mary said apologetically. "Their voices were muffled-like, and most of the time they were talking at each other all at once.

"Anyway, just then that Matthew Trenville comes into the kitchen behind me and taps me on the shoulder—gave me such a fright! I screamed, and he laughed at me," she blushed. "The next thing I knew, the back door slammed and Mrs. Warren came into the kitchen and scolded *us* for making such a racket."

Chan was digesting this account when the girl laughed and pointed toward the treeline near the lakefront.

"Mischief thinks it's a game," Mary said happily. "He loves to tease Mrs. Warren."

Chan looked toward the indicated area and observed the cook shouting—no, he realized—she was calling toward the woods. In a moment, the object of her attention loped out of the trees with a stick in his mouth, tail wagging furiously. The detective watched the scene with some amusement. The woman gesticulated furiously at the dog, who took her criticism in stride and trotted back toward the lodge, grasping his find firmly between his teeth.

"I'd best be tending to my chores," Mary said hastily and scurried to the back door and on into the lodge kitchen.

Mischief the dog and an out-of-breath Mrs. Warren arrived shortly, and the canine lay down on one end of the porch, gnawing vigorously. Charlie Chan greeted her, pointing to the dog.

"The lodge pet has a mind of his own, perhaps?"

Mrs. Warren applied the corner of her apron to her flushed face before replying.

"Mercy me, that dog is a caution," she replied. "Thinks he can run off into the woods and bring back every old stick and bone and carry them into the house," the cook went on, her breathing slowly returning to normal. "And when I try to take something away from him—off he goes, into the woods!"

"Mischief is well-named," Chan observed with a smile, approaching the dog as it continued to chew on what appeared to be an odd-looking bone, a foot or more in length. "But perhaps he answers to some other authority—Mr. Trenville, perhaps?"

Mrs. Warren laughed shortly.

"Not him," she declared. "Half afraid of dogs, that one. No, the only person Mischief will mind is Mr. Clemden."

Chan had coaxed the dog into surrendering the bone. It was blunt on one end, pointed on the other, and discolored from its time in the wilderness, perhaps. With his back to Mrs. Warren, he quickly wrapped the dog's find in a handkerchief and pocketed it—then patted Mischief, who panted toothily in reply.

"A most intelligent breed," he remarked. Mischief acknowledged the compliment with a short bark, but Mrs. Warren shook her head doubtfully.

"Do you really think so, sir?" she replied. "I've often wondered whether he could be trained to behave a little better."

Chan shrugged.

"Perhaps," he conceded, "but already he demonstrates qualities that endear him to this casual acquaintance."

Mrs. Warren snorted inadvertently.

"Begging your pardon," she apologized hastily. "No disrespect intended. Well—I'd best be gettin' back to my chores."

She left detective and dog and went into the kitchen. Chan gave Mischief a final pat, and looked into the dog's brown eyes.

"Pay no attention to Mrs. Warren," he advised the canine. "I am grateful for your assistance and will arrange for a suitable reward—possibly chicken livers?"

Mischief looked enthusiastically at the detective, but Chan knew from his experience with other canines that "joyful exuberance" was this dog's default expression. Even so, he resolved to raid the kitchen later for some appropriate tidbit. Those who assist authority in an investigation should be acknowledged, he reasoned, and Mischief deserved to be recognized for his find.

For Chan suspected that the stain on the bone was evidence of something more interesting than some wild animal's mishap.

It looked a great deal like dried blood, the detective thought. *Human blood.*

Sheriff Fairden was an old hand at following men driving on the region's winding roads. Poachers and trappers who had run afoul of the law never saw his battered pickup truck in their rearview mirror until it was too late, and Fairden often found that the best way to announce his presence was to fire his old Colt revolver into the air.

Trailing Clemden required no great skill, the lawman reflected, since he knew where the caretaker was headed—Raquette Lake. *Another hamlet to tell Chan about*, he smiled to himself.

Fortunately, the sheriff noted, Clemden took the new highway—"new" to old-timers in the area, but several years old now. A few longtime residents resistant to progress avoided Route 28 in favor of the Old Raquette Lake Road, but not Sheriff Fairden. The modern highway greatly reduced the drivetime between the two little towns, and a determined motorist might make the trip in as little as thirty minutes.

The sheriff kept well back of the caretaker's old truck. Clemden's pace was by no means leisurely, but he was setting no speed records today, Fairden thought. The lawman slowed down accordingly, occasionally letting his quarry drive just out of sight.

Through the trees along the highway he caught glimpses of the lakes: Fourth, Seventh, and Eighth—part of the Fulton Chain, named for steamboat inventor Robert Fulton. The sheriff often wondered what this quiet territory would be like today if Fulton had succeeded in turning the lakes into a kind of Adirondack canal route. Just as well that they decided to take that idea a little further south, he reflected. Things up here are better off without all that progress and the people it brought with it, all along the Erie Canal.

These musings kept the sheriff company as he played a kind of hide-and-seek with Clemden's rickety old truck up ahead. With the autumn chill in the air, little activity could be seen on any of the lakes. The hamlet of Inlet was equally quiet as Fairden motored through it.

Arriving in the little settlement, Sheriff Fairden spied the caretaker's vehicle parked outside of Lister's, a rambling pile of a general store on the lakefront that had given the town its name. Across the front of the faded clapboard-sided structure hung a sign with the words "Groceries & Sundries" in large white letters, and under this pronouncement—in smaller lettering—"B. Lister, Prop." The signpainter's art had been unequal to the task, and the owner's initial and last name were so poorly spaced that local wits began calling him "Blister," a nickname that had stuck.

Benjamin Lister was not only Raquette Lake's chief businessman, but also its postmaster, justice of the peace, and recorder of deeds. If and when the little settlement saw fit to convene a chamber of commerce, he would no doubt be its chairman.

Sheriff Fairden eased his truck into a space from which he could see the door to the establishment—and as far away from Clemden's truck as possible. County officialdom had discussed painting official markings on the sheriff's automobile a few years back, and today Fairden was thankful that the idea had been abandoned. At the end of a line of cars and trucks parked in front of the building, his battered old pickup was as inconspicuous as any other vehicle in the vicinity, he hoped.

The minutes dragged by and after what seemed like an hour, Clemden exited the store—empty handed—and drove away in his truck. The sheriff waited only until the caretaker was out of sight before climbing out of his car and making his way into Lister's. While waiting, he had formulated more than one plan of action depending on whether Clemden left quickly or stayed longer inside the establishment.

This was the first of his plans and the most direct. He would enter the store and accost the person or persons who had seen and spoken with Clemden, eliminating mostly those he knew well and other locals he knew by sight.

In other words, he told himself, he would focus on the wildcards in this deck.

Chapter Twenty
WOOLENS AND WATERPROOFS

The bell above Lister's door rang softly as the sheriff made his entrance, but no one looked in his direction.

Usually when Fairden had occasion to stop at Lister's, he enjoyed surveying the store and its wide variety of wares. From floor-to-ceiling shelves lining the two long walls of the establishment, Lister's offerings were displayed and stacked. Everything the residents of the region required seemed to be represented, from canned foods and bottled drinks to weapons, tools, and automobile parts. The effect was vaguely Dickensian, although Fairden would not have used that word. He only knew that the shop and its plentiful merchandise recalled a scene in an old Dickens novel his mother had read to him when he was a boy.

Today, duty cut short his visual tour of Lister's stock.

Fairden sidled up to the counter, where Ben Lister, the proprietor, was talking to a customer—a man of just under medium height and dandified appearance. The sheriff was struck by the citified suit, hat, and umbrella—he had seen such a getup before, at the lodge. This was the man Bainie, the accountant Chan had told him about.

Sheriff Fairden nodded to Ben Lister and tapped Bainie on the shoulder. The accountant wheeled around, a prickly expression on his pallid face.

"I beg your pardon," he said quietly. "Do I know you?"

"This is the sheriff from over the line," Lister explained.

"We have a mutual friend," Fairden told the accountant in a low voice. "Charlie Chan told me all about you—and your, er, project up this way."

A few other customers—locals known to the sheriff—were near to the counter or approaching it. Fairden crooked a finger, and Bainie followed him behind a display of woolens and waterproofs that rose up near a corner of the store.

"Keep your voice down," the sheriff whispered. "Maybe you and I can do each other a favor. I'm looking for the man or men that Clemden, the lodge caretaker, spoke to just now—well, several minutes ago."

A trace of amusement flashed in Bainie's dark eyes, and his thin black mustache curved upward slightly.

"In the jargon of this wild place," he whispered, "we would seem to be two hunters whose prey have crossed paths."

Ben Lister's curiosity had brought him out from behind the counter, and he approached the two men with a quizzical look on his face. Before the storekeeper could speak, Fairden put a finger to his own lips.

"Ben, this fellow and I need to have a private conversation," he explained in a low tone. "All right with you if we borrow your office for a few minutes?"

Lister nodded vigorously, eager to enter into the spirit of this minor conspiracy with the law. He pointed to the door at the back of the store and returned to his post at the cash register.

"Now, Mr. Bainie," the sheriff said, after the two had taken temporary possession of Lister's tiny office, "What did you mean about your prey and mine crossing paths? Who are you after?"

The accountant stood ramrod straight in contrast to the sheriff's habitual slouch. Apart from a cluttered desk—a telephone served as a paperweight on a stack of documents—a single chair was the only other furniture in the little room. Even with the door closed, both men spoke in half-whispers to avoid being overheard.

"Sheriff . . . ?"

"Fairden, Farley Fairden."

"Sheriff Fairden, I think my meaning was perfectly clear," Bainie said with a smile. Like his mustache, it was thin, but there was genuine good humor in it. "You were trailing someone who ended up here—and I think I know who—and I was following a seemingly unrelated person, who also ended up in this wilderness emporium of canned goods and"—Bainie's nose wrinkled comically—"sundries."

"Fine." Fairden retorted. "I was keeping an eye on Clemden, caretaker at the lodge where you're staying. Did you see him talking to anyone in particular here?"

"Fellow with the big beard?" Bainie smiled, broadly this time. "Yes, indeed! This is the interesting part—you'll pardon my enjoyment of this *mise en scène*, but my profession offers few opportunities for drama of this kind."

The sheriff kept his temper in check, but his impatience was clear to the accountant.

"My apologies! I seem to have wandered from the point. You asked—"

"Who Clemden was passing the time with when he was in this store," Fairden said sharply, his voice rising in spite of himself.

"Yes—and I said that was the interesting part of all this," Bainie recalled. "You see, you were trailing Clemden, and I was following one of the men he met with.

"Yantzen. William Yantzen."

Sheriff Fairden blinked. Whatever he had expected, it was not this. A more unlikely pair of—of what, exactly? Conspirators? Conspiring to do what?

"I'll be a—"

"That was my reaction as well," Bainie said dryly. "Rather unexpected. I know very little about the caretaker, but Yantzen impresses me as the black sheep of his family."

"I agree with you there," Fairden replied emphatically. "Whatever's at the bottom of all this, I think young Mr. Yantzen is there—wallowing in it, trying to profit from it, and quite possibly getting rid of anyone who stands in his way."

"There you go beyond my area of expertise, such as it is," said the dapper accountant. "Beyond my commission from Mr. Scanlon, which ended with the death of Walter Merriweather, I have become, shall we say, 'professionally interested' in Merriweather's activities."

"Professionally interested?" Fairden queried. "How so?"

"It seems that certain aspects of Mr. Scanlon's enterprises came to the attention of someone at the Bureau of Internal Revenue," Bainie explained. "Whether their agents approached Merriweather or he went to them first doesn't concern us, but he was cooperating with them.

"They in turn learned of my assignment on behalf of Mr. Scanlon and saw no reason why I shouldn't report the details of my conversations with Merriweather to them as well," the accountant said calmly. "Of course, they emphasized that my assistance would be completely voluntary. If, on the other hand, I refused to cooperate with a federal investigation—"

Bainie removed his gold pince-nez and pulled a handkerchief from his sleeve to polish the lenses. The sheriff noticed the nervous twitching at the corner of the man's eyes and wondered how much of his story was true.

"All very interesting, Mr. Bainie, but I'm interested in the fellow you were following, Yantzen. Did you hear anything of what passed between him and Clemden?"

The accountant shook his head, but his reply was interrupted by a knock at the door, which opened to reveal a familiar face.

"Gentlemen, gentlemen," cried William Yantzen mockingly. "What a pleasure to encounter both of you in this quaint setting. I would apologize for interrupting you, but it seemed to me that I heard my name just now—these rustic walls are shockingly thin—and I couldn't tell whether I was being summoned, or—"

"Oh, you're wanted all right," the sheriff said grimly. "Or you soon will be."

Yantzen laughed mirthlessly.

"Such a wit for a lawman! I assure you, I've done nothing that would interest you or others of your profession."

"Well, then," Fairden retorted, "how about you tell us what you and Zachary Clemden had to say to each other."

"Why?" Yantzen scoffed. "You were spying on us, the two of you—I'm sure you know all about our conversation, and what we had for breakfast, our antecedents, our—"

"We'll get nothing useful from him," Bainie told the sheriff contemptuously. "Unfortunately I couldn't get close enough to make out what they were saying.

"But I will say this," the accountant declared. "It was a very serious discussion—almost disputatious, I would say. Two men with some weighty matter dividing them."

"What about it, you?" Fairden demanded. "You and Clemden—say, that reminds me! How did you come to make the acquaintance of our resident hermit? He don't go in much for socializin', and you bein' a big man from the city and all—"

"I don't see that my social life is any of your business," Yantzen sneered. "Nor is it the business of the law that the lodge caretaker and I exchanged a few pleasantries at this—this trading post.

"Now, since I've taken far too much of your time already, I'll be on my way."

Yantzen opened the door and departed.

Bainie looked at Fairden meaningfully.

"If you'll excuse me I would like to make use of the proprietor's telephone before I return to the lodge."

Picking up the receiver, he indicated the door before dialing.

"This is a private conversation," he emphasized. "I would appreciate it if you would absent yourself."

The sheriff paused in the doorway.

"Don't be too long," the lawman said, scratching his scraggly beard thoughtfully, "I want to call a fellow down at Albany I know from way back."

He grinned at the accountant and winked.

"Can't let you and your federal friends have all the fun!"

Charlie Chan had not been idle during Sheriff Fairden's time away from the lodge. He keenly desired more talk with Mrs. Scanlon in the aftermath of her overheard conversation with the Bryants. The detective mounted the stairs and had turned toward the long hallway when the woman he sought exited her room, closing the door behind her.

"Mrs. Scanlon!" Chan called from the end of the hall. "Please pardon this intrusion, but would you be so kind as to join me for a brief talk?"

Without replying, Mrs. Scanlon marched down the hall toward the landing and stopped there, aiming an imperious gaze at the detective.

"Well? I suppose you have more questions," she sniffed. "It seems to me that we would all be better served if you devoted your time to assisting the sheriff—so that he can bring to book those responsible for killing those two men."

"So pleased that you and I agree," Chan said smoothly, "that my highest priority should be helping local authorities to discover the truth. That is why I very much need a few words with you—if you would be so kind as to join me."

The detective indicated the nook where he and the sheriff had spoken the night before and pulled out a chair.

"Please," he said graciously. "I would offer you greater comfort if it were immediately available, but our conversation will be as brief as possible."

"Indeed," Mrs. Scanlon's single word spoke volumes: a reluctance to speak to one she considered a social inferior, a distaste for the topic of discussion, and a general prickliness that served as her daily armor against encounters with "fools," as she called all those who annoyed her. After uttering the word, she sat glaring at the detective occupying the chair opposite.

Chan made a little show of placing on the marble-top table his ever-present notebook and pencil, flipping through its pages as though in search of something. This exercise concluded, he raised his eyes and returned the woman's angry gaze with a look of determination.

"I humbly suggest that you put aside the anger of the moment," the detective said firmly. "Later you can direct that most destructive of emotions at those responsible for the evil visited upon this locale of late."

Chan's straightforward request mollified the redoubtable Mrs. Scanlon, somewhat.

"I suppose you are doing what's required," she admitted grudgingly. "The whole situation is simply ghastly.

"Very well, ask your questions."

The detective appeared to consult the notebook, then looked up. His face bore no expression.

"When did you last see your former husband, Mr. Scanlon?"

"What on earth does that have to do with—oh, very well! It was many years ago," she said resignedly. "Some meeting at his attorney's office regarding the dissolution of our marriage. Perhaps my signature was required. I believe it concerned increasing support to defray my household expenses. I really don't recall the specifics.

"But it was the last time I saw him," she said firmly. "That, I do recall."

"During the years of your married life," Chan forged ahead, "Did business often require his absence from home?"

Mrs. Scanlon added suspicion to the range of emotions flitting across her face.

"How did you—how could you know such a thing? I hardly see how that bears on your investigation . . ." The woman's voice faded, and her eyes dropped.

"I don't suppose it matters—now," Edna Scanlon murmured. "Yes, he was away for weeks—even months at a time. Business—always business. Or so he said," she added.

The woman sighed.

"You may as well know," she continued. "When I first met Fred Scanlon, he was full of ambition, energy, charm—I was quite a young woman then, and I was impressionable. Naïve, even.

"I loved the man he was then," she said simply. "I cannot say that I love the man he became."

Chan nodded understandingly.

"Blooms of spring wither as seasons pass," he said softly. "Who can turn back time?"

Mrs. Scanlon's eyes were wistful.

"I don't know that I would go back to those days, even if I could."

She shook her head as though to clear it.

"Enough of this," she said determinedly, with something of her typical manner. "It's enough for me to say that Fred changed, and we parted."

"I regret that duty demands I probe this painful subject a little further," said Chan. "Perhaps you could describe his changed nature—what about him was different?"

Mrs. Scanlon's mouth was a thin line; she struggled to maintain her composure. At length, she spoke.

"I wish that I could tell that it was merely a feeling on my part, an emotional impression," she admitted. "But I know that Doctor Collins would agree with me—my husband was not at all well. Physically, he appeared much the same. If anything, more vigorous, more vital than ever.

"It was his mental state that concerned me—concerned both of us, the doctor as well."

Mrs. Scanlon smiled faintly.

"Although I never let Doctor Collins know that I truly agreed with his diagnosis," she said. "We discussed my husband's delusions of grandeur, his fits of mood—all of it—but I felt at the time that I must defend Fred in some way.

"In the end, it made no difference," she concluded. "Fred rejected the doctor's advice and his offer of help. And I left him—or rather, we left each other."

Chan nodded sympathetically.

"Did your husband ever speak of his days at the university where he studied? Did he perhaps mention his membership in some college club or organization?"

Mrs. Scanlon shook her head.

"He very rarely mentioned his time in Albany," she replied with certainty. "I don't recall anything about his studies there—let alone his activities outside of the classroom."

"Did he wear a ring with a symbol on it—as some who graduate from university do?"

The woman smiled faintly.

"During our marriage, Fred wore rings on both hands at one time or another," she recalled. "From the time I first met him it was clear to me that he had a somewhat flamboyant streak. His taste in clothing, for example—he always wore old-fashioned shirts and suits—and rings. He always wore at least one on each hand.

"Except for a wedding ring," she said with some bitterness. "He said wedding bands were 'too plain' for his tastes and refused to wear one. I suppose I should have taken that as a sign of some kind—a portent of things to come."

Chan waited a moment, then spoke with as much sensitivity as possible.

"It falls to me to disclose the current thinking of authorities investigating recent events," the detective said softly. "Unknown man whose body was found under the train—Mr. Scanlon absent from a gathering that he arranged—it is possible that these two circumstances are very much related."

Edna Scanlon stared at Chan unbelievingly.

"I can hardly fathom such a thing," she whispered. "It doesn't seem possible—and who would want to—to make away with Fred?"

"I am overcome with regret," Chan replied, "but again I must reveal to you an unpleasant fact concerning your former husband. Namely, that in his correspondence to me he listed those that he thought were plotting to end his life."

Chan paused for a moment, watching the woman closely.

"Among the names on that list was your brother's, Mrs. Scanlon," he said evenly. "Your former husband's account to me described his distaste for William Yantzen. Do you think your brother could have—"

"Absurd," the woman cut in. "It's true that Fred and Bill never seemed to enjoy each other's company, but—but—my brother has many fine qualities," she declared. "He has been misunderstood by a great many people, and I doubt very much that Fred seriously considers my brother capable of—of—"

"Mr. Scanlon considered not only your brother in that light," Chan interrupted. "Other names were on the list of possible murderers.

"*Your* name," the detective asserted. "*Your* name was on his list."

For once, Edna Scanlon was speechless.

"You say that Frederick Scanlon was 'of unsound mind,' as lawyers put it," Chan went on. "But this giant of the business world wrote that one of those on his list planned to do away with him.

"And now," Chan spread his hands apart, "A man lies dead—and those Frederick Scanlon suspected are here in this lodge."

Chapter Twenty-One

DR. MANSTON'S BOOK

Zachary Clemden motored away from Raquette Lake with a broad smile on his face. His duties at the lodge of late had been taxing: Preparing for the arrival of guests and various seasonal maintenance tasks—buttoning up the place for the winter to come—it had been a lot of work, he reflected. But this time of year a drive to Raquette Lake or Blue Mountain Lake—even over to North Creek—was like a tonic to him.

Except for one battered car in front of him, he had the road to himself. A look in his rearview mirror confirmed that Farley Fairden was no longer with him. Even a law-abiding man notices when the law seems to be following him down the highway. He had wondered if the sheriff was interested in him and his doings when he spotted the lawman's old truck behind him on the drive over. But no, he concluded, Farley was more likely in need of shotgun shells or some other necessity. Even the law sometimes traded at Lister's.

These and other scattered thoughts drifted through the caretaker's mind as he took stock of recent events. *Just one more little chore to take care of before I head back to the lodge, and then—*

Jack Teasdale pulled the handcar to a halt on the tracks well shy of the highway crossing. He was a one-man survey crew this afternoon, not that he had spotted any particular problems along the line. *Soon as this car passes, it's back to the station,* he thought. The old flivver clattered by. Jack waved, but the driver ignored him.

City fellow, more'n likely, the railroad man thought as he started to pump his car the last few feet toward the crossing.

Hearing the sound of another vehicle, he looked up, surprised. A pickup truck was bearing down on the crossing and showed no sign of slowing. Teasdale stopped the handcar with a jerk and caught a glimpse of the driver's face as the truck passed by. It was a friendlier face than that of the last motorist.

By golly, that looked like ol' Clemden—and he was laughin' fit to bust, he thought, amused.

William Yantzen pushed the old car to its limits, but it was both ancient and sluggish. Not that he was in a great hurry; he had received and delivered, and his work was done.

Passing through a place called Inlet, Yantzen steered the little car he had borrowed from the lodge around the edge of a body of water he glimpsed intermittently. The tree-lined highway only occasionally came close to the lake shore. Fourth Lake, a sign read.

He smiled at the memory of his encounter with the sheriff and that other fellow. *Not many brains between them*, he thought contemptuously. *No doubt they thought finding me at that outpost was a great investigative coup*. He laughed in his own peculiarly silent fashion. *They have no idea*.

It was the last coherent thought William Yantzen would have.

Having assured Mrs. Scanlon that the identity of the dead man found in the woods was still—officially—unknown, Charlie Chan retreated to the first-floor parlor where he had earlier encountered the Bryants. Under his arm was the book Dr. Manston had pressed upon him, T. Morris Longstreth's *The Adirondacks*.

Seated in a comfortable chair he immersed himself in the scholarly overview of the great region and its discovery, development, and tremendous resources. A half-hour or more passed pleasantly; the detective was an avid reader.

Chan's eyes gleamed; Dr. Manston's book was the most interesting thing he had read for some time. At length, the detective set the big volume aside and looked around the room. A walnut bookcase on one wall contained both bric-a-brac and a dozen or more dusty tomes, odd volumes shelved there more for "show" than their readability. An old almanac kept company with two dictionaries, a ponderous single-volume encyclopedia, a trove of old magazines, and a slender book that attracted the detective's interest. He flipped through its pages quickly, then closed it and set it aside with Dr. Manston's history book.

He stood, grasping the two books, and looked at the wall opposite where the dead eyes of Mr. Manston's handiwork in the head of a buck stared back at him.

Suddenly, Chan's eyes widened as he realized that the headmount had been damaged in some way. Instinctively his hand crept to the inner pocket where he had secreted Mischief's trophy: a length of bone, he had thought earlier.

No, he realized. Not a bone as such. Setting down the two books, he pulled the dog's discovery out and took a closer look.

It was a portion of a deer's antler. And the big buck looking across the room at the detective was missing a part of its rack. The detective rose and moved swiftly across the room, holding Mischief's find like a priceless object.

Comparing the length of antler in his hand to a small damaged spot on the trophy head, Chan was satisfied with the result. It was clear that the length of antler had been removed from this trophy and one end sharpened to a point—stained with what laboratory testing would surely confirm was blood, Chan was convinced.

Blood of the same type as the unfortunate Walter Merri-weather, the detective told himself.

Pocketing Mischief's contribution to the investigation, the detective retraced his steps across the room. The grim wildlife diorama again attracted his attention, and a thought occurred to him.

Pulling out his pocket magnifying glass, Chan looked carefully at the participants in the little drama—a carrion bird and its meal, the remains of some unidentifiable creature. Dr. Manston had outdone himself, the detective thought with some distaste.

Earlier he had noticed some difference in the two sides of the bird—a slight inadequacy on one of the outstretched wings, perhaps?

Through the glass Chan looked closely at the lesser wing and ran his fingers gently over the area where it appeared that some feathers had been summarily removed.

Pocketing the glass, he had picked up Dr. Manston's book when a shout came from down the hall.

"Mr. Chan? Are you about?" The voice belonged to Sheriff Fairden.

In short order the detective made his way to the Great Hall, where the sheriff and Cecil Bainie stood warming themselves by the blazing fire.

"Change in the weather," Fairden announced. "Colder than it ought to be this time of year, and from the looks of the clouds to the north and west—well, we could see some snow before long."

"I have seen snow only once before," Chan recalled, "far to the west from here—but before indulging in talk of winter beauty, I have much to tell you—"

"And Mr. Bainie and I have a fair amount to tell you, as well," the sheriff replied. "You'll never guess who our friend Clemden met up with in Raquette Lake."

Fairden briefed Chan on Clemden's rendezvous with William Yantzen, and their interview with Mrs. Scanlon's "Brother Bill." Bainie filled in the gaps.

"Most interesting, this meeting of two men seemingly unknown to each other," Chan remarked. "The heated tone of their discussion that you observed, Mr. Bainie, added to character of William Yantzen indicates some hidden business relationship—one that has encountered difficulties, perhaps."

"How do you figure?" Sheriff Fairden asked, his brow wrinkling in puzzlement.

"Mr. Scanlon has written to me of Yantzen as a man who attempts business schemes of dubious virtue," Chan explained. "Caretaker Clemden's years of experience in this locale suggests that he selected a remote meeting place where he and Yantzen could discuss matters of mutual interest—a place where they would be unobserved by those at lodge."

"They sure weren't meetin' up at Lister's for a social occasion," the sheriff grunted. "The other thing I want to tell you—"

"Yes, Mr. Chan," Bainie cut in. "The sheriff was on the telephone for quite some time, and he's been quite pleased with himself ever since.

"I also was able to gather some information that I can share with you later," he added. "I need to collect my thoughts before presenting it to you."

Fairden grinned.

"First, I called a fellow in Albany who works in the department where they keep records of big business doings. They register corporations and keep track of their income for tax purposes," the sheriff explained. "I figured from the looks of Yantzen and Clemden, and everything else that's goin' on here, they jes' might have put something in place to make their dealings at least *look* all legal and above board."

Chan nodded. "A bright idea shines like the sun in spring. Did yours yield much of great interest?"

"Well, I guess you'd say some of my plants sprouted," the sheriff admitted. "Let's see what you make of them."

He cleared his throat, thinking of his tobacco pouch.

"You heard Doc Manston talk about the mining concerns in the Adirondacks—well, it seems our coroner isn't the only person interested in garnets," the lawman went on. "From what my friend in Albany could tell—and he's looking further into the whole thing—it appears that Mr. Frederick Scanlon started a mining company some years ago in partnership with a Mr. Alexander Creighton."

Chan's eyes brightened.

"The missing Mr. Creighton," he cried. "At last he appears, a late bloom in the garden of circumstance."

"It goes on from there," the sheriff continued. "At some point, Scanlon apparently bought out Creighton's interest in the mine—and here's the best part."

Fairden paused to pull out his tobacco pouch and insert a substantial wad in his mouth. Bainie snorted impatiently; Chan showed no impatience, but his interest was clear.

"Scanlon did one more deal that's on record in Albany, and not too long ago," the sheriff said juicily. He looked around for a receptacle for future use. Seeing none, he continued.

"Last transfer of ownership on record with the state shows the mine and its assets going from Frederick Scanlon—"

"Perhaps to Zachary Clemden?" Chan cut in, his face shining with anticipation. "Please pardon the interruption—I am overcome with excitement."

"Don't mention it," the sheriff replied. "But how did you know—"

"Many years spent with fellow policemen have made me more like them," Chan grinned. "Native patience seems to have vanished, replaced by ambition to tread in theatrical limelight. I have become, as daughter Rose would say, 'A big show-off.'"

"I will explain," Chan hurried on, as Fairden opened his mouth to question him further—or to adjust the wad of tobacco lodged in his cheek. The detective could not tell which. "Many questions remain, but some things are now becoming clear.

"Frederick Scanlon writes to a detective he knows only through newspaper stories, asking for investigation of persons he suspects of planning to kill him. Even before his journey's end, the traveling policeman encounters death—but who is this dead man?

"Question still unanswered when death strikes again—this time removing one of those named on Scanlon's peculiar list. And as we speak of this unfortunate event, I am pleased to credit the dog, Mischief, for bringing this to my attention."

The detective drew the pointed length of antler from his pocket and handed it to the sheriff, explaining the four-legged investigator's role briefly.

"When Mischief retrieved this object from the nearby thicket of trees, I was reminded of my late-night encounter with William Yantzen. Clearly he had sought to discard murderous length of antler by casting same into trees. Perhaps county laboratory can determine blood type on sharpened tip—and match same to victim."

Fairden examined Mischief's find, looking up at the detective quizzically.

"I'm a practical man, Mr. Chan, and I'm not questioning your line of reasoning," he said slowly, "but I jes' don't understand—I mean to say, why not fetch a knife from the kitchen? Why would anyone go to such trouble—whittling down the end of an antler that way?"

Chan nodded.

"Choice of murder weapon often points directly to the killer," he explained. "Missing knife, for example, would have led investigators to focus on kitchen and those with frequent access to it. Unusual instrument of death gave no such hint.

"Still," he went on thoughtfully, "if you paint a snake's picture, do not add legs to improve it. Such may be the case here."

Sheriff Fairden stared at the detective."

"You mean the killer mebbe—er—got a little carried away?"

Chan's brief reverie came to an end.

"Just so," he replied. "Carried away for reasons still to be revealed. To continue, accountant Merriweather was dead, and Scanlon had suspected him of tampering with company funds. Scanlon wrote that this keeper of accounts had threatened him, but was that enough for this business magnate to kill his faithful employee and friend from college days?"

The sheriff made a deposit in a spittoon he had belatedly found on the side of the fireplace's raised hearth.

"Not hardly," the lawman declared. "Anyway, it sure seems to me like somebody took care of Scanlon out in the woods—and I reckon we can rule out dead men under trains in the matter of Merriweather's murder."

"Sheriff's keen wit accompanies true observation," Chan replied. "Condition of body in woods means victim was dispatched hours before the unfortunate accountant met his fate.

"Let us, then, consider items found on both bodies. Signet ring in the pocket of the first body bears the same symbol as the watch fob of accountant Merriweather. From Doctor Collins I learn of college organization whose members use this Greek letter, 'final sigma,' as the mark of their membership."

The detective pulled out the two books he had perused earlier and opened the smaller of the two to a page he had marked.

"On dusty bookshelf upstairs I found what I believe university folk call a 'yearbook,'" he explained, holding up a blue-covered volume entitled *The Neon*. "Within this book, which recorded happenings at Albany college for a year early in this century, I discover these words:

. . . it was voted that a committee of three be appointed to wait upon the president of the College, to ascertain his views

*concerning the advisability of reorganizing into a secret society
… the new secret society chose for its name "Eschatos Sigma" and
adopted the Greek letter* ς *for its symbol.*

"Among the names of this group's members," Chan pointed to the bottom of the page and handed the book to his two
listeners, "we find both Frederick Scanlon and Walter Merriweather."

Cecil Bainie yawned.

"Surely their connection comes as no surprise," he objected.
"Two men closely associated in business for some time—it
makes sense that their ties go back to their collegiate years."

Sheriff Fairden started to speak but thought better of it.
Charlie Chan nodded.

"Excellent point—one that concerns us greatly," the detective replied. "Scanlon writes that Merriweather is one
who might plot against him, but it is Merriweather who
dies—while Scanlon—"

"—is dead, too," Fairden cut in. "No question about that."
He hesitated. "Is there?"

"Again, you have touched on the heart of the matter," Chan
said. "Recall that the train made identification of the victim by
sight alone impossible, but the man was already dead before
his unfortunate encounter with a locomotive. Killer hoped
to conceal victim's identity, yet a personal item in his pocket—a ring signifying membership in college group—pointed
to missing Scanlon.

"But consider an alternative view," the detective continued.
"What if killer's intent was not only to make identification of
the body impossible—but to convince police that dead man
was someone missing, a person who could not be accounted
for?"

"Nobody local's gone missing," the sheriff noted, "but I
suppose you're thinkin' of the names on that list—Scanlon's
list of suspects."

Chan nodded.

"All on the list have made their presence known at the lodge," the detective noted. "Only Alexander Creighton remains absent."

"Well-l-l," Fairden said slowly, "we also can't account for Frederick Scanlon—so is he dead or—"

A commotion of voices and laughter approached and entered the room, led by the girl, Clarissa, followed by Gloria Clarkson and Matthew Trenville. Not far behind was Mrs. Scanlon. Seeing the three men in serious conversation, she brought the playful trio to a halt, sharply.

"Miss Clarkson! Please take charge of Clarissa," she said peremptorily. "Either go outside, or—"

"Yes, ma'am," Gloria Clarkson said quickly. "Right away—we were just—"

"It's cold outside," the child complained.

"Then upstairs with you," Mrs. Scanlon snapped. "If you behave, perhaps Miss Clarkson will teach you a game—a *quiet* game," she emphasized as the two headed up the stairs. "As for you, young man—"

Matthew Trenville waited. Whatever the woman's complaint, she was a guest of the lodge; and guests were always right.

"Excuse, please, this interruption," Chan said, "but the sheriff, Mr. Bainie, and I had hoped to see the lodge caretaker—also Mr. William Yantzen. Have you seen either of them?"

"Yantzen, no—not today," Trenville replied promptly. "Clemden—about an hour ago. I think he was going to his cabin."

"Then," Chan directed, "would you please go there and say he is needed at the lodge?"

The young man nodded, donned his coat and hat, and opened the front door.

"Say," he called over his shoulder, "it's really starting to come down—I'll bring in some more wood when I get back."

As if to punctuate the remark, a gust of wind delivered a burst of snow through the doorway before Trenville could slam it shut behind him.

Mrs. Scanlon turned a frosty expression toward the three men.

"I couldn't help but overhear the very end of your conversation just now, gentlemen," she said firmly. "I'm sure that my former husband is very much alive."

"Mrs. Scanlon arrives at a fortunate time for our discussion," Chan said smoothly. "If you would be so kind, please repeat for these gentlemen what you told me of your former husband's tastes in clothing and jewelry."

"First, I want to be clear: I'm sure he's alive," the woman repeated. "If he were dead—well, I would know, that's all. As for the things I said—I told you that he always wore the old-fashioned shirts and suits that were popular when he was a young man. And he always wore at least one ring of some kind on each hand—but never a wedding ring."

"Thank you, so much," said Chan, turning to the two men. "You will recall, Sheriff, that the body on train tracks had no rings on either hand."

The lawman nodded.

"But his clothes," Fairden protested. "Weren't they just the kind of thing Mrs. Scanlon is talkin' about? Looked to me like he had on the kind of old-time fancy shirt that takes a separate collar . . ."

Fairden fell silent. The look on his face went from confusion to realization.

Charlie Chan nodded.

"Dead man was dressed in clothing preferred by Frederick Scanlon by killer who tried to put too-small signet ring on unyielding fingers—placing it in the victim's pocket instead," Chan went on. "You are correct, Mrs. Scanlon, when you say that your former husband is not dead.

"But he is now number-one murder suspect."

Chapter Twenty-Two

A SNOW-WHITENED FIGURE

Mrs. Scanlon's moment of speechlessness was brief. Her disbelief found companionship in a general distrust of this—this "foreign-looking person," as she had described him to the Bryants earlier.

"The very idea! Is that your official view, Sheriff Fairden?" Mrs. Scanlon demanded, not waiting for a reply. "To say that my—to accuse Frederick Scanlon of such a thing when he's not here to defend himself—it's appalling.

"And what about the other man—Mr. Merriweather? I suppose you think that Mr. Scanlon did away with him as well?"

The wrathful woman glared at each of the men in turn. Bainie maintained a stoic silence, and the sheriff grew red in the face.

"Now, Mrs. Scanlon," the lawman began. "No one's accusin' anyone, formally, of anything—just yet," he added lamely. "Inspector Chan and I, we're making progress. And you've been real helpful—everyone here has.

"But I would surely appreciate it if you would be patient for a little while longer, ma'am," Fairden said soothingly. "Fact is, two men are dead—and we're going to get to the bottom of this thing, come hell or high water."

Mrs. Scanlon sniffed.

"There's no need to use such language, Sheriff," she retorted. "I know perfectly well that *you* have your duty to do," she added, eyeing Chan.

"I think," Mrs. Scanlon continued, "that Dr. Collins and Mr. and Mrs. Bryant should be included in this discussion—all the more so in light of your—your remarks just now about my former husband. I believe they are having coffee in the dining room.

"You—Mr. Bainie! Would you please have the goodness to ask them to join us?" Mrs. Scanlon scarcely knew him, but she viewed Cecil Bainie as hers to command.

Muttering under his breath, Bainie went in search of the three. In a few minutes, he returned with them in tow.

"I was just saying to Daniel how dreadfully dull this place is," Mrs. Bryant chattered away at no one in particular. "How nice of you to invite us to join this little gathering. Oh, Sheriff Fairden—are we to be kept here much longer? My husband and I had planned to leave on Sunday, but of course with all that's happened—"

"Muriel, please," her husband broke in. "Everyone knows we're anxious to—that *everyone* here would like nothing better than to leave."

"Well said," Dr. Collins put in. "I assume, gentlemen—and Mrs. Scanlon—that we were invited to join you because matters are progressing—or am I in error?"

"Progress in a murder investigation appears uncertain at times, like the spinning needle of a searching compass," Chan nodded. "Eventually it points toward the truth."

"Progress!" Mrs. Scanlon hissed. "This man," Mrs. Scanlon told the three late arrivals, indicating Chan. "This *detective* has accused Frederick of murder."

Several people spoke at once. Charlie Chan raised both hands, and the room fell silent.

"Someone bears responsibility for the deaths of two men," he said somberly. "Mrs. Scanlon joined our discussion as we spoke of the identity of the man found dead beneath the train. That victim's name—officially—is still unknown.

"But what of Walter Merriweather's killer?" Chan continued. "Investigation points to likelihood of two murderers. Of those persons expected here this weekend, two are absent: Alexander Creighton and Frederick Scanlon.

"At the moment," the detective went on, "one other is also not present: William Yantzen. Sheriff Fairden and I spoke with him a few hours ago at a place called Lister's, in Raquette Lake. None of you, I think, has seen him today?"

No one spoke.

"If you have, or if you think you know where he might be, let us know," the sheriff added. "Truth is, he left Lister's before Mr. Chan and I did—so he should've been back here some time ago."

From outside the lodge came a howling that rose and fell like the call of some animal.

"Wind's pickin' up," Fairden remarked. "Not a good time to be out and about, although I reckon Clemden has enough sense to come in out of a snowstorm. That city fellow, though—"

Not content with wailing from without, the wind sent a whistling gust of frigid air down the chimney. The fire blazed higher as though to meet the challenge, and Muriel Bryant shivered uncomfortably.

The front door opened abruptly, torn from the hand of a snow-whitened figure that brushed ice and snow from its coat and stamped its feet as though to warm them. Zachary Clemden pushed the door shut with his back and pulled off his gloves and hat, using it to wipe snow from his encrusted face and beard.

"Damnation," he gasped. "Came up quick—when I left to walk here it was hardly snowing, but now—"

He looked around the room quickly and dropped his eyes.

"Quite the gathering you have here," he remarked. "Trenville—he said I was wanted at the lodge, so here I am."

"Good heavens, man," Dr. Collins cried, "Come over to the fire and warm yourself. You look as though you could use some dry—"

"Thank you kindly just the same," the caretaker said abruptly. "I'd just as soon stay over here near the door. Best not to track all of the outside into the room."

"Perhaps lodge caretaker has another reason for avoiding some person here," Charlie Chan said sharply. "Maybe you fear standing too close to certain lady, Mr. Clemden?

"Or should I say—Mr. Scanlon?"

The detective's voice rose in pitch, a note of triumph evident, and a momentary silence followed. A half-consumed log broke and fell apart in the fireplace.

The bearded man raised both hands to his face, rubbing it briskly, and then cleared his throat.

"I don't know exactly what you think you're playin' at," he grumbled. "I've heard of the cops doin' this kind of thing, but—"

A woman's voice interrupted the bearded man. Mrs. Scanlon's words were delivered calmly, but her listeners could tell she was in great emotional distress.

"I never really looked at him until just now," she confessed. "One doesn't pay attention to the help in—in a place like this. You understand, don't you dear?" Mrs. Scanlon looked to Muriel Bryant for reassurance, and the latter nodded shakily.

"But then," Edna Scanlon went on in a dazed voice, "when he swore—when he came in and said that single word—I knew. I always took him to task for using that kind of language."

"Lady also observed other tell-tale sign, Mr. Scanlon," Chan cried. "When you put both hands on your face just now, all eyes could see white mark on the finger where you wore a large signet ring for many years—until putting it on the body of the man you killed, Alexander Creighton.

"And where," the detective continued sharply, "is your accomplice—where is William Yantzen?"

The caretaker's eyes gleamed as he returned Chan's steady gaze. A low rumbling laugh emerged from the beard, but there was no humor in it.

"Brother Bill? You know, I never did like him all that much," Frederick Scanlon chuckled grimly. "As for his present whereabouts, I'm afraid I can give you only a general idea."

Scanlon's rasping laugh turned into a snarl, followed by an oath.

" . . . somewhere near the bottom of Fourth Lake, that's where he is—and good riddance to bad rubbish," he snapped.

Mrs. Scanlon uttered a single cry.

"I never did see why you were forever sticking up for him, Edna," her former husband said gruffly. "Although he did do one thing right." He laughed nastily. "Took care of that damned Merriweather with the little sticker I gave him.

"On the whole, though, I'd say he was a no-good, rotten—say, Sheriff Fairden!" the bearded man barked, pulling out a revolver and pointing it across the room. "I hope for your sake that you aren't carrying that horse pistol with you."

Fairden had absent mindedly moved his hand toward the chewing tobacco in his pocket. He smiled calmly.

"No, Clemden—Scanlon—whatever in blazes your name is—that gun is in my old bus, blast the luck. If you're smart, though, you'll put that little peashooter down before you go and kill somebody else."

"*If* I'm smart?" Scanlon scoffed. "I guess I'm smart enough to take myself off to a place you'll never find me—and that goes for you, too, Mr. Chan."

He laughed derisively.

"You and your big reputation—you have no idea how I relished the thought of cooking up this little show and adding the famous Chinese detective to the recipe."

Charlie Chan nodded, his face a placid mask.

"Excellent scheme in the beginning," the detective remarked. "But I came to realize that the troubled businessman's list of those who sought to end his life was filled with opposite statements—much of what you wrote was untrue.

"In fact, some of those you claimed plotted against you, you wished to destroy," Chan went on. "Again, evidence of some flaw in your thinking. Or perhaps, some mental defect that led you to see enemies all around you."

Melting snow on Scanlon's brow merged with beads of sweat on his florid face.

"Mental defect? You—you—I'll show you just how—"

No one could agree afterward on the exact sequence of events, but all were sure of three things: Scanlon raised his gun and fired, Charlie Chan pulled out his automatic with lightning speed and returned the favor, and the entry door opened with a blast of wind, upsetting Scanlon's aim.

"Here's some more wood," puffed Matthew Trenville from the doorway, addressing the room at large. "Say, Clemden—you ought to watch where you're pointing that thing. Good lord, man, are you bleeding?"

The younger man pointed to Clemden-Scanlon's shoulder where a small patch of red was starting to seep through his coat. The revolver slipped from his grasp and fell to the floor as he pushed Trenville out of the way and bolted through the still open door.

"Don't be a damned fool!" Sheriff Fairden exclaimed. The lawman ran to the doorway and shouted into the wind, but growing darkness and the thickly falling snow obscured the fleeing figure.

Charlie Chan joined the sheriff in the entranceway and peered out at the whitely opaque scene. Chan took a step toward the storm outside, but the lawman grasped his arm firmly.

"Can't let you do that, Mr. Chan," he said firmly. "There's not a chance we could track him in a whiteout like this, in the woods at night. His tracks in the snow will be gone jes' about as fast as he can make 'em."

Fairden shut the door with a bang.

"Fellow must have taken leave of his senses," the lawman said resignedly. "Unless he can work magic, he'll be lucky to make it back to his cabin—or anywhere else, 'specially with a bullet in him."

Chan turned to Matthew Trenville, who had deposited his armload of wood on the floor and was still taking stock of the situation.

"I must extend warmest thanks to you for the delivery of firewood at such an opportune moment," the detective said simply. "Your arrival provided a welcome distraction—one that I will long remember."

"Everything happened so fast," the younger man confessed. "I'm still not sure why you're—"

Chan pointed eloquently at the ceiling above them, where Scanlon's errant shot had lodged the bullet meant for the visiting detective.

Chapter Twenty-Three
CHARLIE CHAN EXPLAINS

"The thing of it is, Mr. Chan," Sheriff Fairden objected goodnaturedly, "is that I can follow your trail only so far before I get lost in the brush."

It had snowed all night, and the early morning light shone dimly through the lodge windows—some of which were partially blocked by drifts. Charlie Chan had the attention of the sheriff—who had spent the night dozing before the fire—and the other lodge guests gathered around the dining room table: Monsignor Plevna, the prim Bainie, Dr. Collins, and Mr. and Mrs. Bryant. Only Mrs. Scanlon, Miss Clarkson, and Clarissa were absent.

"Still asleep, the young woman and the little girl," Muriel Bryant had assured the group. "And Edna has finally dropped off, but I'm afraid she was up for much of the night."

Mrs. Glas had wisely left for home before the snow began, leaving Mrs. Warren to provide the morning gathering with steaming cups of coffee and a full pot within reach on a sideboard hob.

Before Chan could reply to the sheriff, Bainie leaned forward and murmured several words in the detective's ear.

"I can speak to that, if you wish," the accountant said, leaning back in his chair with a self-satisfied expression.

The detective nodded, smiling, and returned his attention to Fairden.

"One must set aside all things not essential to most funda-
mental question in any investigation," he replied. "Just as in
wilderness one must clear away brush to find correct trail.

"When we were confronted by two bodies, we asked the
question that Scanlon knew we would ask: 'What third person
killed both Merriweather and Scanlon?' The answer to this
riddle was simple: there was no such person."

Dr. Collins looked up from his coffee with interest.

"So, if I follow you, that fellow Yantzen killed the accountant, Merriweather," the physician said slowly, "and Fred
Scanlon put Creighton on the tracks—to try and convince
everyone that he—that Scanlon, I mean—was dead?"

Chan grinned approvingly.

"Experienced physician makes the correct diagnosis," he
agreed. "You have put in a few words what this detective attempts to explain in many."

"I understand how you might have doubted Scanlon was
dead," Bainie spoke up. "But how could you know that it was
Creighton's body under that train?"

Daniel Bryant, exchanging a glance with his wife, nodded.

"That was what Muriel and I were wondering," Bryant put
in.

Chan smiled and looked around the table.

"Once the unusual Greek symbol provided a connection
between the two murdered men, I thought much about names
in Scanlon's letter to me. Creighton, the business tycoon
wrote, was once his great friend—but they had 'parted ways,'
as Scanlon put it. From being a trusted partner, Creighton had
become a hated rival.

"In this instance," Chan said parenthetically, "Scanlon
wrote true words—unlike other fictions that were designed to
lead investigators down the wrong path.

"Thanks to Sheriff Fairden's pursuit of information from
his state government acquaintance, we learned that a mining enterprise owned by Creighton was acquired by Scan-

lon—who later transferred it to his alter ego, Zachary Clemden."

The sheriff smiled broadly.

"I reckon I owe that fellow in Albany a big favor," he chuckled. "That was a big help, that was." He turned to Chan. "I suppose Scanlon, probably when he was traipsing about in his woodsman outfit, come to find out that garnet mining might be a big payoff?"

Chan nodded.

"Sheriff's contributions to the investigation were valuable," he acknowledged, "And perhaps Mr. Bainie can confirm that Scanlon's accusation aimed at trusted accountant Walter Merriweather was false?"

Bainie adjusted his pince-nez and addressed the group.

"As I informed Mr. Chan, my telephone conversation with the Internal Revenue people confirmed that they were preparing a case against Scanlon. They had long suspected that there was an unusual flow of money away from his business enterprises—and that was his own doing," he explained. "Quite the opposite of his accusation against Merriweather.

"For those of you who don't know," he continued, "Scanlon hired me to investigate Merriweather—claimed that he suspected his accountant of financial wrongdoing. But in fact it was Merriweather who suspected Scanlon of extracting large sums to support some outside enterprise—although he did not know it was a mining venture."

Charlie Chan took up the story.

"As for the origin of Scanlon's garnet discovery, its exact circumstances have yet to come to light," the detective explained. "But as bits of investigation arrived in scattered fashion, like passengers boarding a train, some things became clear—and the larger picture began to take shape.

"This big picture," Chan continued, "I can now describe for you. Some details are from evidence, or deductions based on same. As you have heard, Sheriff Fairden and Mr. Bainie contributed much. Other pieces of this story came from words of Scanlon himself and others.

"Also," he grinned, "healthy dose of detection—plus intuition inherited from ancient heritage."

The sheriff snorted, amused.

"That surely sounds better than guesswork, the way you put it," he smiled. "Let's hear it."

Chan nodded appreciatively and began, ticking off one item after another on the fingers of his left hand.

"First, Scanlon decides he will permanently abandon his real identity and leave blame for business troubles of his own making on the shoulders of others. For years he has siphoned large sums from a company that he no longer fully controls, to fund his mining venture. In the beginning, no doubt he used his own resources, but later he diverts assets rightfully owned by shareholders in the company he founded. To vanish into the character he has created over many years he arranges a gathering at this remote location where he is known only as seasonal caretaker Clemden. There, he believes, he can control events more easily because of his familiarity with the wooded locale.

"Second, he determines that Creighton and Merriweather must die. Creighton, because he knows too much about Scanlon's mining interest; Merriweather, because he holds evidence of Scanlon's embezzlement of corporate funds.

"Third, he solicits cooperation of ne'er-do-well brother-in-law, William Yantzen, promising him a substantial share of mining profits. As a down payment, he gives Yantzen a single rare garnet."

Monsignor Plevna shook his head sadly.

"Wheels within wheels," he mused. "Fred's state of mind, of course, must have exaggerated his sense of the big coup, the magnificent business deal. The whole thing begins to sound to me . . . characteristically elaborate."

Chan shrugged.

"Not so complicated, in a way," he countered. "Embellishments were added along the way—some, because Scanlon favored such things; others, to lead police investigators astray.

"To kill two men and disappear into a new identity, that was his goal," Chan continued. "He obtained readily available sleeping aid and divided it with his accomplice. Yantzen foolishly hid his share in the kitchen pantry so that it would not be found on his person or in his room.

"The day before most guests took the train to Big Moose, Creighton arrived to be greeted by Clemden, who revealed his identity. No doubt hospitality of caretaker's cabin led to offer of liquor, in which Clemden had dissolved enough barbital to render Creighton unconscious."

The sheriff grunted.

"What kind of a man—I guess what we've heard about him was right," he declared. "No sane person would do what you're layin' out here, Mr. Chan."

"A great mind often teeters on the edge of insanity," Dr. Collins put in. "Something—some quirk, some event—must have pushed him over the brink."

A moment's silence descended on the group, then Chan continued.

"To create the impression that Frederick Scanlon had died, Scanlon tried unsuccessfully to place his signet ring on one of Creighton's fingers—leaving traces that were visible to us later."

"To you, anyway," the sheriff murmured.

"Frustrated," Chan went on, "he dresses the unconscious Creighton in a suit of Scanlon's clothing and leaves signet ring, empty wallet, and bird's feather in his pockets. Concealed by darkness, he loads into his snowmobile this grim cargo and hides it in the woods near the place on the railroad tracks where a mortal encounter with the train locomotive was still some hours in the future."

Chan hesitated.

"Here, perhaps coroner's final report will confirm what happened," he went on, "but early examination indicated that Creighton was dead several hours before the locomotive did its work. Either he succumbed to effects of barbitol—"

"Or Scanlon did the job himself," Fairden grimaced. "If this snow ever melts, there might be traces—blood on a rock, mebbe."

"Good lord," Daniel Bryant muttered. Muriel Bryant shuddered.

Chan nodded gently toward his assembled listeners.

"You will please excuse the unseemly details of this explanation," he suggested, "when I tell you that the end of the story is not far off.

"When late afternoon arrives, Scanlon makes his arrangements on the track, and waits for the train. When it stops, and confusion reigns, he is able to board from the rear, as though he was among those already bound for Big Moose station.

"While he was busy in guise of Clemden, guiding passengers to the lodge, Yantzen was entertaining accountant Merriweather in the second floor alcove. No doubt an offer was made over drinks; perhaps foolish Yantzen showed Merriweather the gemstone and promised him a share of the riches in exchange for his cooperation.

"As Scanlon did to Creighton, so Yantzen treated Merriweather. Rendered unconscious by a drugged cocktail, the accountant drops his glass, which breaks. Yantzen attempts to clear away broken glass, and in the confusion he drops the precious stone he had received as preliminary payment."

Sheriff Fairden laughed.

"I'll bet that took some of the wind out of his sails," he smiled.

Chan nodded.

"When I encountered him later, it appeared that the realization had come home to him," he agreed. "It seemed as though he must have hidden the stone in his pack of cigarettes, and he looked for it in vain.

"Still," he went on. "The loss was no matter to a man like Yantzen. He thought of the single gem as a beginning, with much more to come.

"Once the broken glass had been collected, Yantzen managed to position the unconscious Merriweather on the spiky decorations of the staircase top."

"The newel post," Dr. Collins put in. "But the wound in his back?"

"Scanlon had not only provided drug to his accomplice—which he told Yantzen to hide, before and after using it—he gave him a sharpened length of deer antler. Strangely flamboyant Scanlon wanted the dead man executed with a primitive weapon and his body displayed like hunted prey."

The doctor nodded.

"I should have known something was amiss after examining the body," he recalled regretfully, "when I sent Clemden to call the sheriff—only to discover later that he failed to do so. The man was taking every opportunity to thwart all of us."

The detective hesitated for a moment, then went on.

"From wilderness knowledge Scanlon had obtained over the years he provided instructions to Yantzen, how to—"

"Please don't," Muriel Bryant whispered urgently. "I think we know what happened."

"Perhaps Mrs. Bryant and I could be excused," Daniel Bryant suggested. "Come, my dear—let's go upstairs and look in on Edna—and the girls."

Chapter Twenty-Four
THE BEAUTY OF SNOW

The men around the table rose respectfully as Muriel Bryant left the room with her husband. They were still standing when, from the kitchen, a tearful Mrs. Warren emerged with a freshly brewed pot of coffee and a tray of breakfast rolls, fresh from the oven. She deposited both on the sideboard and turned to face the men standing around the table.

"I've heard much of what you folks were discussing about Clemden—Mr. Scanlon," she said in a strained voice. "Begging your pardon, I wanted you to know something that—that—Monsignor Plevna already knows, I think, since he knew Fred as a younger man."

The cleric shifted his stance uncomfortably.

"Mrs. Warren, there's no need to—"

"No, Monsignor, with respect—I think there *is* a need," the woman objected. "A need to set things straight. Not that it will make any difference, after all this time, to me. But the girl may have some rights in the matter.

"I'll be brief," Mrs. Warren continued, clutching the folds of her apron and shifting her gaze from one man to the next, around the table. "Mr. Scanlon and I were acquainted when he was a young man. I was little more than a girl.

"He spoke to me of how we might have a life together, despite our different upbringings, but in the end he couldn't or wouldn't keep his promises. I was a young working woman with no prospects, no parents . . . " Her voice drifted into a brief silence.

"It's an old story, I suppose," she sighed. "He left me, and not long after met and married a woman from a very old, well-established family. I have no doubt that the match made possible all his success, his great vision of himself as a big man of the world."

She paused.

"There was a child," she said quietly. "I don't believe that he ever knew, or cared. I was in no position to—to—heaven help me, I gave her up for adoption." Her voice trembled, and then she continued.

"The only saving grace of the matter is that, in a way, she's come back to me now, almost grown, and a sweet girl she is, I'm happy to say."

Charlie Chan gazed sympathetically at the cook.

"Mary—the girl you scold in the kitchen—you treat her with a firm hand so that your mother's love for her goes unsuspected," the detective said kindly.

"That's it exactly, sir," Mrs. Warren said gratefully. "She doesn't know, and maybe there's no need for her to know—but if someone were to approach Mrs. Scanlon...maybe something could be done for Mary, money for an education perhaps."

The doctor and the priest exchanged glances.

"I'm sure that the Monsignor and I can help," Dr. Collins said firmly. "And there's no need for anyone outside this room to know what you've told us."

"Thank you, Doctor, and my thanks to all of you," Mrs. Warren said. "I'll be going—but if you should need anything, I'll be in the kitchen."

The men resumed their seats, digesting the cook's revelation. After several seconds of silence, Fairden addressed the detective.

"I'm still tryin' to take it all in, and that's a fact," the lawman admitted. "Big businessman wanted to disappear for good and all, probably had some more of those little green rocks squirreled away somewhere for future expenses, and he figures to kill the two men who had any idea what he was up to.

"What gets me, though," he went on, "is that Scanlon had that no-good Yantzen time Merriweather's killing so that nobody would suspect *him*—because they thought he was already dead!

"Damnedest thing I ever heard of," he drawled. "But why get you involved, Mr. Chan?"

"Overconfident Scanlon thought that a detective celebrated in newspapers but unfamiliar with the Adirondacks would leap to incorrect assumptions—and help confirm his supposed death."

Sheriff Fairden snorted.

"Well, he sure got that wrong," he chortled. "Calling you in, assuming you'd jump to the wrong conclusion—that was his biggest mistake."

Chan acknowledged the compliment with a slight inclination of his head.

"His largest error was an incorrect assumption that he could outwit all who investigate wrongdoing—detective from far-off islands, but also experienced coroner and dedicated sheriff who uphold law and order in this beautiful region," the 'detective from far-off islands' said firmly.

Dr. Collins cleared his throat uncertainly.

"Scanlon—is there any sign of him?"

Sheriff Fairden shook his head regretfully.

"I reckon he tried to make it to his cabin, and that's the first place I'll check," he assured the physician, "but it snowed at least a couple of feet overnight—and he had a bullet in him.

"It might be better if he didn't make it," the lawman said flatly. "The newspapers would say it was another 'tragedy at

Big Moose Lake.' And no jury would take kindly to an outsider—'specially one pretendin' to be a local."

Chan shrugged.

"Rich men can afford clever attorneys," he pointed out. "Maybe Scanlon will recall how a sudden uncontrollable rage took hold of him, and the moment of passion forced him to do unthinkable deeds—acts that he now greatly regrets."

"You jes' never know what a jury will think," admitted the sheriff. "Lawyers talk at 'em, fill their heads up with fancy words like 'premeditation,' and it's hard to predict how much of that talk will stick with twelve honest men.

"Still and all," he went on. "I do believe the version of events you jes' told us, Mr. Chan, is what happened—jury or no jury."

Chan nodded.

"Truly, enlightened men do no dark deeds," he quoted. "Ancient wisdom still holds true. Scanlon possessed great wealth, influence—even power over others. But in the end the real nature of things—and some measure of enlightenment—all these things were beyond him.

"When the lamp has no oil the wick is wasted in vain."

The beauty of snow, like beauty itself, is in the eye of the beholder.

Clarissa—and to a lesser extent, Miss Clarkson—saw the newly whitened woods outside the lodge as a playground, and after a hasty breakfast they plunged into its possibilities with enthusiasm.

Sheriff Fairden—and to a lesser extent, Charlie Chan—looked at the frozen landscape and thought of the loose ends still to be secured before the investigation could rightly be called complete.

"As I said to you not long ago, you are sheriff," Chan reminded his law enforcement colleague brightly. "To you belongs the glory of solving these strange crimes, but yours is also the responsibility for gathering up final pieces of evidence—and determining whereabouts of chief suspect."

The two men were struggling through the drifts that separated the lodge from the caretaker's cabin. Charlie Chan had packed his single suitcase in hopes that the sheriff could find a way to transport him close to civilization. The detective's thoughts had turned to home, and he was unwilling to wait for a thaw to ease his journey.

"Thanks for reminding me," Fairden grumbled. "I do have an idea about how we might get you out of this predicament, but we also need to check jes' the one place that Scanlon would make for—wounded and runnin' from the law."

"His cabin?"

"Yes, sir, it's barely possible, but we got to check."

The sheriff glanced at his companion, whose winter garb seemed more appropriate for a city sidewalk than an Adirondack trail.

"You know, neither one of us is dressed for this kind of hike," the lawman said with a laugh, "but you sure seem to be takin' it in stride."

Chan gasped as he stumbled over a hidden obstacle, possibly a tree root.

"Compliment that I will cherish in days to come, when I repose in the shade of a tree that blooms in year-round warmth of Honolulu," he replied, rising and brushing snow from his overcoat and shoulders.

"I sure do thank you for all that you've done," the sheriff exclaimed as the two resumed their hike. "I never would've untangled this thing myself—that Scanlon fellow sure is a deep one.

"Part of me, though, thinks he would've got clean away with it," Fairden mused, "if he'd kept things simple."

Chan smiled, slightly out of breath from his stroll in the snow.

"Complicated mind of Scanlon could not stop adding flourishes to his plan," the detective replied. "His Greek college organization ring—he tried unsuccessfully to place it onto his victim's finger to strengthen the impression that it was Frederick Scanlon who lay dead in the woods.

"When he found it would not fit, despite his best efforts, he placed it in Creighton's pocket. He knew Merriweather carried watch fob with the same symbol linked to a more ancient inherited timepiece. In this way, he reasoned, police would connect the two men and think the dead man under the train was Scanlon—fraternity brother of Merriweather."

Fairden snorted.

"Well, that part of his plan worked—till it didn't," he admitted. "Thanks to you, Inspector.

"But say," he recalled. "What about those feathers? I suppose he had some fancy reason for those, too."

Chan smiled, his eyes glinting in the sparkling light of the snowy landscape.

"While removing antler from animal in upper room of lodge, he noticed bird in diorama and plucked two black feathers from it—more dust to throw in the face of investigators. Most likely he knew that a black feather in some cultures is an ill omen, but in others it predicts the opposite outcome. Placing one on the body of Creighton, he instructed Yantzen to do the same when dispatching the unfortunate Merriweather.

"Same kind of false trail he presented," the detective said, taking a deep breath, "by sending a communication that promised his noon arrival at lodge. His troubled mind surely delighted in thoughts of made-up clues eagerly considered by investigators."

"Fellow who thinks like that," the sheriff grumbled, "has taken leave of his senses."

The two men had come to a halt.

"There she is," Fairden exclaimed, pointing ahead. "It don't look like much, but it may be your way out."

Obscured by a covering heap of snow, "she" was Clemden's snowmobile, next to the caretaker's deserted cabin.

"The way I figure it," the sheriff explained, "is that we need to get you to Big Moose station, first. No tellin' how widespread this snowfall was—sometimes a mile or two in one direction or the other makes all the difference.

"But that's beside the point," he continued. "I jes' need to get you to somewhere the trains are runnin', now or later. And I don't suppose Mr. Scanlon—dead or alive—will mind if we take this for a little drive."

"What of Mrs. Scanlon and other guests?" Chan reminded him. "They also are anxious to depart."

Fairden chuckled.

"They'll keep," he replied. "You're my first priority, and after things settle a bit the rest will follow.

"Howsomever, we'd best make sure of Clemden first, before we drive off in his snow buggy. No smoke from the chimney," he observed, "but let me take a look through the windows—jes' to see if he somehow made it back here in the storm."

The sheriff waded through the snow to and from the side of the one-room dwelling and returned, shaking his head.

"Well, he made it," he said grimly. "Then again, he didn't—in a manner of speaking."

"Scanlon is dead?" Chan said quietly.

Fairden nodded.

"Reckon we better go in and take a look, but he's dead all right."

The door was wide open, and the snow had drifted inside the single room. The dead man was lying frozen in the snow inside the door, and a small toolbox—its contents scattered—was upside down next to him.

"Once I get you squared away," the sheriff told Chan, "I'll have to go for Doc Manston—even if he did say he needed time to catch up on his work."

While the lawman went outside to see what could be done with the caretaker's snowmobile, Charlie Chan made a thorough search of the cabin and its contents. A small notebook rewarded his efforts. Then he looked once again at the door knocker and strike plate he had admired on their previous visit.

With tools that lay in the snow beside the dead man, the detective discovered what he had been looking for. The unusually thick strike plate was, as he had suspected, a kind of small wall safe. Opening it roughly, Chan was rewarded by the sight of a small burlap bag closed at its top with knotted twine. He squeezed the little gunny sack, feeling the tiny objects within thoughtfully, and pocketed it.

The detective seated himself on the single chair available and leafed through the notebook. Time passed more quickly than he had realized—or else the sheriff worked more rapidly than expected.

Suddenly a series of minor explosions and a kind of clattering came from outside the cabin, and Fairden entered the room. He kicked aside some of the drifted snow and, with some difficulty, pushed the door shut to keep out the noise.

"Got 'er started, but she needs to warm up a bit. Find anything?"

"Journal of Frederick Scanlon, which I entrust to you," Chan replied, handing him the notebook. "It seems to confirm much of what we knew. Strange man planned most aspects of killings and instructed his confederate accordingly.

"In this diary he describes how a great beast's head on the wall gave him the idea for fashioning an unusual weapon from its antlers. He writes of gathering two black feathers in the same room—he thought that they might puzzle the police. One he planted on unfortunate Creighton's body; the other he gave to Yantzen to place on the body at top of stairs—a body displayed like the trophies throughout his lodge."

The sheriff grunted.

"Should've been a guest in the Utica asylum years ago," the lawman declared. "I don't see how he kept so many people from finding out what he was really like."

"Also in his notebook," Chan went on. "Meticulous in all things, this careful businessman pasted an item on its inside cover that will interest you."

"What's that?"

"Receipt for false beard and other items of hair—mustache, eyebrows, even a wig—made by New York theatrical costume company," the detective grinned. "Fake fur concealed Scanlon's features so effectively that even his former wife did not recognize him—as long as he did not approach her too closely . . ."

"And underneath that he was probably growin' his own," the sheriff speculated. "Anyway, from what I gather it had been a good many years since Mrs. Scanlon had seen her husband, so—"

"Pardon, please, but here is something Dr. Manston may find of great interest, if my assumption is correct," the detective went on, handing over the little bag. "I would advise caution in opening it—"

Fairden had already unknotted the twine and was looking into a substantial handful of green gemstones, garnets, which sparkled even in the dimly lit cabin.

"Scanlon's savings account," he murmured. "Well, well."

There was a knock on the cabin door.

"Let's leave things here as they are," Fairden advised, "and entertain our caller outside."

The sheriff opened the door, and he and Chan slipped out through the doorway. A small delegation greeted them: Matthew Trenville, Gloria Clarkson, and her charge, Clarissa. The little girl giggled as she received some words of caution from the other two and ran toward an unblemished patch of white to make snow angels on the ground.

Fairden pulled the door shut behind him.

"Saw you two making for the cabin," Trenville explained. "I figured that you might be helping Mr. Chan make a quick getaway in this pile of machinery—" He indicated the near-by snowmobile, which was idling loudly.

"—and I, that is *we*, didn't want you to leave without saying goodbye."

"And, perhaps, without accepting heartfelt congratulations from this weary traveler?" Chan grinned questioningly.

"I told you he would already know!" Gloria Clarkson smiled at her new fiancé. "Yes, Mr. Chan, I guess I'm going to become a woman of the wilderness—unless I can convince Mr. Trenville to consider life in a city larger than Eagle Bay."

General laughter greeted both possibilities, and the two men shook hands with the bridegroom-to-be.

"One thing I've been meanin' to ask somebody," Sheriff Fairden said awkwardly to the little group, "not that it's any of my business, but that little tyke, Clarissa—"

"Well, there's no harm in telling you," Miss Clarkson said shyly. "Mr. Chan already knows that Mrs. Scanlon was thinking of adopting Clarissa from the home—the orphanage where I work.

"But she told me yesterday that she has decided not to go through with it."

"So Clarissa will return to the home to await some future possibility?" Chan inquired.

Matthew Trenville grinned.

"Miss Clarkson and I plan to make application ourselves," he said happily. "And if we're lucky—"

"It would be unusual," Gloria Clarkson admitted, "but I think, given the circumstances, we have a good chance of starting a family with Clarissa in our new home."

"After a short honeymoon, of course," Trenville interject-ed.

"That's the best news I've heard in quite a spell," the sheriff exclaimed. "Well, all aboard for Big Moose," he continued, raising his voice over the noise of the snowmobile engine. "You ready for a little ride, Mr. Chan?"

The two men boarded the rattling, backfiring contraption, and Charlie Chan waved to the three young people as the snowmobile slowly pulled away down the trail toward the station.

THE END

ACKNOWLEDGEMENTS

My thanks to all those who have embraced the *Charlie Chan Returns* series: readers, reviewers, old friends and new. As always, the encouragement of my academic author-spouse Patricia Swann sustains my efforts. Nick Burns continues to bring to bear his years of publishing and marketing expertise, and NKB Publishing's role in the revival of a beloved fictional character cannot be overstated.

None of this would be possible, of course, without the author Earl Derr Biggers and Chinese-Hawaiian detective Chang Apana, whose remarkable career provided the inspiration for the creation of Charlie Chan.

ABOUT THE AUTHOR

John L. Swann has been a writer for much of his professional life. He has worked in broadcast journalism—as a reporter, anchor, news director, and talk show host in radio and TV—and in public relations and marketing. A native of the rural Midwest, he lives in New York state with his wife, Patricia.

Read the first three mysteries in our series
Charlie Chan Returns

Death, I Said
Violence and death upend a
quiet university campus in
1930s San Francisco.

The Tangled String
Thievery, death, and
blue-blooded family
skeletons at a Boston hotel.

Beyond Murder
Drug smuggling and a sinister
conspiracy overshadow the birth
of Chan's first grandchild.

With wit, wisdom, and intuitive intellect, Charlie Chan will
crack the case and unmask the guilty.

**Available at Amazon.com, BarnesAndNoble.com, and
booksellers everywhere.**